Readers love
Jake C. Wallace

Jerricho's Freedom

"Wallace is an excellent world builder, and he succeeds here again, creating a whole other society of demons with their own sets of rules and laws. The characters were engaging and relatable."

—Joyfully Jay

"The excitement never let up and bowled me along to the very last page, and my biggest complaint about this book is that it ended."

—Sinfully: Gay Romance Book Reviews

A Chance for Us

"Intense, fast paced, action driven and a bit of romance to boot are all phrases that best describe this wonderful novel. I highly recommend it to you."

—The Novel Approach

"Well written with amazing details that grips the reader from start to finish."

—MM Good Book Reviews

Dare to Love Forever

"This is absolutely delightful. I was hooked by the first chapter & didn't stop reading till… the end. I love the world Wallace builds."

—Alpha Book Club

"This author has a way with the smexy that should be considered dangerous… There isn't much more you could ask for in this story and if you couldn't tell already I loved it!"

—Diverse Reader

By JAKE C. WALLACE

Happily Ever After Isn't Easy
Jerricho's Freedom
Soul Seekers

NEW VAMPIRE JUSTICE
Dare to Love Forever
A Chance for Us

Published by DREAMSPINNER PRESS
www.dreamspinnerpress.com

JAKE C. WALLACE

HAPPILY EVER AFTER ISN'T EASY

Published by
DREAMSPINNER PRESS

5032 Capital Circle SW, Suite 2, PMB# 279, Tallahassee, FL 32305-7886 USA
www.dreamspinnerpress.com

Happily Ever After Isn't Easy

Cover Art

ISBN: 978-1-63533-401-2
Digital ISBN: 978-1-63533-402-9
Library of Congress Control Number: 2016958609
Published May 2017
v. 1.0

Printed in the United States of America
∞
This paper meets the requirements of
ANSI/NISO Z39.48-1992 (Permanence of Paper).

This book is for my mother, Beverly.
Without you, I wouldn't be the person I am today.
Your influence, your actions, your beliefs, have shaped who I am,
made me a nonjudgmental, accepting person.
You taught me the lessons that are most important in life.
I am so lucky that you are my mom. I love you.

CHAPTER 1

GABE REYNOLDS wasn't sure how he'd let the same shit happen to him again. He had to either be the most gullible, trusting guy on the planet or the biggest idiot. Life was supposed to get better, *be* better, be easier. He hadn't expected his life after his divorce to be all hearts and flowers immediately, but he'd paid his dues, right?

Twenty-one years with the wrong person, the wrong gender, living the same lie day in and day out, those had been his dues. He'd stayed even when the relationship had been little more than a roommate arrangement. He'd taken his duties seriously, tried to make it all work, done that noble thing, but nobility doesn't equal happiness. He hadn't even been the one to end it. But when the divorce fell into his lap, he'd run with it. Well, run was a strong word. He'd hidden for a while, then limped, all the while wondering how to start over, how to come out of that dark, cold closet. Almost three years later, he was no better off than he had been before the divorce.

Focusing back on the computer screen, he reread the private message on Facebook again, had the words memorized by then, each one a reminder of the chance he'd taken and lost.

I'm sorry, Gabe, for everything. Sorry for jumping in too soon after Jeff. I really wanted this to work….

Gabe swallowed hard. There had to be something wrong with him, maybe something that told others he had excess baggage and wasn't worth the hassle. He wasn't young anymore. His body was slightly overweight, saggy in important places, because he loathed exercise and loved carbs, and at forty-three, his metabolism had slowed to a crawl. But he never imagined he'd be starting over at that late age with the need to impress anyone else.

According to all those gay romance books, gay guys were supposed to be hard, chiseled, Adonis-like creatures with thick hair and strong chins, beautiful eyes and washboard abs. They were firefighters or cowboys or shape-shifters or vampires or dozens of other things more interesting than him. Gabe could only tick the box next to the thick hair, and even that was sort of a plain ashy brown color, longer on top and cropped close to his head on the sides. Even his eyes were a nondescript brown. Damn, it had been so much easier in his teens. What he wouldn't give to have that skinny, practically hairless, bony twink body (without the acne and the raging hormones, of course). But without that body, he was too shy to go out and meet men. Shouldn't he be able to go out, get his flirt on, and then in one heart-stopping moment meet his soul mate and live happily ever after? Even men believed in fairy tales. Yet his happily ever after was currently residing in the toilet with his marriage, one unrealized dream relationship, and his self-esteem.

I know you said you thought about me all these years, hoped one day we could be together again and happy....

He might not have been happy in his marriage, but he'd been content and complacent and sexually unsatisfied and frustrated and—oh, who was he kidding—fucking miserable, but he'd managed to bury everything deep inside without having a heart attack or an ulcer or stroke—yet.

Okay, so maybe his self-esteem had taken a hard hit (his wife had gotten pregnant by the furnace guy), and he was a bit rusty in the dating realm (his last date was in 1990). Add to those the fact that he was a middle-aged gay man in a small town in northern New York after his heterosexual marriage had crashed and burned. What was supposed to be easy had become Mt. Everest. And Gabe had become an even lonelier and more confused man than he'd ever been during his sham of a marriage. At that point he'd wished for easy, begged for easy, dreamed of easy.

He rubbed his temples as his stomach twisted in knots. For two weeks, he'd basically gone to work and then home to his little cottage, floundering, wallowing, whatever the term, in the broken remnants of his dream relationship with Tim, the one future light that had allowed him to keep his sanity while living a lie.

I wanted us to be those boys we once were, totally in love and ready to experience life together. Life had been so easy back then, and for a moment, I wanted that uncomplicated forever love....

Gabe now knew that happiness and love were fleeting concepts that weren't within his grasp.

But I had been foolish to think that we could recreate that past given all we've been through. The past is over, and I'm too lost in the now to be anything to anyone....

Maybe someday Tim would be ready, but Gabe was done with relationships and their empty promises. Maybe someday Gabe's heart would mend and he'd figure out how relationships worked and how to keep one. Until then….

I'm sorry I can't be your happily ever after.

GABE SIPPED his bland black coffee minus the hazelnut creamer and sugar and grimaced. An amused chuckle pulled him from his morose thoughts.

"Why're you torturing yourself with that plain crap?" Betsy smiled over her own cup loaded with cream and sugar. Her chipper attitude that morning rained on his pity parade.

Gabe placed his cup on the table, sighed heavily, and looked up at his younger, cuter, blonde-haired half sister across from him at his kitchen table.

"You'll understand when you're over forty and just being within the general vicinity of sugar and fat makes you gain weight."

She gave him an unimpressed grunt. "Hey, you're talking to a woman here. We start gaining curves and weight at puberty, and after that it's all downhill. Men? You get more distinguished and handsome as you age. We women just get old. And you're not fat."

Gabe raked his hand through his short hair. When he lowered his hand, he narrowed his eyes at the few strands still wrapped around his fingers. Maybe the thinning part would come sooner than he thought. Next would be gray hairs. *Can't escape them forever.*

"No, just pleasantly plump, right?"

Instead of the laugh he'd hoped for, Betsy only returned a contemplative look of sympathy that turned his stomach.

"You're really being hard on yourself. I know Tim did a number on you, but don't let it rule your life. He's not worth it."

Gabe shook his head. "I'm the one who's apparently not worth it." He hadn't made the grade and had failed to get Tim.

"Oh my God!"

Her outburst startled Gabe. His knees hit the table, and his coffee sloshed over the rim of his cup.

"That man's an egotistical, self-centered ass. He played you, used you, and when he was done, he dropped you. He's changed, I told you that, but… I know you wanted it to work."

Gabe shrugged indifferently. "Maybe if I was a few pounds lighter, more exciting and interesting—"

"Enough." She raised her hand determinedly. "You're a good person and smart, good-looking"—she narrowed her eyes as if daring him to contradict her—"successful, respectful, respected, and so damn noble at times you should be royalty. You stayed in a marriage for over twenty years because you spoke some vows in a church, even though your marriage sucked and you were unhappy. And even when your ex stomped all over those vows and cheated, got pregnant with another man's kids, the ones you'd been trying to have, you forgave her, stayed civil, and gave her practically everything you owned. Now go ahead and tell me you're not good enough."

The thin line of her lips and the weight of her defiant stare kept any arguments to the contrary from falling from his lips. Dismayed, he gazed into his dark, lifeless, boring coffee and thought if he were less like that coffee and more like a caramel latte with chocolate and whipped cream, he'd have Tim.

"I wish I was as confident as you describe." And half as pragmatic.

Betsy banged her fist against the table and the cups jumped. "If I ever get my hands on Tim, I'm going to strangle him."

"It's not his fault," Gabe said halfheartedly, unable to meet Betsy's eyes.

While Gabe truly believed the whole excruciating event hadn't solely been Tim's fault, the callous conduct of the man he'd loved since he was a teenager had sliced deep into his heart. As if the pain were physical, Gabe reached up and rubbed his palm over the ache that had settled beneath his sternum.

The silence reigned long enough that Gabe looked up. Man, Betsy hadn't looked at him with such vehemence since she was a teenager and he'd drilled her dates when they came to pick her up. Some ran and never returned. He shifted in his chair. The waves of anger radiating from Betsy threatened to knock him over.

"Car."

"Huh?" Gabe had lost the course of the conversation.

"I'm going to run over him with my car, back over him, and do it again."

Gabe snorted with amusement. "Careful, Bets. Your horns are showing."

How he wished he could be like her—strong, independent, self-confident, assertive. Able to be alone, without a man, and not care. The woman was a retired Army sergeant and now a federal probation officer who could kick ass and manage to cow the most hardened men and women.

Betsy reached across the table and laid her hand on Gabe's clenched fist. Her touch settled him. Internally, chaos reigned and his mind rarely rested, overwhelmed with the pain and sorrow and upheaval Tim had left. If Betsy really knew what a mess Gabe had been, she'd definitely shoot Tim with her required sidearm. The sleepless nights, lying in bed until the wee hours of the morning, the inability to focus on even mind-numbing tasks like TV or reading. The black cloud had settled over him like a second skin. Oh, and don't forget the crying—fucking crying like a heartbroken teenage girl. He hadn't even cried when his grandfather died. Luckily, his well of tears had dried up. One more morning facing his bloodshot, swollen eyes in the mirror and Gabe might have begged Betsy to put him out of his misery.

Betsy sipped her coffee filled with cream and sugar. "What about Patrick? Whatever happened with him?"

Another failure. Gabe had met Patrick on an online dating site while weeding out those only looking for hookups. Gabe wasn't built that way, no matter how desperate he was to get physical with another man.

When he didn't answer, Betsy said, "I mean, when you talked about him, you sounded happy. I know that his being in South Carolina was a bit of a barrier, but you seemed to have a lot in common."

"Except for the attraction." No matter how much they had in common, there had been no spark. No rush of excited sexual energy or frenzied need to get closer to the other person you couldn't get close enough to. "I just wasn't physically attracted to him."

Betsy chewed on her lip. "Maybe the attraction would have come in time. Sometimes people become friends first, then fall in love."

He knew she was right, but at the time he'd truly been waiting for that one person who rocked his world. "I know, and I screwed up, but what's new. He moved on and met a great guy, and they're living together. So you see I wasn't the one for him."

"Okay, I give." Betsy stood and picked her purse up from the floor. "Listen, I have to get going, but remember, Gabe, I'm not the evil one here. That man strung you along and played you. He's had how many relationships in how many years? Most people have a few bad relationships, but the man hasn't been able to keep anyone. There's a reason for that." With her point made, she kissed his cheek and left.

Tim said he wasn't happy with anyone else because he'd never gotten over me.

And Gabe had bought that hook, line, and sinker, because he'd never gotten over Tim. His first love. His only love. Gabe had eventually come to love his wife, but as a friend. But Tim Nolan? Gabe had loved Tim, real, sappy, gooey heart love, since he was fifteen. The moment Tim with his blond hair, ocean blue eyes, and golden skin had sauntered onto that Lake Champlain beach, Gabe's confusion and doubts about his sexual orientation had been allayed. Definitely one of those aha (or maybe oh shit) moments.

Gabe had quickly become friends with the charismatic, gregarious, and touchy-feely Tim. His overuse of those guy-approved touches like back slaps and the arm-over-the-shoulder hug that lingered too long had been maddening. Gabe was sure fate had been trying to drive him insane with the number of hard-ons Tim had inspired. For nearly a year, Gabe had jerked off under the covers, in the bathroom, even in the darkened woods on their camping trips. All the while, thoughts of touching Tim, kissing Tim, ran through his mind. The torture finally ended when in one heart-stopping moment, Tim kissed him. Because it was 1989, their boyfriend status had been secret until they'd graduated. That's when everything had fallen apart.

Gabe's phone rang, pulling him from the past. He ignored the annoying noise, which thankfully stopped. When the ringing started again, he grabbed the cell.

His ex. "Hi, Karen."

The sobbing wasn't anything new but still squeezed his chest painfully.

"Hey, what's wrong?" He stood and dumped his black coffee into the sink and set the cup down. Fuck black coffee.

"G-Gabe. I don't… I don't know what to do…."

Gabe picked up his keys on the counter and headed to the front door.

"It's okay. We'll figure it out. I'll be there in about twenty minutes."

He sighed as he pulled on his jacket and locked the door behind him. He could be gone for hours.

CHAPTER 2

STILL TRYING to shake off the old memories of Tim, Gabe sipped at his gas station coffee flavored with hazelnut creamer and real sugar. Saturday night generally was a night where his loneliness threatened to engulf him whole. This was a distraction. On his way to Karen's, he'd had an epiphany. If he had to be alone, then the only person his body had to please was himself. A few extra pounds and crow's-feet wouldn't do him any harm.

He pulled up outside of the large Queen Anne-style house in town he'd shared with Karen for eighteen years. That house was now occupied by her husband, Randy (the furnace guy), and their adorable twins, Mikey and Maddy. Children had been one of two things Gabe had been unable to give his ex-wife.

They'd been unable to conceive, a mystery to the doctors they'd seen. Dozens of tests and no reasons were found as to why Karen's eggs wouldn't accept his sperm. Little buggers just couldn't get in. Gabe figured those eggs had known "gay" sperm when they'd seen it. This was his inside joke. Of course, when he'd shared that with his one gay friend, Marty, the look of horror had been priceless. The lecture about gay stereotyping and gay rights not so much. Gabe couldn't even do gay right.

Despite trying everything short of in vitro, there were no babies for them. By that point, their marriage had disintegrated beyond repair. A child wasn't going to fix their eroding relationship. There came a time in most people's lives when living without someone to love and who loved you back wasn't acceptable anymore.

The second thing Gabe had been unable to give to Karen was his heart. That had belonged (probably still did) to someone who didn't want it, had stomped the life out of it and left it a hollow echo of its former self. Worse yet, Tim had taken every ounce of hope Gabe had hidden with him all those years in that closet. Now Gabe wondered how he was supposed to retrieve that missing hope. Maybe the point was to get that hope back. Maybe the point was to let go of a dream he'd clutched tight for over twenty-five years.

Letting go was like stepping off a cliff when you didn't know how far down the ground was—an utterly terrifying drop that brought your stomach into your throat and tried to choke the life out of you.

He wasn't sure if he was ready to step off that cliff yet.

He rang the doorbell and heard the pounding of little feet. He set his coffee down and crouched in readiness.

The door opened, and Mikey shouted, "Unca Gabe!" as he flew at him. Gabe caught him in time for a shrieking Maddy to barrel into him. Barely keeping his balance, he lifted them both.

"Hi, guys." Just holding the twins filled the ache in his heart. Even though they weren't his, he'd come to love them. "What's up, my little monkeys?"

"Mommy sad. She cry." Mikey's large brown eyes showed their concern.

Maddy nodded in agreement, her blondish curls bouncing around her shoulders.

"I know. Where's Daddy?"

"He work." Maddy touched his face and rubbed at his whiskers. For some reason, she always touched his face, and the action endeared her to him even more.

"Okay." He set them down and picked up his coffee. "I'm going to check on Mommy. Where is she?"

"Her room." Mikey raced into the living room and plopped onto the couch in front of the TV. Two toddlers alone was a recipe for disaster.

Maddy was more resistant to leaving Gabe.

"Did you guys have any lunch?"

Maddy shook her head. Quieter and more reserved than her brother, she generally needed more comforting than he did.

"I'm going to check on Mommy, and then I'll come back and make you some mac and cheese, okay?"

She grinned and joined her brother on the couch. Gabe pulled off his jacket, hung it in the entryway, and then headed upstairs to their old bedroom. When he knocked, there was no answer, so he peeked around the door.

"Karen?"

The room was dark, the shades blocking most of the daylight. He flicked on the overhead light. Karen was under the covers, her head buried beneath the pillow. Gabe sighed and went to the bed.

"Karen. You need to get up. The kids are downstairs by themselves, and Randy isn't here." He pulled back the covers. "Come on."

She blinked up at him, her shoulder-length blonde hair tangled around her face. Her eyes were swollen and red. Damn, she looked bad. When had he last spoken with her? Last week? No, two weeks ago, and then she'd been good, stable, the bipolar depression responding to her new meds. He rarely went longer than a few days without checking on her, but he'd been too wrapped up in his own despair.

"Where's Randy?" Her confusion was apparent.

"Maddy said he's at work."

Her eyes widened. "Oh God, he left this morning. What time is it?" She sat up, her eyes scanning the room frantically. "What're you doing here?"

He frowned. "It's after eleven. You called me crying about thirty minutes ago. Don't you remember?"

She shook her head, then nodded. "Yeah, I do." Tears immediately began to course down her cheeks.

"Did you take your meds this morning?"

When she was in the depressive phase of her illness, she tended to forget to take them, which only made her worse. And she was definitely in that phase right then.

The confusion was apparent on her face. "I… I don't remember."

Gabe ran his hand over his hair. His ex-wife had been diagnosed as bipolar at the beginning of their marriage, but with medication and counseling, the extreme highs and lows hadn't been as frequent. Since the birth of the twins, though, those episodes were becoming more frequent. Randy worked long hours and wasn't there to support Karen. The limited amount of times when Gabe did see him, Randy said very little to him. While Karen's husband had always been civil, Gabe got the feeling Randy viewed him as a threat to his marriage. Seemed odd since Randy had been the one who'd cheated with Gabe's wife.

"I need to get the twins some lunch. Why don't you get into the shower? Here. Drink this." He handed her his cup of coffee, which she took. "What time will Randy be home?"

"I don't know." That question nearly had her sobbing again.

"It's okay. Shower and come downstairs, and I'll have some lunch ready. Can you do that?"

Her breath caught, and she nodded. He patted her arm and then went down to the kitchen. He pulled out a couple of boxes of macaroni and cheese and set a pot of water on the stove. Waiting for the water to boil, he got out what he needed to make cheese sandwiches, the twins' favorite.

Maddy came into the kitchen. "What doin'?"

Gabe boosted her up onto the counter. "Making lunch. Mommy's in the shower and will be down soon. Can you open the cheese for me?" He handed her a slice of wrapped cheese. As he dumped the noodles into the boiling water, she quickly pulled open the wrapper, even managing to get the cheese slice out in no more than two pieces.

He smiled as she laid the slices on the bread. At one time having kids in that house had been his dream. Little ones to teach, play with, and love. At least the large house had kids running around, even if they weren't his.

He set Maddy onto the floor. "Go tell Mikey to come and wash his hands. Lunch is almost ready."

She raced off, yelling to her brother. Gabe knew Mikey would be too engrossed in his show to come anytime soon. Once he had the mac and cheese ready, he'd seek them out. While he waited for the noodles to cook, he pulled out Karen's med box. He'd set her up with the box after the birth of the twins. At the time, the doctor had labeled her depression as postpartum, but Gabe had known different. Almost three years later and she wasn't doing much better. He hated to admit it, but she was worse. He didn't want to think what that meant for the family's future. As a mental health counselor, he knew what severe mental illness could do to a parent, a spouse, and their children.

The two-week pillbox showed that Karen had missed over 50 percent of her meds over the last two weeks. Just one missed dose could throw her off and lead to regression into the illness. He'd have to talk to Randy, which he so didn't look forward to doing.

Karen came into the kitchen, hair wet, in a T-shirt, sweats, and the old, tattered sweater he'd given her for Christmas ten years ago. When she saw Gabe with her med box, her tears started immediately. Gabe didn't say anything. He filled a glass with water and handed her the dose of meds she'd missed that morning.

"Thanks."

She sat at the counter and held the glass of water tightly in her hands.

Gabe mixed up the mac and cheese and called the twins. The kids raced into the room and simultaneously shouted, "Mommy!"

Karen bent down and hugged them both. "My babies. I'm so sorry I wasn't down here. It won't happen again. I promise. Come and eat what Uncle Gabe made."

Gabe helped them to wash their hands and plopped them onto the stools at the counter. As they ate, the kids filled him in on preschool and everything they could remember. Gabe loved to hear their views of the world and how big everyday things were in their eyes.

By the time they'd finished eating, the twins' eyes were drooping. Gabe helped Karen put them down for their nap. Then he cleaned up the kitchen and living room. Karen sat in the rocking chair next to the fireplace. Already she looked better, the food and meds having done her good. Gabe sat on the couch across from her.

"You're missing your meds, Karen. You know you can't miss one dose."

She nodded. "Sometimes I get so busy, and I forget. The kids just need so much attention, and the housework… I get so overwhelmed sometimes. And Randy works so much."

Gabe couldn't imagine the energy needed to raise twins, especially when Karen was in her forties. Randy was seven years younger, but he worked long hours as a repairman.

"Have you been seeing Dr. Nemer?"

She looked away and bit her lip. He knew the answer. Gabe pulled out his phone and, without asking, found her psychologist's number. He knew he'd get his voice mail since it was Saturday.

"Charles, it's Gabe Reynolds. I'm with Karen, and she needs an appointment to see you as soon as possible. You can call her. If you can't get her, please call me. Thanks."

Monday Gabe would call Charles, Karen's psychologist, again. They had worked together over the years and were good friends. Gabe was surprised he hadn't contacted him about Karen missing her appointments.

"Thanks." She swirled the tea in her cup. "I didn't mean to let it get this bad. When I feel this… sad, I can't do anything."

He knew how debilitating her illness could be, but she had to keep herself well. "You have two small children. They were alone when I came here. What if…." He clenched his fists. "What if one of them got hurt or sick and you weren't there."

Her chin quivered. "I know. I love them so much. I...."

He exhaled. "I love them too, Karen, even if they aren't mine. I just want them to be safe."

Her eyes widened, and she opened her mouth but then appeared to stop herself. "I'm sorry, Gabe. I'll try harder."

Gabe touched her knee. "I know how hard this is. I can talk to Randy—"

Fear flashed across her face. "No, please, don't say anything to him. He's already upset that I'm having such a hard time. Just give me some time to get myself back together. I can do this. Please, Gabe."

Her reaction wasn't surprising, but that fear.... What was she afraid of?

"Okay. But I'm going to check on you every day. And you're going to let me take the kids for a few hours after work to give you a break."

"We can talk about it. I'm gonna go and lay down with the kids. They should sleep a couple of hours." When she stood, Gabe noticed how thin she was when her sweater fell open. He was glad she'd eaten something for lunch. "I'm sure you have something planned with Tim."

A stab to the chest. "Um, well, Tim and I aren't together. It didn't work out."

"But you seemed so happy last time we talked."

He pursed his lips. "I'll tell you about it another time. Get some rest."

She nodded and went upstairs. He took one last look around his old house, shut and locked the door, and then climbed into his car. Another reminder of Tim and what he didn't have. Since his teens, so much of Gabe's thinking and fantasies had centered on Tim. Now Gabe's mind had no idea how to think without Tim there, the neural pathways etched deep and possibly set for a lifetime. Gabe moaned. Tim would never truly be gone. If only he could get the man out of his head, let him go, move on. Work on Monday would be a welcome distraction.

CHAPTER 3

AT NINE o'clock Monday morning, Gabe stepped into the Westport Youth and Family Center, where he was a counselor/case manager/ janitor. With limited funds, the center ran on a shoestring budget, which was ironic because shoestrings, wire, some duct tape, and crazy glue were what held most of the building together. Gabe wasn't the handiest guy, but he was free and willing to try.

"Morning, Gabe." Alicia Morgan was at the receptionist's desk, the phone cradled between her ear and shoulder as she typed on the computer. Alicia was the other counselor/finance manager/receptionist. With a weary sigh, she said, "It's a five-alarm day."

Gabe tried to suppress an eye roll and a groan. Several teens already sat in the waiting area, including Gabe's client Travis. Seated off in a chair by himself, with his knees pulled to his chest, black hair hanging in his eyes, the teen's forlorn expression indicated something had gone wrong in one of two places—home or school (where he should have been at that moment). Gabe guessed school.

Gabe shifted his bag to his other shoulder and grabbed the contents of his in-box. "I see I have an early start."

Alicia glanced over her shoulder in Travis's direction. The sixteen-year-old picked at something on his battered shoe. When no one was looking, he appeared vulnerable and lost. Once he noticed someone was watching, the concrete barriers would go up and the bravado would appear. Travis was small for his age and tended to use less socially acceptable ways to appear larger, tougher, and intimidating.

Gabe walked over to the teen. "Travis, you need to see me?"

Travis didn't speak. He jumped up, already wearing that mask of a scowl, and preceded Gabe into his office, where he flopped unceremoniously onto the old futon. Gabe went to his desk, unpacked his laptop, and hit the Power button. His dinosaur of a computer at work was so old he was surprised the antique didn't require foot power to work. He checked his schedule for the day, his e-mail, then opened some reports he needed to complete. All the while Travis sat, messing with his shoelace. They played this game each time Travis came unannounced. His impromptu visits always meant something had pissed him off.

"I'm never going back to school."

Ready to talk and it had only taken thirty-three minutes. Gabe rose and rounded the desk, then sat in the chair across from Travis. The kid struggled every day to conform to rules and a social system where he didn't fit. Most adults had written the kid off, but Gabe had caught glimpses of the lost little boy behind the posturing and hard attitude. Unfortunately, the world kept beating that boy back into his shell. Gabe feared that eventually that boy would disappear.

Gabe waited for him to continue.

"I couldn't do gym today, and Coach Wilson was out. There was a substitute."

Damn.

Travis's scowl deepened. "When I said I couldn't play, the sub, Mr. Sawyer, got all up in my face, demanding an answer why. I… I couldn't tell him that. I said Coach Wilson lets me sit out if I need to and gives me extra credit to work on or something else to do."

Travis rubbed his palms in an agitated motion over his legs, as if working up to something big. What had the substitute done to this kid? Gabe sat forward to give Travis encouragement to continue.

After a minute, Travis went on. "Today was touch football. I… you know I can't. Not with so many people."

Gabe finally spoke. "Did you see Ms. Massier?"

Travis shook his head. "The principal wasn't there today."

Gabe had worked so hard to create a support system around Travis at school, and one ignorant sub had gone and blown it all out of the water. Travis's mother had sexually abused him as a boy. Convicted for the abuse, she was currently in jail, which was ironic since Travis was the one who'd lost his freedom. Touches from those he didn't trust implicitly freaked him out. He had slowly come around to where he could handle inadvertent touches in crowds. Anything more was hard for him.

Gabe took a deep breath and released the air slowly. Anger wouldn't help the situation. The lack of awareness of the pact with the coach by the substitute wasn't what angered Gabe. It was the fact that he'd dismissed Travis before the kid could explain. Gabe grabbed his school ID. He visited the school so often the principal had given him his own. Didn't hurt that she was his best friend as well.

"Why didn't you go to the quiet room?" The room was Travis's backup if he was too upset to stay in class.

Travis jutted out his chin and puffed out his chest. "Because if I stayed, I was gonna punch somebody. He told me I was lazy." He crossed his arms, which resembled defiance, but with Travis the stance was more of a protective measure.

Gabe clenched his jaw. To hide his reaction, he turned to grab his coat and car keys. When he turned back, he'd managed to return to his neutral counselor face. Travis stood, knowing that despite his "never" comment, school was where he was going.

Gabe accompanied Travis to the office, explaining the situation to the assistant principal, Mr. Woods, then ushered a much calmer Travis on to his current class. Gabe entered the gym, where a group of noisy students were playing basketball. By the bleachers, a tall and—oh shit— muscular man in a tight blue T-shirt and body-hugging shorts stood watching their progress. The parade rest stance, stiff posture, and closely shorn black hair screamed military. That explained the asshole part.

As Gabe approached, the stiff man turned in his direction. Despite the glowering, Gabe was taken aback by the light hazel eyes framed with long dark lashes, the squared chin, the highly arched eyebrows, the full, kissable—

Gabe nearly stopped in his tracks with that thought. Only once in his life had Gabe experienced that gut-wrenching, immediate, heated attraction to another man, and that had been Tim. Now he could add this gorgeous, hard-muscled man to that list.

The man narrowed his eyes impatiently when Gabe failed to speak. "Yes?"

"Mr. Sawyer?" Gabe tried to deepen his voice. He felt miniscule next to the larger man, who had an undeniable air of authority.

Mr. Sawyer's eyes perused Gabe harshly from head to toe, as if sizing up the enemy. His body was eerily still. It was frightening and exhilarating at the same time. "Yeah."

Such an extensive vocabulary.

Gabe cleared his throat, struggling to rein in his raging attraction. He was there for Travis. "My name is Gabe Reynolds. I'm with the Westport Youth and Family Center and a counselor liaison with the school. I'd like to talk with you about Travis Parker."

The man's scowl remained. "Who?"

That question threw a bucket of water on Gabe's attraction. He bit hard on the inside of his cheek to retain his professional composure. "Travis Parker. You refused to let him sit out of class today."

Recognition flitted across the man's chiseled features. "As you can see, I'm in the middle of a class." He turned away, summarily dismissing Gabe with the action. That only boosted Gabe's resolve.

"Mr. Sawyer, I understand you're a long-term sub, so it's important we clear this up before Travis's next gym class. If you could give me five minutes, I'm sure we can resolve this misunderstanding."

Mr. Sawyer turned back to Gabe, raising an eyebrow, as if surprised by Gabe's insistence. Damn, if that cocked eyebrow wasn't sexy. After giving his whistle a sharp blow, Mr. Sawyer instructed the students to run drills. He walked away without further addressing Gabe, who could do nothing but follow the rude man into the office.

Mr. Sawyer leaned back against the desk, crossed his massive arms and legs, and waited. On his left bicep, the bottom of a black tribal tattoo peeked from under the sleeve of his tee. Tattoos definitely did it for Gabe. Endeavoring not to fidget nervously, Gabe clasped his hands behind his back, twining his fingers together.

He cleared his throat, praying his voice didn't squeak. "Travis has an understanding with Coach Wilson about certain gym activities he's uncomfortable with. In return, Coach Wilson gives Travis assignments to complete. I'm sure you weren't aware of this arrangement."

Mr. Sawyer rose to his full height. If they were outside, Gabe thought he'd probably block out the sun, which wasn't true since Gabe was only a few inches shorter. Why did the man feel so large?

"So while the rest of the class follows orders and participates, Travis breaks off from the group and does as he pleases?"

Follow orders?

Gabe feigned bravado in the shadow of the intimidating substitute. "Travis has certain issues I'm not able to discuss with you, but understand Travis isn't doing this to be difficult or to defy 'orders,' as you put it. He's working hard to overcome these barriers, and a little understanding from others goes a long way."

Mr. Sawyer frowned, and two dimples popped out on his cheeks. "Coddling kids maintains their weaknesses. Avoiding situations will not strengthen their character or allow them to rise above and become the best they can."

Said like a product of the military.

Gabe's heart rate increased, a warning his calm facade was in danger of cracking. "And calling them lazy will? This isn't boot camp, Mr. Sawyer. It's high school, and despite your errant beliefs, tough love doesn't cure everything. You have no idea what Travis has endured. If you did, you'd see strength of character that rivals anything your military beat into you. He's a survivor who hasn't quit even when the rest of the world has pretty much given up on him."

By the time he'd finished speaking, Gabe's hands were clenched into fists at his thighs and he leaned closer to the other man.

Mr. Sawyer continued his pointed stare at Gabe, who battled to maintain his position and not cower. Sweet Jesus, those hazel eyes were looking right through him.

Without removing his perpetual scowl, Mr. Sawyer relented. "Okay, Mr. Reynolds. I'll allow Travis to decide if he wants to participate in the assigned activities with his peers. In return, he'll complete assignments that I deem are replacements for his absence."

Why did that statement trip all kinds of warning bells in Gabe's head? He should have questioned what Mr. Sawyer meant. However, Gabe knew when to back down and call it a draw. He'd have to keep a close eye on Travis. Maybe visit his assigned gym class a few times. Check in on Mr. Sawyer.

Yeah, that part was 100 percent about Travis.

"I appreciate your willingness to help Travis. He's a good kid and really needs people on his side." Gabe tentatively held out his hand.

Mr. Sawyer eyed the appendage in much the same way Gabe imagined he would assess a weapon pointed at him. Deliberately, Mr. Sawyer extended his hand while keeping his eyes trained on Gabe's face. The warm palm slid against Gabe's skin, and fingers wrapped Gabe's hand tight in an almost painful grip. That heat zinged through Gabe's body and flipped his stomach, flushed his skin, which felt too tight, not to mention what was happening in his groin. In Mr. Sawyer's eyes, Gabe saw something akin to a challenge, but a challenge of what? There was a definitive physical attraction but—

"Yeah, well, next time call and make an appointment," Mr. Sawyer said gruffly, then left the office.

He couldn't stand the egotistical ape. Resisting the urge to let Mr. Sawyer know just what he thought about him, Gabe quit while he was ahead.

WHEN HE returned to the office, he remembered to touch base with Charles about Karen. That morning he'd called Karen at 8:00 a.m. and reminded her to take her pills and to eat. Her tone concerned him, but he had to admit she sounded better than she had on Saturday.

"Hello, Gabe. How're you?" Charles's tone sounded guarded.

"I'm good. You?" Gabe sat at his desk.

"Can't complain. I received your message and spoke with Karen. She'll be coming in tomorrow."

Gabe fiddled with a paper clip. "She's not doing well, Charles. When I went there on Saturday, she was in bed and the twins were alone downstairs. I checked her meds, and she's missed over half of them in the past two weeks."

Charles exhaled noisily. "I was afraid of that. Mary has been calling and trying to reschedule her missed appointment several times without success."

Gabe crushed the clip between his fingers. "Why didn't you call me? I could have made sure she made her appointments." Could have pulled his head out of his ass and done something other than pine for Tim.

A pause. "Gabe, you know I can't discuss Karen's case with you, much less tell you when she isn't making her appointments. The release she signed for me to talk with you expired quite a while ago."

Gabe would make sure she signed another one soon. "I need to make sure she's taking care of herself. The twins mean the world to her, and if something happened to take them from her, I don't know what she would do." When her depression worsened after the birth of the twins, Randy had taken the babies to his mother's to give Karen a break. Karen had accidentally taken too many meds in a short period of time and had needed to be hospitalized. While she said she hadn't meant to harm herself, Gabe hadn't been so sure.

"Karen is your ex-wife. Shouldn't her husband be taking care of this?"

"Do you see him calling you? He isn't making sure she takes her pills. He works long hours, so I doubt he's helping with anything in the house, including Karen. I've been trying to make sure she's doing what she needs." Well, except for the past two weeks, that was.

"She…. Damn it, Gabe, she didn't tell me any of this. To hear her speak, this guy is Prince Charming, who dotes on her and treats her like a queen. How can I help her if she isn't telling me the truth?"

Gabe pinched at the bridge of his nose. "It's probably what she wants to believe. We both know this affair and the resulting kids were during a manic phase. She had to live with me for over twenty years. I was emotionally unavailable and in the closet. Randy was a way out, a way to get the love and affection she needs. They barely knew one another when they got married."

"Tell me what I'm dealing with when she comes in."

"If I had been walking into someone else's house on Saturday, I would have called child protective services. I couldn't do that to her, which is why I'm doing everything I can to get her back to a functional level."

"Okay. I'll get her to sign the release at her next appointment. Just so you know, I'm going to push her for the truth about her husband and current level of depression. I'll do a suicide assessment as well. If I even suspect those kids are in danger, I have to do something. But I promise I won't do anything until I speak to you, okay?"

Gabe blew out the breath he swore he'd been holding since dialing Charles's number. "Thanks. I really appreciate that."

"Sure. Talk to you tomorrow."

Gabe hung up ready for a drink, but it was only eleven thirty. As he opened a report he needed to write, his mind went back to Mr. Sawyer. He didn't even know his first name, but he couldn't stop his mind from wondering how those hard pecs would feel under his palms.

"Shit." He so needed to forget the annoying, handsome man.

CHAPTER 4

THE NEXT morning Gabe checked in with Karen before heading to work. Afterward, Gabe made a second cup of coffee before heading to work. He'd tossed and turned, the issues with Karen and Travis and Mr. Sawyer keeping him up most of the night. He trudged through the morning with mind-numbing weariness. Tuesday afternoons had always seemed to beat him down, but since Tim, the effect had tripled. He looked forward to a few quiet hours to focus on progress notes. He was on his third cup of coffee of the day and could feel the twitchiness in his muscles from the caffeine. Maybe he should lay off the legal stimulant, but then he'd probably fall asleep at his desk.

The shrill ringing of his phone practically brought him out of his chair. He rubbed at his forehead, trying to moderate the rapid beating of his heart. He reached for the phone and checked the caller ID.

Julia Massier, the school principal.

Gabe exhaled wearily. "Hey, Julia. I'm assuming since you're calling my office line this isn't a social call." The chuckle he tried for fell flat.

A heavy sigh. "No, Gabe, I'm sorry. It's not. Travis got into an altercation in gym class. He's in the quiet room."

Gabe rubbed at the burgeoning knot at the back of his neck. "Is he going to be suspended?" Travis's father would flip if that happened again. Like most everyone else, the man was nearly at the end of his rope with Travis.

"I'm still sorting out what happened. I'm heading down to talk with Mr. Sawyer. Would you care to join me?" Gabe's snort brought a titter from Julia. "I heard you met our substitute gym teacher yesterday."

Gabe grunted at the word. The gorgeous man had definitely "substituted" for Tim lately in his fantasies. The idea of seeing Mr. Sawyer after the nefarious thoughts Gabe had been having was unnerving.

"Yeah, I met Mr. Personality. Recruiting from the military now, Julia?"

It was Julia's turn to snort. "He's actually good for many of the students who need strong direction. He may need to work on his people skills."

"What people skills?"

"I think you two got off to a bad start. Really, he's a nice guy. I like him, and you know that many of my teachers I can take or leave. Give him another chance."

Gabe wasn't so sure about that. "I'll be there in ten minutes."

"SERIOUSLY? YOU thought that was a good idea?" Gabe had practically shouted. He gripped the edge of the windowsill to keep from strangling the clueless man.

Mr. Sawyer stood across from Gabe in Julia's office while she attempted to referee the confrontation. Gabe had insisted on speaking with Travis before the meeting. The kid was a wreck, terrified of both his father's reaction to the fight and the principal forcing him to return to gym class.

"Gabe." Julia held up her hand. "Let Brandt finish."

Gabe gritted his teeth so hard his ears hurt. The arrogant, self-righteous... Jesus... good-looking asshole.

"What I thought was I had two men unable to see eye to eye. So I paired them up and required them to work together."

Gabe took a brave yet idiotic step toward Mr. Sawyer. The man looked as if he were ready to throttle Gabe. "No. What you did was pair one of the school's biggest bullies with the kid who's been his main target for years." How Gabe wished he could wipe that smug look off that handsome face.

"Now wait, Gabe. I think the concept was a good one. Actually, this school could use some team building between the students." Julia raised her hand again to stop Gabe's protest. She should just carry a stop sign. "However, in this case it did backfire."

"Because Travis didn't put in the effort." Mr. Sawyer crossed his arms, accentuating his large chest. "Gregg tried to get him to help, but the kid refused."

"Because Travis couldn't build your bridge or whatever you had them doing, he's at fault?" Gabe's voice rose with his growing irritation.

"No. Travis hit another student. That's why he's at fault."

Gabe's rage grew arms and legs, taking on a life of its own. He was a professional, but Mr. Sawyer evoked high levels of emotions in Gabe that he rarely experienced, lust being at the forefront. "Did you even talk with Travis? Get his side of the story?"

Silence, and then Mr. Sawyer shook his head. "He ran out of the gym, but several other students corroborated Gregg's story."

Gabe's fingers clenched at the fabric of his pants to force his hands to stay down. "Those students are Gregg's friends, and they'd say anything to back him up. There's your team building for you. They've got each other's back. Too bad it was at the expense of another team member. And I'm sure none of them heard Travis being called a… 'fag.'" Gabe hated that slur.

Mr. Sawyer flinched at the word. At least he'd had some sort of reaction.

"Yes, Mr. Sawyer, on top of all the other shit Travis has had to deal with, he's gay. He once made the mistake of showing interest in another boy, who he thought was reciprocating. Instead that boy told the entire school, and now Travis has to deal with the homophobic attitudes of not just some students and parents, but even some teachers. Are you one of those people, Mr. Sawyer?"

"Gabe." Julia's caution didn't halt Gabe's need to know which "Travis" category the substitute was in, pro or con.

Mr. Sawyer's eyes narrowed with a fiery rage that should have scared the bejesus out of Gabe, but he was too high on anger for any fear.

"I'm not a homophobe, Mr. Reynolds. In fact, it's a character flaw I find intolerable. Hate breeds fear and intolerance, which weaken the strongest men. A group is only as strong as its weakest member."

Gabe crossed his arms. "Nice speech. Bet they taught you that in the service. How about telling us how you really feel?"

Mr. Sawyer stepped closer, close enough that Gabe could feel the heat radiating off his body. "What a man or woman chooses to do in their private life is their own business. I measure a person by their integrity, respect for others, and fulfillment of their duties. Not by whom they choose to sleep with."

Gabe's breath caught. That heady, musky, all-male scent drew Gabe in as much as those mesmerizingly sharp yet sexy eyes.

"Okay." Julia's voice brought Gabe back to the room. "We have two issues here. There will have to be consequences for punching Gregg. I won't suspend Travis, but he'll have in-school suspension. As for Gregg calling him a… fag"—she hesitated to say the word—"that's a violation of our hate prevention policy, and we have to decide if we give him in-school or out. I vote for out, but then I'd like to ship him off to another school."

"Wait." Gabe knew what that would mean for Travis. "There's no one to back up Travis's claim that Gregg called him a fag. If you suspend Gregg, you'll not only make Travis out to be a snitch but open him up to all kinds of retaliation."

"While I agree, Gabe, something has to be done. I've never known Travis to say something happened that wasn't true, and I won't tolerate that hateful language in my school. You know I can't." Julia glanced meaningfully at Gabe.

As friends, she'd experienced firsthand what some people in town had called Gabe when he'd come out. Hateful and nasty slurs ignorantly spewed his way that had nothing to do with Gabe as a person. Those words had hurt worse than a stab of a knife, but what had cut him to the core was the mistrust. Some parents had refused to allow him to counsel their children, as if he'd recruit them to the gay side or, worse, was a sexual deviant. As a mental health professional, he could rationalize and theorize their attitudes, but as plain old Gabe? Plain old Gabe had never understood what he'd done to deserve their viciousness and hate.

"While you might not agree with my methods, Mr. Reynolds, what appears to be needed here is some character training. The Seven Core Army—"

"This isn't the Army." Gabe rolled his eyes in a less than professional manner.

"I'm very well aware that this isn't the Army."

God, how could Gabe dislike someone and be so attracted to him at the same time? Add to that the man was straight and you had Gabe's twisted life.

Mr. Sawyer went to the whiteboard and wrote "LDRSHIP. The Seven Core Army Values." He pointed to each letter of the acronym. "Loyalty, duty, respect, selfless service, honor, integrity, personal courage. All values we strive to personally attain and teach every kid. In the Army, soldiers live these values every minute of every day. Not just on the job."

Julia cocked her head. "I like the idea, but how do you turn it into something that's not just another lecture to zone out?"

Mr. Sawyer actually cracked a rueful smile. "As they do in the Army, with some basic training."

Gabe could only think that Brandt's idea was going to be a disaster.

WITH TRAVIS squared away and happy with in-school suspension,
Gabe left the school. As he climbed into his car, he received the call from
Charles he'd been dreading.

"Hi, Charles."

"Hey, Gabe. Karen just left. I have a signed release, so I'm not
going to mince words. I'm really concerned. She's highly depressed.
I couldn't assess any immediate threat; however her delusions of her
marriage and current level of functioning are disturbing. Despite my
pushing her to admit her statements weren't as truthful as she said, she
continued to claim what she was saying was true. Even confronted with
the fact that I was aware of what was possibly happening in the house,
she continued to get quite angry that I was challenging her."

"You think she believes what she's saying?" A scary thought, which
could point to a deeper psychosis than he'd originally thought.

"When I was with her, I didn't notice any extreme anxiety,
disorganized thoughts or speech, or hallucinations. Despite the crying
and lying in bed, there was no indication that she was anything more
than severely depressed. I got the impression that she might believe
what she's saying. Although she could also be protecting herself from
having to admit her marriage is failing. I had her psychiatrist, Dr.
Warner, meet with her, and he adjusted her Klonopin, as well as adding
Seroquel, which hopefully will address the acute episodes. I'm hoping
with following the medication routine and seeing me twice a week, we
can turn this around."

Great, another pill to keep track of. "So where do we go from here?"

"I'll be seeing her twice a week until we can get past this. She
will check in with Dr. Warner once a week. I told her that it's important
she come to these appointments and take her meds regularly to avoid
anyone questioning if the children are safe with her. She needs support
and low stress. Taking care of twins is stressful enough for someone who
is mentally stable. I told her to relay that to her husband, but I'm not sure
if she will."

He'd have to speak with Randy if Karen would let him. "Thanks,
Charles. Let me know if there is anything I can do."

"You got it. Talk to you later."

Gabe wasn't sure he could take any more excitement and decided to head home.

EXHAUSTED, GABE was thrilled to be home. Despite being worn out, his nerves thrummed with an uneasy energy. His meeting with Mr. Sawyer hadn't gone as he'd expected. While the man was utterly annoying and bristly, Gabe also found him to be forthright and respectable. He had that definitive leadership aura that drew people in and compelled them to follow. Right then Gabe was ready to follow Brandt anywhere and throttle him at the same time.

After a quick shower to clear off the grime of the day, Gabe crawled naked onto the bed and stretched out beneath the cool air of the ceiling fan. The breeze raised goose bumps across his arms and belly. Running his warm palm across his stomach, he wondered how rough Mr. Sawyer's—Brandt's—hands would feel. Damn, he yearned for the roughness of large hands stroking and rubbing and fondling him. Gabe pressed hard against a nipple and applied friction. He loved it rough, craved being forced, wrists held down, facedown on the bed, being slammed into from behind. Tim was the only one who'd fulfilled all those needs. But Gabe was sure the powerful, muscle-bound substitute gym teacher could easily handle him.

Gabe hissed as he pinched his nipple. Reaching down, he palmed his balls, rolling and teasing them before he would allow himself to touch his cock. After wetting a finger in his mouth, he reached between his thighs and ran the moistened fingertip over his tight, sensitive opening. His hips bucked at the sensation. Tim had been his last fuck, over two months ago. Patrick eight months before that. Gabe's need was high and bone-deep. Pushing the finger in without hesitation, Gabe groaned, then wrapped his other hand around his precum-slicked cock head and squeezed. His knees pulled up with the intensity of the sensation.

Quickly he added a second dry finger with the first, relishing in the burn. He scissored and stretched his hole, as if opening himself for a lover. Nerve endings fired and lit up his entire body. Spitting into his palm, he rubbed the overly sensitive skin of his throbbing cock, tired of having only his hand for a sexual partner. But this wasn't his hand. Brandt was stroking his prick, his massive fingers stretching Gabe's hole, pegging his prostate, working him into a heated frenzy, pushing him to that all-important orgasm.

"Please."

Gabe's ass clenched around the invading fingers. Brandt pulled hard on his cock, and Gabe reveled in the friction. As his balls drew closer to his body, the pleasure spread throughout his torso and legs. A shiver of recognition of what was to come raced from head to toe. Gabe raised his hips off the bed as Brandt's fingers fucked his hole hard and fast. Gasping, Gabe hung on the edge for one breath-stealing, bliss-filled moment as every muscle in his body stiffened with the promise of mind-shattering pleasure.

"Brandt." The name rushed out on his breath.

Gabe moaned and clenched his teeth as he fell into warm waves of ecstasy. Ropes of creamy cum lined his stomach, chest, and chin. Afloat, he convulsed and shook with one of the most explosive orgasms he'd had in years.

Chest heaving and muscles aching, he reveled in the postorgasmic haze until he recalled the name he'd uttered, the ghost man who'd brought him off. Brandt. Not Tim. The realization knocked him off-center, challenging his belief that only Tim could fill his needs. Not only had Tim been replaced in his fantasies, he'd been replaced with a straight, exasperatingly annoying man. Gabe groaned, wondering just how far from normal his life could get.

Chapter 5

WEDNESDAYS GABE ran three different lunch groups for students at the school who needed support. His last group of kids had just left. Julia had asked him to meet her before he headed back to his office. He stayed away from the gym and looked around every corner to avoid running into Brandt. Just as he was about to make the trek to Julia's office, his phone rang.

He answered. "Hi, Karen." The sounds of crying children reached through the phone. "Karen?"

"Gabe." He wasn't sure, but she sounded as if she was crying too. "Randy's worked late every night this week. I haven't gotten a break. The preschool's been closed because of a pinkeye outbreak. Is there any way you can spend some time with them? Give me a chance to catch my breath?"

Gabe headed back to the group room to get his coat and bag. "I don't have any appointments scheduled at work this afternoon. Let me take them to the playground, and get them dinner."

"Thank you. You don't know…. Just, thanks. I'll have them ready."

Gabe hung up and headed to Karen's. Within thirty minutes, he was back at the school, which had the best playground in the area, with a pair of excited twins. The kids had been cooped up all day due to their school closing. Luckily, the kids' eyes hadn't shown any signs of the infection.

"Slide!" Mikey bolted when they rounded the building. Maddy chased after him in her purple princess dress that she'd put on over her clothes. They both climbed the ladder to the slide.

"Be careful." Gabe positioned himself at the bottom. Mikey came down first, his arms raised over his head.

"Unca Gabe. Watch!" Maddy sat on the slide and raised her arms, imitating her brother. Her blonde curls flowed behind her as she giggled the entire way down.

"Yeah, Maddy!" Gabe scooped her up and spun her around, then set her down as she laughed.

Maddy went back up the slide as Mikey raced to the wooden jungle gym, smiling wide. Gabe grinned as he ran circles around the structure until he decided to climb the rope ladder that went to the top. The jungle gym was huge, with bridges, slides, an imitation rock wall, and poles to slide down. Large enough for a couple of classes of children. Luckily, they would have the playground to themselves until recess.

Maddy joined her brother on the jungle gym. Gabe sat on one of the benches, grinning as they played. Every once in a while, they yelled for Gabe to watch what they were doing. They were such sweet kids, and he never hesitated when given the chance to spend time with them.

"Cute kids."

A shiver raced over Gabe's skin, telling him exactly who was behind him even before turning. Brandt.

"Huh?" Jesus, could he be more lame? "I mean, sorry, I didn't hear you."

The corner of Brandt's mouth lifted. Damn, without his scowl he was even more gorgeous. Brandt pointed to the jungle gym. "I said you have some cute kids. Twins?"

Gabe opened his mouth and almost thanked him. He'd almost believed he could be their dad, and his heart had joined in the joy. "Yeah, they're twins. But no. They're my ex-wife's kids."

That brought a look of confusion to Gabe's face. "Doesn't that make them yours too?"

Gabe snorted. "Ask the furnace repair guy." More confusion on Brandt's face. Gabe wiped at his forehead. "I'm sorry. They aren't mine. My ex is remarried. Her current husband is their father."

Brandt cocked his head, appearing curious. "And you have the kids that belong to ex and her husband at the playground. Seems like there's a story there."

"You have no idea."

Gabe realized they were having a civil conversation instead of squaring off and shouting. Maybe Julia hadn't been far off when she said Brandt was a nice guy. Gabe was ready to bid the substitute teacher good-bye when Brandt plopped onto the bench next to him… very close next to him. Gabe froze, unsure what to do. His mind said run as he recalled jacking off to visions of the guy the night before. His heart raced, his skin tingled, and his groin warmed. Talk about hard up. When he shuddered from his proximity to Brandt, he was ready to kick his own ass. He had to get over that attraction, which was purely physical. Had to be.

They both settled back against the bench. Maddy waved to Gabe from the top of a tower. Gabe smiled and waved back. Mikey wrapped his arms and legs around one of the poles and slid down. The kid had no fear.

Brandt turned to Gabe. Even his inquisitive look was sexy. "So, Mr. Reynolds, you're hanging at the playground on a Wednesday afternoon. Sounds like fun."

Gabe felt small sitting next to Brandt, more like a student than an adult. Strange, because Gabe was only a few inches shorter than Brandt. Bulk was where he and Gabe differed—about fifty pounds of bulk. Strong. Strong enough to hold Gabe down and—

Gabe coughed and ran his hand through his hair.

"You okay? You're a little jumpy, Mr. Reynolds."

More like a teenager getting a boner over the school jock. Oh, those had been fun times. Seemed as if twenty-five years hadn't passed.

Wiping his palms on his thighs, he feigned a smile. "Sorry. I'm a bit distracted."

Distracted and attracted. Which would more than likely get him a beatdown. He sat back, sucked in his gut, and pushed out his chest for all of ten seconds. Exhaling, he tried not to focus on his out-of-shape body. Brandt was like Rambo or something.

"And, please. Call me Gabe."

The corner of Brandt's lip lifted, the amusement reaching his eyes. "Brandt."

Gabe knew he was grinning like a fool and dialed his reaction back a bit. "And actually, this is fun for me. I—"

Brandt lifted his hand. "I think you misunderstood." He looked to the kids with an expression that bordered on melancholy. "I love kids. Especially this age. They're so bright-eyed, curious, ready to take on the world." He snorted. "Too bad that world isn't as magical and wondrous as they believe it to be. But still…. You get to see it through their eyes, as if everything is brand-new. Gives you hope. It's quite amazing."

For a moment Gabe was sure if he looked at Brandt the man would see a sappy, lust-struck expression on his face. Any man who loved kids, well, tick another box in the Brandt column for Gabe.

"Do you have kids?"

"No. Was married to the military. Plus, I never really felt settled enough to take that step. I didn't want my kids to grow up without me." Brandt leaned back on the bench, still watching the twins. "Are you from Westport?"

Gabe got the feeling that the kids subject was off-limits for some reason. "I grew up here, went away to college, but came back. I love the lake and the mountains. Couldn't stay away."

"Where'd you go to school?"

"Northwestern."

"Go, Wildcats."

Gabe nodded and laughed. "Yeah, go Wildcats. Not that I was much into the sports side of college. More of a library dweller."

"Can't say I was a library dweller, being in the military. Joined when I was eighteen. But I've done my fair share of studies. Never been on campus. All of my degrees I earned online."

"So more than a trained government monkey?" Not that Gabe had ever felt that Brandt wasn't intelligent.

Brandt's brow creased, and Gabe feared he'd gone too far. "There's more to this awesome body than being a well-honed government weapon." His grin dazzled Gabe. "I took advantage of being the best I could be and grabbed hold of their military college opportunities a few times over."

"A few times?" Gabe turned on the bench with interest, his nervousness fading.

"Bachelor's in education with a minor in psychology. Master's in sports physiology."

"Hence, the subbing in phys ed."

"Yeah. I'm not sure what I'm looking to do. Just getting back into the civilian life." Brandt looked away, and a shadow crossed over his face. As quickly, the expression was gone. "Anyway. Here I am. And you said you're a counselor?"

Gabe nodded. "I work at the youth and family center in town. My caseload is kids around eight to eighteen. We're located up by the library."

There the conversation fizzled, but Gabe had something more he needed to say. "Listen, I know we clashed from the start. I tend to get a bit territorial when it comes to the kids I work with." Brandt would probably make fun of him for backing down or not persevering or some soldier crap.

Brandt held his gaze, but Gabe had to look away to catch his breath.

"You're persistent. Standing up for something you believe in is admirable. Like you said, Travis needed someone on his side. I guess I forgot what high school was like. Was treating the job more like the military." Brandt appeared contemplative. "I've spoken with some of the kids you work with, and they hold you in high esteem. You're making a difference to them."

Gabe felt his cheeks warm, and he ducked his head. "Not sure how much of a difference. The funding for the center keeps getting cut. We lost a counselor position last year."

Brandt sat forward, his gaze softer than Gabe thought his gruff exterior could obtain. "You're doing good work. Work that needs to be done. I may be all for forming character and being the best, but that doesn't help these kids get over crappy shit that happens to them when they're young. I've known a few men and women who've eaten the end of their guns, and not because of what happened in the military. Believe me, if you help one person avoid that, your time is well spent." Brandt sat back and wiped his hand over his mouth.

"Thanks. And I'm sorry for those you knew. We had a student here a few years ago complete suicide. He wasn't a kid I was counseling, but still I wish... I wish I could help them all."

The mood had become dour. Gabe was tired of living in the depressive rut of his life. He needed to work on moving on. "So can we call a truce?"

Brandt offered his hand, and Gabe slid his against the warm palm again. Brandt's shake was firm. "Truce."

Again their gazes locked, and Gabe knew why he was caught but figured a forthright, self-confident man like Brandt was used to looking others in the eye. That was why he maintained eye contact. Gabe had to keep his expectations realistic.

As if on cue, Mikey raced to them, hands cupped and held out before him. Gaze fixed on his palms, Mikey nearly impaled himself on Gabe's knees. "Whoa, there. Whatcha got?"

"Capetiller."

"Caterpillar." Gabe watched the fuzzy insect wend its way onto the sleeve of Mikey's jacket. Maddy raced over, hid beside Gabe, and eyed Brandt warily. "I want you to meet my friend Brandt. He's a teacher at the school. This is Mikey and Maddy."

"It's nice to meet you both. That's a great caterpillar."

"Yup." Mikey's eyes were wide. Wonderment covered his entire face. "Take home?" His wide-eyed hope went right to Gabe's heart. He wanted to give him everything.

"Probably best to let him go. He probably has a family, and they'll miss him." Gabe was also sure Karen wouldn't appreciate the insect in her house. "Why don't we put him back where you found him so he can find his way home." Given the sad look on the kid's face, Gabe prayed there wouldn't be a meltdown.

Brandt saved them from the impending tantrum. "We can find some nice leaves for him to eat, okay?"

Mikey's eyes lit up. "He eat leaves?"

"Oh yeah, they love leaves. Big, green, juicy ones. Come on."

Mikey followed Brandt past the jungle gym, and they stopped at the edge of the woods. Maddy clutched Gabe's arm, her gaze following them as they went.

"Do you want to watch them let the caterpillar go?"

"Uh-huh."

They arrived just in time for the caterpillar to climb off Mikey's hand.

Brandt crouched down to Mikey's level. "See. He likes the leaf you chose for him."

Mikey smiled wide. "He my friend."

Brandt laughed, his smile wide. "Oh, you're most definitely his friend now." Brandt raised his hand. "High five."

Mikey smacked his hand, then jumped up and down. "My friend." Over and over, he sang the words.

Maddy pulled on Gabe's hand. "Hosey wide."

Gabe groaned. "I would, honey, but my old back wouldn't be too happy." The last time he'd given them horse rides, he'd spent the night on the heating pad.

Brandt turned his back to Maddy, knelt, and then looked over his shoulder. "Hop on, Princess Maddy. I'll be your horse."

Maddy shook her head and, in all seriousness, pointed to the ground. "Hosey down."

Gabe tilted his head back and laughed. Brandt raised a brow. Maddy, having lost her shyness, went behind Brandt and pushed on his back until he was on his hands and knees.

Brandt looked to Gabe. "Footman, can you help Princess Maddy onto her horse?"

"Why certainly." Gabe lifted her onto Brandt's back. She giggled as he started to move and whinny like a horse.

"Me! Me!" Mikey tried to climb on.

"Whoa, horsey." Gabe lifted Mikey, and he sat behind Maddy.

"Go!" Maddy kicked her feet and squealed as Brandt crawled around the jungle gym. Mikey shouted for him to go faster and then said something about dragons. Brandt stayed in character, neighing and following their direction to go this way and that. And damn if Brandt wasn't ticking more boxes.

The bell sounded for the end of the period, and Brandt stopped. "That's my cue. I have to get back inside."

Both kids let their disappointment be known as Gabe removed them from their horse.

Gabe stuffed his hands into his pockets. "Thanks for being the horse. If I got on my knees, I might not get back up for a while. Happens when you're old."

Brandt easily rose from the ground. "Pfft. You're far from old." He turned to the kids and held his hands up. "Thanks for the fun." The kids each slapped a palm. "Maybe we can do this again, soon."

Gabe met Brandt's gaze, and for a moment he was trapped like a fly in a web, lost in the depth of those almond-shaped hazel eyes. He forced himself to look away and shuddered. He definitely wouldn't turn down another playdate.

"Good to see you again, Gabe." Brandt saluted and jogged toward the school. Gabe drew in a deep breath and released the air slowly. Why was life so unfair?

"Okay. To the car. We're going to the diner."

The kids shouted their approval and raced Gabe to the car, and they were off to their favorite place to eat.

A COUPLE of hours later, they pulled into the driveway of his old house. Randy's truck was in the driveway, and Gabe's gut clenched. Randy probably wouldn't be thrilled he had the kids. Mikey ran through the front door. Maddy had passed out in the car, and Gabe carried the princess into the house. Karen met him inside the door.

"Hey. She's out like a light."

Gabe shifted the sleeping Maddy into Karen's arms. "Thanks, Gabe." She had whispered. Had that been for Maddy's sake or so Randy wouldn't hear? "I'll call you tomorrow."

Gabe looked into the living room, but he only saw Mikey playing with his trucks.

"Is everything okay?" Despite Randy not being fond of him, he generally said hello when Gabe was there.

"Randy's tired. He just got home. I'm going to give the kids a bath and get them to bed. Give him some quiet."

Gabe raised his brow. Quiet? He barely spent time with them as it was. "You have an appointment tomorrow?"

She nodded. "At nine. Again, thanks."

Gabe had no choice but to leave. He leaned forward and kissed Maddy on the head. "Bye, Mikey."

Karen visibly flinched with the volume of his voice. Gabe might have done that on purpose.

"Bye, Unca Gabe." Mikey waved, then went back to pushing his monster truck.

Gabe went to his car, thinking about what Karen had told Charles about her marriage. Randy was well-known in Westport. No one had ever said a bad word about him, so Gabe wasn't concerned that he was hurting Karen. But something was going on between the two of them. The worry wanted to settle in, but he wouldn't allow it to take residence. His afternoon had been good, and he was going to enjoy escaping his mourning for Tim. Even if that feeling wouldn't last.

He smiled as he drove home, memories of Brandt playing with the kids fresh in his heart. Someday he had to find someone he actually had a shot with. Until then he'd live in his fantasies.

CHAPTER 6

FRIDAY AFTERNOON arrived with little fanfare. Thursday night, Gabe had stopped at the house hoping to catch Randy, but not surprisingly, he was working late. Gabe had to admit Karen's affect had been good. The kids had appeared well cared for, the house had been clean and dinner on the stove. Gabe hoped she was finally heading out of the depression.

The last few days had been uneventful. Gabe tried not to revel in that peace, because the moment he relaxed, the world would end. With the weekend almost upon him, Gabe was looking forward to leaving the workweek behind and Brandt with it. He'd foolishly allowed himself to fantasize about the ex-soldier to the point that he'd spaced out during a counseling session. He needed to get a grip and leave thoughts of Brandt behind.

At the end of the school day, Gabe checked in with Travis. The usually sullen teen had a glint in his green eyes and a slight smile on his lips. Missing were the two dominant states he generally vacillated between—the me-against-the-world scowl and the lost, lonesome boy. He'd expressed gratitude to Gabe for talking the principal out of suspending Gregg. The beatdowns probably would have been massive, he'd told Gabe. He had to agree.

From Travis's reaction, gym class was going better for the kid. His admission that Mr. Sawyer wasn't a bad guy had raised Gabe's eyebrows. Travis rarely had much to say about anyone. He went on to rave about some kind of obstacle course and team-building activities. A rare wide grin had split his usually stoic features as he'd boasted about his team coming out on top three times already. Though initially wary of Brandt's methods and his assertion that positive results would follow, Gabe couldn't ignore the turnaround in Travis about gym class. Could it all be attributed to some modified military training? Gabe wasn't totally convinced, even given Travis's complete one-eighty. But he had to give credit where credit was due.

As Gabe shut off his computer at the end of the day, his cell phone rang. Thinking Betsy was calling to check in, he answered without looking at the caller. "Hello."

"Hey, Gabe."

"Ahh, Julia. Happy Friday. Since you're calling my cell, I'm guessing you're not on official business?" He tensed, waiting for the world to end—or at least his quiet Friday night.

"All is calm on the school front. A few of us from school are going to the Wooden Nickel for drinks. I need your buffer skills." The pleading in her voice was undeniable.

While Julia enjoyed getting drinks with her coworkers, once alcohol loosened lips, she—being the principal—often became the target of every gripe and complaint from the overworked and underpaid staff. Gabe was there to change the subject or offer a distraction. He wasn't in the mood to wrangle drunk teachers and ruin his good mood. But when he thought of how Julia had never failed to come through for him, he couldn't say no.

Gabe sighed, rubbing his hand over his gritty, fatigued eyes. "What time?"

"Six thirty. Thanks, Gabe. I owe you one."

"Let me go home and get cleaned up. I'll meet you there."

One drink and then he was going home.

AT SIX twenty-nine, Gabe parked in the lot behind the Wooden Nickel. The bar was just outside of town and a popular hangout for the older crowd. Gabe went straight to the bar and ordered a Switchback. The dim lights and lack of windows belied the bright sunshine he'd just left. In the corner, the jukebox played low enough for comfortable conversation. A few regulars hung at the bar. Because he was so early, the place was practically empty. Stan, the bartender, pointed Gabe to the back room, knowing why he'd come. A larger than usual group crowded around a few tables. Taking a drink from his beer, Gabe navigated round empty tables to the group. He recognized most of the teachers and administrators. Some of the faces were new.

"Gabe, glad you could make it." Tomas Young, the school superintendent, rose and held out a hand.

Gabe shook his hand. "Nice to see you, Tomas. It's been a while."

Tomas laughed heartily. "The wife is out of town with the kids, so I'm walking on the wild side. I might even stay out until ten."

"I might not make it that long." Gabe already wished he were home. Julia waved him over and pulled out the chair she'd reserved for him. Gabe pointed in her direction. "I'm being summoned." Gabe patted Tomas on the shoulder and rounded the table. He plopped into the chair.

"Thank God you're here." Julia's face was flushed, and there were two empty glasses in front of her. A full one was in her hand. "We got here a little early. Speaks to what a shitty workweek it was."

"I hear ya."

Gabe surveyed the woman who'd been his friend for over ten years. Her golden blonde hair, usually pulled into a tight, no-nonsense bun, lay loose and soft along her shoulders. The top few buttons of her gray dress shirt were undone, revealing ample cleavage she never allowed to see the light of day in school. Not a petite woman, she resembled the curvy pinup girls from the forties. Her wide light gray eyes were inviting and friendly.

Gabe took a drink of his beer. "So where's Dave number two?"

Julia waved her hand in the air. "Work, home, somewhere."

"Uh-oh, is there trouble brewing in the 'D' paradise again?"

Julia threw him a look of spite.

Gabe held up his hands. "Sorry. I can't help it if you jumped on the D train and didn't get off. Or is it the Dave train now?"

Julia slapped his arm. "Could you cut out the D crap? There weren't that many."

"Six in a row, the last two having the same name."

"Okay. Maybe I'm in a rut."

"Try a crater, but hey, I'm on your side. So is Dave number two going to make it?"

She sipped her drink. "That remains to be seen."

Gabe tipped his beer at her. "Doesn't sound good for D two."

"Yeah, well, what about you? You look like shit." She crinkled her brow.

"Leave it to you not to mince words." Gabe shrugged a shoulder. "Same old. Karen's having a hard time, so I've been helping with the twins."

Julia gave him a speculative look. She liked Karen, understood their situation, had been there for the past ten years. She wasn't afraid to tell him he was too involved with his ex.

"Let's just not talk about that. I really need a break."

Julia nodded and lifted her glass of wine. "Yes, let's hide from life for one night."

Gabe clinked his beer with her glass. A conversation happening down the table caught his attention.

Tish Lambert, high school English teacher, spoke in her thick Brooklyn accent. Her black hair was teased as high as humanly possible. Her bright red lipstick exaggerated the paleness of her skin. "I went into the gym the other day, and he's got them building these towers in groups. You could tell he picked the groups. He had the jocks working with the nerds and the stoners with the achievers. A-ma-zing."

Dan Smyth, the science teacher, snorted, the wrinkles at the corners of his eyes more apparent with his amusement. He was the same age as Gabe but a bit rougher around the face.

"This morning, when I left my classroom, I heard the loudest noise coming from the gym. So I headed across the hall to break something up, you know? When I get there, I see two kids climbing the ropes, and the rest of the class is screaming at them to get their asses to the top." He leaned forward as if ready to divulge something in secret. "You know who one of those kids on the ropes was?"

Tish shook her head, her helmet of hair not moving a bit. By now most of the table had quieted to hear the conversation about the new substitute gym teacher. "Randal McKinley. And get this. He beat Derek Louis to the top."

A chorus of guffaws and gasps of disbelief sounded from around the tables.

"No way. Little Randal McKinley beat macho man Derek Louis to the top?" Allison Stone, the special ed teacher, asked. The look of amazement on her young face mirrored those of the others.

"How the heck did he do that? A stiff wind could blow the kid over." Julia's eyes were wide as she sipped at her mixed drink, having gone to something harder than wine.

"Never underestimate your opponent or the effect of having a team on your side." From behind Gabe, that deep whiskey tone sent chills racing up Gabe's spine. His hand clutched his beer bottle as he wavered between excitement and dread that Brandt was there.

"Ah, Brandt, glad you can join us." Julia plastered a huge grin on her face as she turned to greet him.

Several of the women around the tables—married and single—placed that same goofy grin on their faces. Apparently the new substitute had the same effect on the women as he had on Gabe. Christ, he wasn't going to make it through the night.

"There's an empty chair right here." Allison patted the vacant seat beside her. Her doe eyes shone up at the man who probably would have a good six inches on her. That chair put Brandt practically across from Gabe. As Brandt rounded the group of tables, Gabe noticed how his black button-up shirt pulled tight across his chest, and envisioned those tight jeans doing the same across his ass.

Sitting, Brandt greeted each person he knew and received an introduction to those he didn't. Gabe pulled at the label on his bottle and, when it was his turn, looked up confidently. The intensity in those hazel eyes never failed to stir butterflies in his stomach and make him catch his breath.

"Reynolds." Brandt gave him a curt nod.

"Sawyer." Gabe dipped his chin, trying to hide what he knew amounted to nervous excitement on his face. So much for forgetting the man.

"We were just talking about what you're doing with your classes. I believe it's been very effective so far." Tish leaned closer to Brandt, her blooming cleavage apparent even from across the table. Wow, she was subtle.

Brandt appeared to lean away from her. Did the woman unnerve him? "Well, it's only been a couple of days, but the kids are really getting into the spirit. Actually, I have Gabe to thank for the inspiration."

Gabe choked on his beer hearing his name fall from those perfect lips. "Huh?" A couple dozen eyes, trained on Gabe, caused him to shift in his seat. "I mean, you're welcome."

Brandt cocked that eyebrow, which definitely had a direct connection to Gabe's groin. Gabe could swear he saw a twitch at the corners of Brandt's mouth.

Gabe started on the second beer that had magically appeared in front of him. Talk continued around him as he consciously worked to avoid Brandt's gaze. Soon he finished the second beer and started on a third. He glanced to Julia, who gave him a knowing look. At this rate, he was heading for a good drunk. Heaven knew he was due.

As the night progressed, the bar filled to capacity, the volume of the music increased, and Gabe started to relax. Across from Gabe, Brandt tried to converse with others while the two single women on either side of him kept him busy with thousands of questions.

"How long were you in the Army?" Allison gazed at Brandt with great interest. The only thing Gabe had ever seen her interested in were her shoes. He'd bet his left nut that the ones on her feet cost more than he paid for rent in a month. Definitely a sign of her daddy's money and not her teacher's salary.

"Seventeen years." Brandt took a sip of his Saranac.

The answer surprised him. Brandt's youthful appearance, in Gabe's estimation, had placed him near thirty. Seventeen years in the Army had to place him in at least his midthirties.

"That's close to that magic twenty," Dan said. "Why not stay the course?"

A subtle twitch in Brandt's jaw contradicted the composed exterior. "Just time to get out." He shrugged and chugged what remained of his beer.

Gabe wondered what his story was. Betsy had stayed in the service for eight years. Seventeen years spoke of someone in it for the long haul, someone who thrived on the regimented lifestyle, believed wholeheartedly in the mission, lived and breathed the military. Now he was subbing in a high school gym class. Didn't fit.

Gabe remained outside the fringe of the conversations. Commenting when asked but mostly listening. Every so often, he would catch Brandt's gaze and become locked in his pointed stare. As their eyes met again, Brandt raised his Saranac to his lips and took several long pulls. Gabe watched the glide of his Adam's apple, imagined that throat swallowing and squeezing around his cock. Intently, Gabe stared as Brandt lowered the beer and, with what seemed great deliberation, swept his tongue along his sweet lips. Gabe's enthralled gaze followed as the pink muscle glided from one side of his mouth to the other. Balls, he was getting hard. And drunk.

Glancing up again into those absorbing eyes, Gabe startled, realizing what he'd been doing. Jumping up, he knocked the table with his thighs, tipping some of the drinks. A chorus of protest went up.

"Hey, big guy. Take it easy." Julia grabbed her teetering drink. "You okay?"

Gabe nodded and only managed to mutter, "Bathroom."

Gabe rushed to the men's room and locked himself in a stall. He pressed his sweat-sheened forehead against the cool metal of the door and let out a ragged breath. The night was going so horribly wrong. He envisioned Brandt meeting him in the parking lot and cleaning his clock for his conspicuous gawking. He was going to have to avoid him for the rest of the night.

After relieving himself and washing up, he circumvented the table and went to the bar. He hadn't meant to drink anymore but couldn't bring himself to leave. When Stan set the beer down, Gabe reached for his wallet.

"I've got it. And give me a Saranac." Brandt laid the money on the bar.

Someone really hated Gabe.

"Thanks." Gabe tilted the bottle to him and then drank half. His throat had never been drier, and with the buzz he had going, he feared he'd say something stupid.

Brandt picked up his beer. "Shoot a game of pool?"

Gabe couldn't halt the bark of laughter. "Me? I can't play when I'm sober, much less with a buzz."

Brandt lifted the corner of his lips. "Well, I guess I'll just have to take advantage of you while you're drunk."

Gabe's mouth dropped open, and he knew Brandt hadn't meant the innuendo he'd heard.

"Come on. Table's open."

Reluctantly, or maybe not, Gabe followed Brandt as he wove through the crowd to the pool table, eyes glued on that luscious ass, which confirmed his earlier theory of those tight pants. Why was he torturing himself like this?

CHAPTER 7

BRANDT PUT in his quarters and racked the balls. All Gabe had to do was keep from staring and he'd be fine.

"You're gonna have to break. I suck at that too."

Brandt smiled. "Just playing for fun. Don't get your panties in a knot."

Gabe chuckled and tried to relax. Around them, people shouted to compete with the loud music. However, Gabe was so focused on his pool opponent that the noise was a distant rumble.

Brandt broke and ended with solids. He lined up his next shot and sunk that ball. When he moved in front of Gabe and bent over to line up his shot, ass front and center, time seemed to stand still. Gabe flushed, turned on his stool, and gulped down his beer.

"Here." Brandt held out the cue stick.

Grateful for the distraction, Gabe walked around the table, assessing his options. Brandt sat back against a stool, arms and legs crossed. His gaze was like a heated beam on Gabe, bringing back his nervousness. He shook his shoulders and decided to go for cool and unruffled.

As he lined up his shot, Brandt spoke. "I had fun on the playground the other day. Those kids are great."

Gabe snapped the cue, and the ball bounced off the side of the hole and actually fell in. "Yes." He surveyed the table. "That they are."

"But you said they aren't yours. You don't have any kids?"

Gabe checked the angle of the shot with his stick. "No. My ex and I weren't able to have kids."

"How long were you married?"

Gabe kept his head down and took a shot. Another striped ball obeyed and went into the pocket. That was good. Keep him occupied. "Eighteen years." *Long years.* "Together since college."

Actually, he'd grabbed ahold of the first girl interested in him and held on tight. What had ended his relationship with Tim at the end of high school, had crushed Gabe's dreams of being with Tim forever, was Tim outing Gabe to someone they knew. And then everyone had known. The shit had hit the fan at home.

"That's too bad it didn't work out. I don't mean to pry, but what happened?"

Gabe lined up another shot. "I could say the furnace repair guy, but really our marriage had been over long before he came along." Another shot and a miss. He handed the cue to Brandt and hopped back onto his stool.

Brandt grabbed the chalk and rubbed the blue cube over the end of the cue. "So, the furnace repair guy is their father?"

"Yeah. She had an affair, and lo and behold he gave her what I couldn't. Even if she had gotten pregnant by me, at that point we were merely roommates. We kept trying until the end, but…. Well, anyway, you're real dad material. The twins couldn't stop talking about 'Bwant' at dinner."

Brandt sank two solids with one shot and laughed. Such a sweet sound. "If you happen to hit the playground again, let me know. I play a mean dragon."

Gabe grinned wide, but that faded quickly as he remembered he couldn't crush on the man.

Another ball down and Brandt continued his table domination. His muscles bunched beneath his black shirt, the sleeves pulled up over his massive forearms.

"So, even though your ex cheated, you're on good terms? I mean, you're taking the twins and spending time with them, so you must be. And I can tell how much they love you."

Gabe didn't want to get into Karen's mental illness. Besides, he barely knew Brandt. "Like I said, we really were just going through the motions. Her cheating didn't hurt. It was the fact that she had children with someone else…." Gabe felt like there was a fist around his throat. He coughed as tears burned his eyes. Shit.

He jumped off the stool. "I'm gonna hit the head." He was off before Brandt could say a word. Every time he drank, there was that moment when the good buzz turned bad and his emotions took over. That meant it was time to head home. He returned to the table and grabbed his jacket. He bent to whisper in Julia's ear. "I have to go. I'll call you tomorrow."

She grasped his wrist and gazed up at him, her expression taut with worry. "Are you okay? You seem off."

"I'm just tired." Don't forget horny and confused and guilty for sneaking out.

She surveyed his face for a moment, looking for some clue, and then smiled weakly. He would definitely be hearing about his quick departure later. "All right, but call me tomorrow."

Gabe nodded and kissed her cheek. Giving a general wave to the table, he headed for the front door, the opposite direction of the pool table. Gabe stepped out into the cool night air. Man, he'd been suffocating in there.

Making his way to the parking lot behind the bar, Gabe passed the covered patio used for outdoor parties. Movement out of the corner of his eye caught his attention. In the darkness, Brandt leaned casually against one of the posts. Shit.

Apparently he'd known about Gabe's plan to bolt. Ignoring any fear of retribution for staring, Gabe stopped for a moment, waiting for Brandt to approach him. When Brandt didn't move, Gabe went to his car, pulled out his keys, and hit the button to unlock it. As he reached for the door handle, a hand covered his. Gabe yanked his hand away as if he'd been burned, and turned reflexively, ready to defend himself. Adrenaline flooded his system, ready for the fight-or-flight portion of the evening.

Brandt loomed dangerously close. The security light at the back of the lot cast shadows across Brandt's expressionless face. It was really quite unnerving.

"Brandt. You scared the shit out of me."

Brandt actually smirked. "Sorry. I didn't realize how quiet I was being."

It was Gabe's turn to cock an eyebrow. "Yeah, well, there's no need to use your stealthy superpowers on me. I'm just a harmless middle-aged man."

Brandt frowned. "Middle-aged? Again with the old. You're like what, thirty-five or thirty-six?"

Damn, if that had been a line, Gabe would have fallen for it. "Uh, not quite that young."

Brandt narrowed those hazel eyes at Gabe. "You said you were heading to the bathroom. You didn't say you were leaving."

Gabe clenched his fist, his keys digging into his palm and bringing some clarity to his head. "I didn't realize the time. I usually don't stay out so late. Sorry. I asked Julia to tell you good-bye."

Brandt was still, too still, but then shifted on his feet and looked around the parking lot. His pink tongue came out again to swipe his bottom lip, only this time it appeared to be more of a nervous gesture.

Brandt stepped closer and leaned against the door of Gabe's car. Even relaxed, he looked stiff and uptight.

"I wanted to ask you something."

Gabe swallowed hard around the egg-sized lump in his throat. "Ask me what?"

Brandt shrugged. "I was hoping we could grab a coffee or possibly dinner sometime."

The statement took Gabe with unmitigated surprise. "Grab what?"

Brandt flashed a smile. Balls, that was nice. "Coffee or dinner, you know, that meal at the end of the day. You and me sometime, unless I read you wrong."

"Read me wrong?" *He can't be asking....*

Brandt motioned between them. "You and me…. The attraction."

Gabe felt his eyes widen and without thought stepped back. "Oh shit. You think I'm gay?"

"You're not?" Confusion mired Brandt's expression, but then he took another step toward Gabe, closing the distance between them.

Gabe took another step back. Was Brandt asking him out? Was this a trap? Get the gay guy to hit on the straight guy and then call foul. He thought of Travis's interest in the boy who'd outed him to the entire school and just how dangerous attraction to the wrong person could be.

"No… I mean, yes. I'm gay. What of it?" Gabe took a final step back and ran into the chain-link fence encompassing the lot. Trapped like a rat, a gay rat, by the huge scary cat.

Brandt stepped up and stood toe-to-toe with Gabe. Their bodies—their groins—were inches from one another. All available oxygen whooshed away as Gabe's heart beat relentlessly against his ribs. Brandt raised his oversized hand and, with surprising gentleness, grasped Gabe's chin. Electric sparks raced along Gabe's nerves, sending tingling zigzags throughout his body. Gabe pushed his hips into the fence to prevent his burgeoning erection from accidentally brushing against Brandt. Those gentle fingers lifted Gabe's chin higher and angled it to the side. Brandt's lips came closer. His dark eyes hooded and then closed when their lips met in an uncertain touch.

Hell, Brandt was kissing him!

Brandt's tongue ventured out and traced the seam of Gabe's lips. Lowering his lids, Gabe reveled in the warm caress as heated breath feathered across his face. Gabe wrapped his fingers around the links of the fence to stop himself from climbing Brandt and rutting against him.

The pressure on his lips intensified, and Brandt's probing tongue sought entrance to Gabe's mouth. Willingly Gabe opened, and their tongues immediately tangled in an erotic dance. And—oh, God in heaven above—Gabe's cock throbbed inside of his jeans. He fought to keep his hips from bucking forward. As the kiss hit about an eight on the Richter scale, Gabe's chest heaved as he panted into that luscious mouth. What had started as a shy, tentative kiss had quickly escalated into an increasing battle for domination. Gabe would gladly surrender to Brandt's forceful will if he gave Gabe what he needed. Without forethought, Gabe released his death grip on the wire of the fence and placed his wrists next to his ears, palms up.

Breathlessly, he commanded in between kisses, "Grab my wrists."

Brandt complied but tried to pull Gabe's arms down. Gabe resisted. Gasping wildly, Gabe glanced up at Brandt. His gut clenched with the burning heat in those sensuous eyes.

"Hold them there."

Brandt took a moment to catch on, then pressed his palms against the insides of Gabe's wrists and wrapped his long fingers around the wire of the fence. Gabe tested the movement of his trapped wrists. Not a centimeter of give. Gabe closed his eyes and, with a guttural groan, rejoiced in the feeling.

Yes, fuck, yes.

Brandt whispered into his ear, "You like that, do you? Like being restrained… held down?"

The question rushed more blood to Gabe's already engorged cock, and his hips bucked forward as a whimper left his throat.

"Oh yeah, you do."

Brandt growled, lining up their bodies, joining thighs, chests, stomachs, groins. Thoughts chased one another around Gabe's head. Wire from the fence dug into his shoulders, back, and buttocks as he was effectively pinned beneath the massive body, and sweet Jesus, he loved it all.

Pushing his aching erection into Brandt's groin, Gabe sought the necessary friction to get himself off. In response, Brandt pressed his muscular body harder, squeezing the air from Gabe's lungs, making a deep breath impossible. The lack of oxygen caused Gabe's head to swirl, intensifying the euphoric high. Lips trailed kisses down his neck, and teeth worried his skin. What was Brandt doing to him? Any minute Gabe was going to come in his pants. He wished he could claim his last cum-soaked pants had been in his teens, but making out with Tim during their reunion, he'd released over twenty-five years of pent-up frustration.

Fuck, Tim.… Get out of my head!

"Brandt." Gabe's whispered word was as much of a reminder of who he was with as his need for release.

Lips returned to his ear. "I've gotcha. Let it go, Gabe."

Hearing his name in that husky, lust-soaked voice increased Gabe's frenzied thrusts. His cock chafed against the inside of his underwear and jeans. Riding that knife's edge, he was so close but couldn't fall.

The hands around his wrists tightened. The body against his pushed with greater force, cutting off all air. Brandt's hard cock dug into Gabe's pelvis. Heaven. He had to be in heaven. Wave after wave of ball-twisting pleasure shook his body, filling every cell. Close, he was so close, so close.…

"Come on," Brandt whispered.

Gabe let out a barely audible cry, and the euphoric bliss detonated with white-hot heat from his balls, like an exploding star. Lights flashed in the darkness behind his eyelids as his muscles convulsed with his release. Endorphins rushed his system, drugging him. For a moment, Gabe floated, sated, in the amniotic warmth of his orgasm, weightless and content, at peace. One at a time, his senses returned from their fractured state. A shushing noise filled his ears. The cold air chilled his sweat-dampened skin and hair. Shudders jolted through him. His cheek rested against Brandt's hard shoulder. Brandt's strong arms wrapped gently around Gabe, effectively holding him up as he worked to catch his breath. Tears—fuck. He was crying.

Gabe scrambled on wobbly legs, falling back into the chain-link fence that swayed beneath his force. His fingers grasped the wire to hold himself up.

What the fuck did I do?

"Are you okay?"

No, I'm not okay. He was embarrassed and confused.

Gabe looked about wildly, wondering who had witnessed the mind-numbing bliss that had dismantled him and torn him apart. The parking lot was still empty, but how could he…? What did he…? *Home. Have to get home.*

Concern stretched across Brandt's face. "Gabe, don't leave. Let's talk."

Gabe didn't know what to think, what to do. He wouldn't be a one-night stand. Couldn't be. He saw himself heading down the same path he had with Tim.

"I gotta go," Gabe mumbled. He rushed past Brandt, trying to keep his balance since his equilibrium was for shit.

He wiped away any evidence of his unacceptable tears with the back of his hand. Yanking his keys from his pocket, he was in the car and had the engine roaring when Brandt knocked on the window. Ignoring him, Gabe slammed the car into reverse and left the person who'd just knocked his world off its axis. With him, Gabe carried enough humiliation for that entire world.

CHAPTER 8

GABE STARTED the shower, then peeled off his clothes. The heat of the spray did little to relax his hunched shoulders and quivering muscles. Brandt had thrown him so far off-center, he no longer felt like himself, as if he didn't fit inside his own skin. The inability to process and compartmentalize the experience, which had expanded to fill his every thought, was unnerving.

He'd sworn off relationships, and that was the problem. What he'd done with Brandt had, more than likely, been the beginning of a one-night stand. Brandt stirred so many emotions, kicking up their dust until they swirled about him and threatened to choke the life out of him. Despite that, he hadn't felt so alive in…. Well, never. His entire being thrummed with a soul-deep resonance that threatened to lift him from the dark pall he'd been cloaked in for so long. Why did it feel like he'd just found something special in a darkened parking lot behind a bar?

No. The only thing people found behind bars were quick fucks. Gabe was still raw and inflamed from the loss of Tim, and now Brandt had burrowed beneath Gabe's skin. The magnitude of what he was feeling expanded and crowded his insides. With Brandt, he'd only be heading for another broken heart. He'd latch on to the guy and expect something more where there was nothing. Man, he had to be the stupidest gay man alive. What he'd found since coming out was that many gay guys weren't relationship material, and if they were, they weren't relationship material for him.

The hot water beating on his back morphed into an icy torrent, carrying with it a reality that stung just as great. Muscles that had attempted to relax now bunched and contracted in the cold. Gabe forced himself to shut off the water as his teeth chattered. He grabbed a towel and mechanically worked to rid his body of the wetness. In the mirror, he caught sight of his haunted stare. Exhausted but wired, he was ready to jump out of his skin while feeling too tired to move.

Lucky enough to live far from his neighbors, Gabe dropped his iPhone into the dock and cranked up the volume, attempting to drown out the obsessive thoughts ravaging his skull. Lying on his bed, he pulled the pillow over his head, trying to focus on anything other than Brandt.

His phone vibrated. Gabe pulled the pillow off his head, fearing to even look at the phone. Brandt didn't have his number. Julia knew he'd gone home. Could be Karen, and that thought had him checking his phone. It was Karen.

"Hey, Karen. Are the kids okay?"

"Yes. They're sleeping."

The tremble in her voice wasn't something he could ignore. "What's wrong?"

Her sigh was troubled. "When you found out I was cheating on you, did you feel really bad?"

Gabe sat up and leaned against the headboard. "I don't understand what you're asking."

She sniffed. "I cheated on you. It felt really terrible, I know that now, and I'm so sorry."

"Karen, we were… our relationship was practically over. I was a gay man trying to be straight, trying to do the right thing, but I lied to you. I couldn't love you like you needed, like you deserved. I don't blame you."

Another sniff and he heard her blow her nose. "I didn't know how horrible that could feel. How everything you believe in can be pulled out from under you. It's the worst feeling in the world."

Gabe frowned. "What're you saying, Karen?"

"I think Randy's cheating on me." Her sobs grew louder.

"What makes you think that?"

"He's never home. He works late and on the weekends."

"Did you ask him about it?"

"No, but he doesn't want me anymore. We never have sex. He doesn't even sleep with me most of the time. I know there's someone else."

Gabe pinched the bridge of his nose. "Did you see Randy with someone else or hear him talking to someone on the phone? Maybe see texts?"

"No, but why else would he be gone so much? I don't think he loves me anymore." Her sobs increased.

"You should talk to him, Karen. Tell him how you feel."

"He won't listen. All he does is come home, play with the kids, and go to bed. I don't know what to do." She was past the point of being able to listen.

"I can tell how upset you are. You feel like your husband's pulling away from you, and that hurts. When you're this upset, you aren't thinking clearly."

"I know he's cheating. What should I do?"

"Are you in bed?"

"Yes."

"Are you lying down?"

"Yeah." She hiccupped and released a trembling sigh.

"Good. Just relax. I know you want to talk about Randy, but right now you need to get some sleep."

He couldn't focus on Karen and Randy. His head was too busy spinning with what he'd done with Brandt.

"Why do I keep choosing men who don't love me?"

Gabe heaved a sigh, and his heart broke for her. Her mental health was precarious, and her marriage was hitting a rocky road. And why did he feel guilty for all that? "Randy loves you. Marriages go through rough patches, sweetie. You'll both get through this. Talking is the first step. I can help you if you need me to talk with both of you."

"I don't think he'd talk to you."

"Okay. Maybe you could both see Dr. Nemer. There's lots that can be done. I know it feels hopeless, but it'll work out."

She didn't say anything to that.

"You okay?"

She sighed, her crying having ceased. "I'm going to go to sleep. I'll call you tomorrow. Thanks."

"Okay, good night."

Gabe put his phone on the table and rubbed at his temples, wishing he could sleep as well.

GABE HAD shut his cell phone off last night to stop the nerve-strumming sounds from the incessant texts and calls. Betsy, Julia, a number he didn't recognize. The only person he spoke with in the morning was Karen. After getting some sleep, she assured him that she was okay and taking her meds. She had also talked with Randy, and they were going to talk that night. Gabe was able to relax finally.

Throughout Saturday, he stayed home, working through a myriad of emotions and feelings that were trying to drown him. He'd puttered around the house, unable to focus on one activity for any amount of time. Thoughts of Tim and Brandt continually battled to be recognized. He'd lament why Tim didn't want him one moment and then wish he had Brandt's number the next. Then he'd spent time listing the reasons why neither of them would want him. The roller-coaster ride was long and bumpy and filled with loops that made him dizzy. Add in Karen's issues and the roller coaster was ready to go off the tracks.

When Sunday morning arrived, his consistent inactivity and movement found him exhausted, despite doing nothing more physical than walking around the house. He wasn't sure his mood could get any darker. God, could he even remember the last time he'd been happy? Yes. One night, while on Facebook, a message from Tim had popped up. His butterflies had grown spikes that night.

"How're you doing?"

"Good, Tim. How are you?"

"Not so good. Relationship with Jeff ended. Kind of messy. It's not easy, is it?"

That night had been the start of many late nights of messaging, commiserating, talking about the past, the present, and even the future. The thrill of reconnecting with Tim, the comfort of getting to know him again, had energized Gabe. The love of his life was single again, and Gabe had received that rare gift of a second chance. Because of his terrified reluctance to come out as a teen and his rebellion against Tim when he'd been outed, he'd lost the one person he'd cared for, loved. Gabe had been in the position when they'd reconnected to give Tim what he'd failed to give the first time around. Too bad their reuniting had all gone to shit, twice.

And then he'd met Brandt. Even after the rocky start, he was hooked by the intriguing man. Gabe had been positive that he was straight. He was gay, gorgeous, a good man who loved kids, and everything Gabe thought he wanted. Everything he'd thought Tim was… or who he wanted to Tim to be. Tim had been his chance at happily ever after, but that would have been too easy, right?

As he thought of Tim and his lies and deceptive behavior, Gabe's anger grew. Brandt had asked him out, and because he feared being rejected as he had been by Tim, he'd run. Overreacted was more like it, when he'd assumed the man only wanted a good fuck. But didn't relationships start with a date? If Brandt had asked him out, then he was definitely interested in something more. If he'd only been after a one-night stand, he would have taken advantage of the situation right then.

A loud banging on the front door startled Gabe from his reminiscing. He wanted to ignore the banging, but there was another bang, and a deep voice yelled his name. Gabe held his breath. *No, it can't be.* Had he imagined it?

Bang. Bang. "Gabe, if you don't open this door, I'll bust the fucking thing down. I know you're in there!"

Gabe groaned, clutching his head. This was miles beyond his capacity to deal with right then. Come back in a week and maybe he'd be ready.

Bang. Bang. Bang. "I've been trying to call you since Friday night. Open the door. I need to talk to you."

Bang. Bang. Bang. Bang.

Ignoring the noise wasn't going to get the door-banging jackass to go away. He dragged himself off the couch and shuffled to the door. Through the frosted glass, he could see a large, dark outline. Inhaling deeply and blinking a few times, Gabe unlocked the bolt, brusquely turned the knob, and yanked the door open.

A bright, shining grin greeted him. "About time, Gabe. You look like shit."

Gabe frowned. Tim was on his porch. A week ago that might have excited him, brought him hope. Right then, much like the night before, Gabe's world shifted. "What do you want, Tim?" Gabe did little to hide his annoyance. He gripped the doorknob, resisting the urge to slam the door in his ex's face.

CHAPTER 9

WHAT THE fuck? Gabe blinked. Tim was the last person he'd expected to ever see again. Tim stuffed his hands into the pockets of his jeans. The black turtleneck sweater and white North Face vest only accentuated his fit body. No wonder he'd looked elsewhere after Gabe. Tim could have anyone. Time had been more than generous with Tim. Wrinkles were limited to those slight crinkles at the corners of his blue eyes and mouth when he smiled widely. A touch of gray at the temples of his dark blond hair looked like highlights. His nose had become more defined, eyebrows fuller. Just looking at him was like a sucker punch.

"I tried to call you a few times, but you didn't answer. And you're not on Facebook anymore."

You're the reason for that.

"Been busy. In fact, I was just heading into the shower. Got a busy day."

Tim shifted and then looked down, seeming to study the trainers on his feet. When he looked up, there was a heart-stopping anguish coloring those blue eyes. "Can you spare a minute to talk? I really have some things I need to say to you. Please?"

For a moment, Gabe could see the young boy he'd known, the one he'd fallen in love with, and didn't that just stab right through him. Sighing, Gabe stepped back, allowing Tim to pass, cognizant to keep his distance. When they entered the living room, Gabe didn't offer Tim a seat. Crossing his arms, Gabe stood behind the couch and waited for Tim to start.

Tim paced for a moment, then faced Gabe. "I want to apologize for the way I've acted. After Jeff and I split, I was… broken. I jumped in with you too quickly. I was looking for anything to get rid of that pain. I was a real mess."

Actually, what Gabe had seen of Tim had been smooth, enticing, and willing. "So you're telling me I was a mistake?"

Tim's eyes widened as he shook his head. "No, Gabe. It was just… too fast. Jeff and I had only been broken up for a little over a month after being together for over three years, and... I felt so lost, and I guess I was looking for something." Tim looked to the floor again.

Gone was the cocky, smug, and self-confident persona Gabe knew. He couldn't ignore the shake in Tim's voice, the tormented expression, the hunched shoulders. Tim appeared more of a mess now than he'd ever been. Twinges of guilt were quickly replaced with the memory of Tim reaching into Gabe's chest and yanking out his heart—twice.

Gabe rubbed at his sternum from the physical pain. "Tim, you said things to me that were total bullshit. Crap about want and need and love and fate and the future. You gave me every indication that you wanted to be in a relationship with me, to try again, and then what did you do? Fucked me and turned your back on me. You said you needed time—six months—and when I tried to back off and be your friend, you told me that you didn't play games, when it was you who was playing them." Gabe took in a deep, shaky breath.

"I... I couldn't... I was fucked-up."

"So fucked-up you were with someone new within a month?"

Tim narrowed his eyes. "I messaged you and asked how you were. You said you were involved with that Pat guy."

After being kicked to the curb by his high school boyfriend, Gabe had been all too happy to tell Tim he was involved with another man.

Tim shrugged. "So I found someone else."

"So much for pining over me." Gabe snorted. "By the way, that lasted a long time. A few weeks?"

"You're not so innocent here, Gabe. I loved you and wanted to be with you, but you locked that door so tight no one could get in." Tim's anger flared. He wasn't playing the martyr anymore.

"Are you talking about your 'request' when I was eighteen to come out when you did? I was terrified, Tim. Just a kid who knew he loved another guy, but to tell everyone, my friends and family, my parents? I didn't have understanding, progressive parents like you. I probably wouldn't even be out now if my father hadn't died. My mom only speaks to me on holidays, and then only if I call her. I begged you to give me some time, begged you to wait for me, but you loved me so much that you told the girl with the biggest mouth in the school about me, then ran off to college and never looked back." That well of pain had been capped for far too long.

"You said that you forgave me for that." Tim sounded almost accusatory.

Gabe schooled his face into a hard mask. "I guess I'm taking it back. I would've said anything to have you again, anything to keep you with me. It definitely wasn't enough. I even gave you a second chance, or have you forgotten so soon?" Gabe turned away and sniffed, quickly wiping away a stray disobedient tear.

Not once, but twice, Tim had come, using the same script. The loneliness after Patrick had eaten Gabe alive and he'd just wanted—needed—it to stop. And hadn't that mistake ended with Tim leaving Gabe again with the remnants of his already battered self-esteem further tattered and torn.

"I know I fucked up, Gabe. I'm sorry I—"

Gabe spun around, unable to hear any more lies. "I don't believe you. I don't trust you! I don't know if I can ever trust anyone not to use me as a doormat again. Karen cheating on me and then you dumping me twice, and now—"

He cut himself off before the name Brandt could fall from his lips.

Tim didn't seem to notice. "I told you I was messed up, that I didn't know what I was doing. I was a fucking mess inside and I…." He trailed off.

"You used me," Gabe growled.

Tim shook his head as if it would negate Gabe's words. "No. I wouldn't hurt you on purpose. I love you."

Those three words. He'd waited twenty-five years to hear those again, and now they were hollow and a meaningless representation of a life he'd yearned for and lost. With that, he realized Tim was too late. Three strikes and he was out. Something had changed since meeting Brandt.

Gabe looked into those blue eyes and mourned the loss of that boy he'd known—hopeful, wide-eyed, silly with dreams, and in love. Sure, he still lusted after Tim, but Gabe was through with the self-deprecating behavior that only resulted in the demolition of his self-worth. The awareness of what this visit had become slammed into him—the end of his love for Tim and a future that was never going to happen. Gabe no longer feared saying good-bye to Tim and closing the door on that part of his life.

Gabe rubbed at the back of his neck. The knot of tension that had always been there began to dissipate. Sighing heavily, he walked around the sofa and sat wearily on the arm. He was still tired. And with the anger fleeing, he had to deal with the reality that he was partially at fault.

"I'm sorry too, Tim. When you told me about breaking up with Jeff, I knew you were hurting, and I chose to ignore that. Instead of talking with you and helping you with the loss, which is what the counselor side of me had planned to do, I drank too much, spilling my guts about what I've wanted since we were eighteen. I know I scared you when I told you all that. But the way you treated me after was the most painful shit I've ever had to deal with. I didn't deserve it."

Tears that had filled Tim's eyes now spilled over and ran like tiny rivers down his face. He maintained silent eye contact with Gabe. This was way past hard.

"That was bad enough, but then you came back and pretty much did the same thing again. Christ, I was a mess—have been a mess. A sniveling fool, drowning in self-pity." He let out a dry chuckle. "I'm surprised Betsy didn't have me committed."

He shook his head at how supportive his sister and Julia had been. Two strong and patient women holding him up like a pair of crutches. Without them, he would have faded away into nothing. Drawing on his own strength, the time had come to stop relying on those crutches he automatically reached for when things went badly. And Tim had gone worse than bad. Now Gabe's thoughts were of another man, a man who woke something inside of him that he couldn't ignore. Could something happen there? Could he find happiness with someone else? Would that sexy, buff guy want to date an old, soft, and foolish man? God, he hoped so. He really wanted to find out.

"It's over, isn't it?" There was a slight hitch in Tim's voice.

Gabe looked up. Tim's blue eyes mirrored the loss Gabe felt. "Yeah. It is."

Tim wrapped his arms around his middle and nodded. "I could see it. Could feel something different from the moment you opened the door. You just didn't seem so...."

"Desperate?" Gabe chuckled morosely.

Tim cracked a brief, waning smile, then quickly lost it beneath his misery. "In love."

A lump formed in Gabe's throat as he consciously allowed the truth to set in. He wasn't in love with Tim anymore.

Tim took a hesitant step closer to Gabe. With Tim's distress, Gabe noticed hidden lines that previously weren't visible Like a time-morphed photo, Gabe noticed that possibly Tim hadn't been as untouched by time as he'd once thought. Or possibly Gabe's rose-colored glasses had been removed.

"Did I kill it? Did everything I put you through kill your love for me?" Tim's eyes turned glassy again.

Gabe thought his answer would be yes, but instead he said, "No. Maybe what I thought was love all these years was only the ideal of what we might have had. I always thought, if I could just get you back, then everything would be perfect. But we're both different people than we were back then. Changed for better or worse, I don't know." Gabe shrugged and then looked up at Tim, into those lovely blue eyes. "You didn't want me then, and you don't want me now."

Tim attempted to protest, but Gabe cut him off. Standing, he took Tim's hands into his. None of the electric sparks he'd experienced with Brandt were present. It was like holding the hands of a friend, and that was both upsetting and comforting at the same time.

"Last time we were together, you said I was like coming home. Well, as adults, most of us go back home, get some love and comfort, but we always leave again. We don't stay there because we don't belong." Gabe allowed a tear to continue its journey down his face, leaving a cold, wet trail. He deserved those tears, had earned them, but this was the last tear he'd shed for Tim as a lover. From here on out, Gabe hoped he would slip into the role of friend.

"I don't want to lose you." Tim squeezed desperately at Gabe's hands.

Gabe shook his head, overwhelmed and unable to fathom the loss as well as the relief. The twenty-five-year siege on his heart was ending. He could move on. "You won't lose me as a friend. You were the first best friend I ever had. I think it's time we work on that relationship, don't you?" Gabe found it easier to pull his mouth into a light, melancholy smile.

Tim drew in a shuddering breath, pulled his lips into a thin line, and nodded. "I think we could do that. Just… just give me some time. I promise I won't abandon you again."

Gabe wanted to trust him, but the ball was in Tim's court. Gabe could only be there if and when his friend was ready. Tim dropped his hands hopelessly, and Gabe could tell the man was losing a battle. Soon he would crash, much like Gabe had Friday night. He felt for Tim but couldn't be the one to comfort him.

"I should go. And again, I apologize and hope that someday you can forgive me."

Gabe followed Tim, and when they stopped at the front door he opened it for him. Gabe stepped out onto the porch with his new "old" friend. Tim stopped just before the stairs, then turned to Gabe, who rubbed at the coldness on his bare arms.

"Is it okay if I hug you good-bye?" A hopeful yet exhausted smile emerged on Tim's face.

Gabe opened his arms wide, and Tim stepped in. Gabe rubbed his hands over Tim's back in a comforting gesture. A week ago, having Tim in his arms would have been the sun, the moon, and the stars all rolled into one, but now it wasn't enough.

Tim pulled back slightly and raised his hand to Gabe's cheek. Fingertips caressed his skin as Tim stared into his eyes.

"Good-bye." Tim lowered his lips for a kiss. With the soft touch, Gabe was transported back to the darkened parking lot, Brandt's lips brushing against his, the almost animalistic claiming of Gabe's heart and soul. Gabe allowed the kiss to continue, imagining Brandt was with him. When he opened his eyes to Tim, he felt his disappointment in his chest.

Gabe stepped back and cleared his throat. "So what're you going to do now?"

Tim leaned against the railing and crossed his arms. "Go home and sulk. Try to get my head together. Maybe I'll take a vacation. Go sit on a beach somewhere. Cabo sounds good right about now."

Gabe didn't want to go the counselor route, but he had to say something. "You've jumped from one relationship to another. You said yourself they never last any longer than a few years." God, why had Gabe thought he'd last forever with Tim? Betsy had been right. He couldn't stay in a relationship. "Take some time to get to know who you are and what you really want without someone else in the mix."

Tim shook his head and smiled ruefully. "Always the counselor, Gabe."

"No, that's friend advice."

"I haven't ever really been alone. Shit. That sounds scary. Don't know if I can do it."

"You can't be yourself in a relationship if you don't know who you are. From what you told me, you get with a guy and you try to be who he is or what he wants. That can't work because you're playing a part, and you can only keep that up for so long."

Tim looked away, his gaze over the field surrounding the house. Gabe let his advice sink in, waiting for Tim to either accept or dismiss his opinion.

"Fuck," Tim whispered.

A car came down the drive, and when Gabe saw that it was Julia, he swore in his head. She hated Tim for what he'd done to Gabe. He was going to head her off but didn't make it down the steps before a red Mustang pulled in beside her.

Brandt.

CHAPTER 10

JULIA EXITED her car with a scowl, but Gabe turned his attention, smiling wide as Brandt stepped out of his car. That dazzling smile was more than he could take.

"Hey, Brandt." Almost as an afterthought, he said, "Julia."

Brandt's eyes went to Tim, and his smile faded. "Hey. I just wanted to see if you were okay after the other night. You weren't answering your phone."

Tim snorted. "Or his door."

Julia eyed Tim. Gabe would never hear the end of it. Tim stepped up and threw an arm around Gabe's shoulder, then planted a kiss on Gabe's cheek.

Brandt's expression morphed from one of surprise to understanding. "Okay… yeah, I'm glad you're okay. I gotta head out."

Gabe shook off Tim's arm and scowled at him. "Brandt, wait!"

Gabe ran down the stairs and into the driveway as Brandt's Mustang backed away. Gabe clenched his fists at his sides, fire roaring in his gut. He spun and glared at Tim.

Tim was smart enough to look repentant.

"What the fuck were you doing, Tim?"

Tim backed up. His eyes were wide, and his mouth gaped and closed. "I don't know. I just…. Shit, I'm sorry, Gabe."

"Sorry? Seriously, I just got done telling you we were over and you turn all macho and act like you're staking your claim when another guy shows up."

Julia stepped tentatively onto the porch but was silent.

Tim crossed his arms. "Is he…. Are you seeing him?"

Gabe gritted his teeth. "Why should that matter? You can't just play with people like that. Friends don't do shit like that."

Tim seemed to deflate and rubbed at the back of his neck. "I don't…. I really want you and—"

"No, you don't. If you really wanted me, then you would have stayed with me the first time. What I said earlier, I meant it. You need to stop with the relationships. You're pretty fucked-up, Tim, and it's only going to get worse. You really need to get some help before you have no one left in your life."

Gabe turned and walked to the other end of the porch, taking in deep breaths. Then he chuckled. The last time he'd been so angry was the day he'd met Brandt. That brought a smile to his face and an ache to his chest.

"Tim, I think you'd better go," Julia said. Gabe was surprised she hadn't lit into him as well. Why was she being so nice?

"Yeah. Okay." He walked down the stairs, and when Gabe looked to him, his head hung low. He got into his car and drove away.

Gabe rubbed at the throbbing in his temple.

"Brandt was worried about you. He asked me for your number at the bar Friday night. Said he needed to thank you for something. Then last night he called me all panicked because he couldn't get ahold of you. I couldn't reach you either, and when I called Betsy, she said the same. So when Brandt called me this morning, I told him we should come over, and jeez, Gabe, could your life get any more fucked-up?"

GABE RUBBED at his forehead and listened as Julia ranted about Tim, and this time he couldn't defend the man, so Gabe sat back and let her get it all out.

"I can't believe the nerve of him! He's broken your heart over and over without a second of concern for your feelings. He's heartless, and I seriously have to question your sanity and ability to make good choices when you let him into this house, much less back into your life the second time he came crawling back." If this were a cartoon, steam would have been pouring out of her ears by now. "He's heartless and self-centered and only cares about himself. He knew what he was doing on that porch. Good-for-nothing…. Ugh!"

Gabe sipped his coffee. A splash of creamer and one Splenda. A good compromise, he thought. That wasn't the sign of someone who couldn't make good decisions, right?

Who was he kidding?

A loud, exasperated sigh caught his attention. "Listen to me when I'm ranting."

Gabe couldn't stop the wry grin that crossed his face. Julia was pissed while Gabe's ire had fizzled out, leaving only the pain of betrayal. "Tim came here to apologize and, yes, try to get back with me. I spoke with him because I needed to tell him I was done with him. Which I did. We'd agreed to be friends. Of course that was before he was a dickhead. Maybe someday if he gets his head out of his ass and realizes he's ruining all his relationships, maybe then we can be friends."

She pursed her lips. "Why can't you ever stay mad at someone for more than five minutes? I swear I could go kick the shit out of something right now and still be pissed, and here you are sipping coffee, all relaxed. It's really quite disturbing."

Gabe grunted. "I'm far from relaxed. I might not be mad, but Tim meant a lot to me, even if it didn't work out. But that part of my life is over. I have to move on."

Gabe turned the words over in his mind to get used to the idea. Was he okay with that? More than he realized. A dull ache, a sense of loss, but not the feeling that something was missing. But that wasn't entirely true, because something was missing. Another person was crowding out Tim in the missing category—Brandt.

"So Brandt was worried about me? Why?"

The snort-like guffaw from Julia was a sound Gabe had never heard before—even in nature. His misguided attempt to throw Julia off was transparent.

"So you're going to play the stupid card? Good, because that's how you've been acting for the past year. Before that, I'd only suspected you were just this side of insane for staying in that sham of a marriage. Now you've added stupid into the mix. At least you're growing."

"Ouch." Gabe smirked at her harsh assessment.

She narrowed menacing eyes, effectively erasing the smirk. "You know I don't mince words and don't sugarcoat the truth." That was the one thing Gabe appreciated about Julia. He needed to hear the truth even if that truth hurt. "And I've spent years dealing with teenagers who try to hide the truth from me, and I've developed a good bullshit detector. So don't even try. I know something happened between you and Brandt on Friday night. I mean, Monday and Tuesday you were at each other's throats, and then Friday night, well, Friday night he asks me for your phone number after you abruptly leave and then proceeds to drill me for any info about you that I was willing to spill. I swear to God, he was like a teenage girl with a crush." She leaned back, and even though she crossed her arms, Gabe could see the crinkles at the corners of her eyes, which told him she approved that something had happened.

Gabe pushed his spoon around the table, wanting to tell her everything, but he wasn't sure what had really happened. He shifted uncomfortably, thinking of the mind-blowing orgasm with Brandt in the goddamned parking lot. Could it have meant more to Brandt than just sex as well?

Julia's hand covered his. It was highly reminiscent of Betsy's act of comfort last week. Those two women were always taking care of him. He owed Julia—both of them—the truth.

"Hey, you can tell me if you want, but you don't have to. I want so much for you, Gabe. You deserve someone in your life. Brandt's a great guy. Respectful, a bit gruff, but once you get past the rough exterior, he's a guy who cares enough to push people to be their best."

Raptly attentive to the spoon, Gabe thought of the playground, and how he'd turned into a big kid around the twins. "Friday night Brandt followed me out to the parking lot. I may have kind of been lusting after him since we first met, and well, we talked a few times. I was really starting to like him, but I didn't know he was gay until he kissed me." A warm blush crept up his neck and into his cheeks.

A giggle followed by another unladylike snort came from across the table. Gabe was the one to narrow his eyes now.

Julia waved a hand and tried to cover her smile with the other. "Sorry. Go on."

"He asked me out on a date."

Julia sat forward, that silly, girlish grin splitting her face. "And you said yes, right?"

Gabe bent over and banged his forehead against the table. "When he kissed me, I freaked and ran away." He wasn't telling her about the orgasm Brandt had given him.

"You ran away?"

He sat up and sighed deeply, rubbing at the throbbing, which had doubled. "I freaked, okay? After Tim, I… I'm afraid to be rejected, and I hate that feeling."

"Damn, you really like him, don't you?"

Gabe nodded, perhaps a little too enthusiastically. "I do. You should have seen him on the playground at the school with the twins the other day. He was outside with his gym class and saw us. He spent his free period playing with Maddy and Mikey. It was really sweet." The memory brought a sappy smile to his face, but he shook his head in defeat. "Anyway, I'm sure he was only interested in a roll in the hay. That's what many of the gay men I've talked with want. Besides, he could get some really hot, successful guy. I don't want to be a placeholder until then."

That comforting hand that had been resting on his moved and lightly smacked him aside the head.

"Ouch." Gabe rubbed at the sting.

"That's for being an idiot." She grimaced, massaging her palm. "And for having such a hard head, but you deserved it. He clearly likes you. I told you that he was acting like one of those lovestruck teens I have running amok in the high school. Brandt probably is more embarrassed that he kissed you when you had someone else, which you don't. So just call him and go on that date."

Gabe wasn't so sure. The threat of rejection ate at his gut with razor-sharp teeth. Perhaps he should go back to being alone. That was easy. This was tooth-pulling hard and just as agonizing.

"Listen, someone looking for another one-nighter doesn't interrogate your best friend about every minute detail of your life. He doesn't worry about you all weekend and get ready to break your door in if you don't answer." She paused. "And he looked hurt seeing Tim acting like he owned you."

Gabe ran a hand through his hair.

"Call him, Gabe."

Gabe only nodded reluctantly. *This might take some alcohol.*

LATER THAT night, Gabe sat on his back deck, sipping wine and turning his cell phone over in his hand. He contemplated his next move. Definitely needed to make the call before he was drunk. Last time he'd been in a drunken stupor and spoken with someone for whom he had feelings, he'd confessed his undying love to Tim.

Gabe shook his head in a thought-clearing gesture, because Tim, who had been the center of Gabe's entire gay universe, would no longer have the starring role in his life. It was beyond fathomable. The script had been rewritten, and the lead had been recast with a tall, dark-haired, hazel-eyed ex-soldier, who would no doubt reject the part after Gabe's idiocy. Damn, if that didn't feel like getting his insides yanked out through his ass.

Earlier, Gabe had listened to the messages he'd missed from Julia, Betsy, and Brandt when he'd shut his phone off Saturday. The messages from Betsy and Julia had been firm and calm since they both knew Gabe and his tendency to bug out every so often. Gabe had called Betsy earlier and assured her he was fine. Brandt, well, his messages had gone from worried to a sort of panicked rambling by Sunday morning. If Gabe had bothered to listen to his messages on Friday night, he would have heard Brandt in a playful tone saying that he wanted to see Gabe again, and then, in a softer tone, telling him how sorry he was that their first time had been as uneventful as a rutting against a fence. If only Brandt knew how life-changing that rutting had been.

Gabe blew out a breath and chugged the rest of his wine. Only one glass, so he was safe to call. Searching his contacts, he found the newly saved number. He warred with himself, part of him hoping Brandt would answer and part of him hoping he wouldn't. His gut was tied in a knot, and damn if he didn't feel like he was going to throw up.

"Just call the man," Gabe encouraged himself.

Hitting Call, he cleared his throat. As the number of rings increased, his heart fell a little. A beep and then Brandt's commanding tone sent a shiver through Gabe as he instructed the caller to leave a name and number.

At the second beep, Gabe did his best to harden his voice and sound confident. "Hi, Brandt, it's Gabe. Listen, I know I screwed up Friday night… and this morning. I'd really like the chance to explain. Please, call me back when you can." Unsure of what else to say, he paused, then said, "Talk to you soon."

Hitting the End button, Gabe put the phone down, trying unsuccessfully to ignore it.

CHAPTER 11

TWO DAYS later and still no word from Brandt. Should he text him? Would that be odd? What were the rules on texting someone you'd had an orgasm with but who wouldn't call you back? Gabe hadn't tried to call again for fear he would look like a stalker. His concentration was for shit. Each time his phone chirped or rang, his stomach did a somersault. Each time the call wasn't from Brandt, Gabe feared he'd been right and the man had only been after a quick shag. Of course, Julia didn't hesitate to remind him he was an idiot and to go and see Brandt. She'd even offered to speak with Brandt on his behalf, but Gabe assumed that would only piss the guarded man off more.

The time had come for some tactical maneuvers. Gabe didn't have a reason to see Brandt. Travis's issues in gym had disappeared, and he'd actually been having fun in class. And he was glad for that. Gabe hoped that experience would spread to the other areas of the teen's life. The kid deserved so much more than life had given him so far. Without an excuse to go to the gym, Gabe turned to his next tactic—nonchalant attack.

Coordinating that attack with Julia, Gabe staked out the school parking lot with Brandt's Mustang in full view. He clenched his cell phone in his hand as he waited for Julia to text him when Brandt was coming out of the school. He would "just happen" to bump into him and start a conversation. Gabe was always at the school, so being there wouldn't be odd.

Within the confines of his car, Gabe's heart hammered in his ears, the sweat from his palm gathered on his phone, and if his rate of breathing increased much more, he'd fog up the windows. Gabe glanced at the clock—three thirty-five. The staff meeting for teachers was supposed to end at three thirty. Any minute Brandt should emerge from the school.

Gabe had rehearsed dozens of times—in the shower, the car, in front of the mirror, in between appointments at work—exactly what he would say, and in an instant, that all fled from his head. Panicked, he tried to focus on his memorized speech, but every word deserted him. The phone in his hand vibrated.

He's coming out now.

No! He wasn't ready. What would he say? Glancing through the windshield, he saw Brandt exit the building, followed by…. Shit, Tish. Her top was tighter and skirt shorter than ever. Man, the high school boys must have been popping boners left and right. They walked close together, and then her hand rested on Brandt's forearm, and he was… laughing?

Suddenly, Gabe's resolve turned vengeful. *That's e-fucking-nough of that!* Gabe bolted from his car and reached Brandt just as he approached the Mustang with Tish still in tow.

Brandt gave a closemouthed smile when he spotted Gabe. Gabe flashed him a nervous smile. "Hey, Brandt." He hated how his voice cracked. "Tish."

"Gabe," she said in her nasally tone. "So, Brandt, let me know about that dinner, okay?"

"Sure."

"Talk to you soon, Brandt." Her smile was all teeth and so transparent. Gabe could practically hear the ticking of that "biological clock" he'd overheard her lamenting over at the bar after she'd had a few too many.

"See ya, Gabe," she barely managed before walking off. He waved halfheartedly.

Brandt pulled his keys out of his pocket and unlocked the driver's door. "Hey, Gabe. How's it going?" Brandt's expression was flat. He wasn't being warm or cold. He was just being nothing.

Gabe stepped forward and resisted putting a hand on Brandt's arm. How could he be so close and not touch him? "I'm good. You?"

"I'm good too. You have something at the school?"

Gabe's mind raced. *Reason! Alert! We need a reason!* "Oh… umm… I'm meeting J-Julia." *Apparently this is rocket science.*

Brandt nodded with what appeared to be satisfaction with his answer, and Gabe felt like a fool for lying to him. He wasn't good at it anyway.

He chuckled. "Okay, that's not true."

That brought an amusing confusion to Brandt's face. "No?"

Gabe dug his hands deep into the pockets of his pants, playing with the keys. Why was he so dang nervous? "I wanted to talk to you. I called you the other day and left a message."

Gabe was getting a strange vibe from him. While he'd screwed everything up by running and then Tim pulling his bullshit, Gabe didn't think he deserved to be ignored.

"Sorry, I didn't get a chance to call you back."

"It's okay. I wanted to tell you that what you said the other night, about the attraction between us, I did notice it." *Felt it in every cell of my body in fact.*

Brandt looked unsure, more than hesitant. "Listen, I have to be honest here. I'm not after a quick fuck. I don't play around. I know men who do, and it's just not me."

Gabe couldn't breathe. "You think… you think I'm looking for a fuck?"

Brandt's brow rose. "Well, yeah. I saw you with that guy. And it's okay. You're looking for something different. I can't say I'm not disappointed."

Gabe couldn't stop the laugh that came out of him. And unfortunately, it sounded less amused and more unhinged. "Oh God. I can't believe this." Gabe swiped his hand over his mouth. "That is so far from the truth. If you were serious about the date—"

"Of course I was. I wouldn't have asked if I weren't." Brandt frowned, and Gabe feared he'd pissed the man off.

His reaction took all the humor out of the situation. Gabe had to fix this. "I'm sorry. I didn't mean to laugh. What I want to do is apologize about Friday night and freaking out on you. And what you saw on Sunday wasn't what you think it was. I want to explain it all, but not here in this parking lot." Gabe paused when he realized what he'd said. He lowered his voice and looked down as he twisted his hands in front of him. "I mean, what we did in the parking lot at the bar, I loved it."

A moment of silence caused Gabe to look up, and Brandt was biting at his bottom lip. "Really? Because I thought…. Damn, I thought I'd misread you and forced you to do something you didn't want to." Brandt chuckled dryly. "I've felt so bad and avoided your call because I thought you were going to let me have it. I was really scared that I hurt you."

Jesus, could their assumptions have been any more off base? "You didn't, really. What we did was intense, and I've never felt anything like that before." Gabe tried to convey his sincerity. "Can we just talk and I'll explain?" If his heart beat any harder, it was going to explode or he was going to stroke out.

When Brandt smiled, Gabe exhaled and his muscles unclenched. Sweet Jesus, he'd missed Brandt, and realized the constant ache beneath his ribs hadn't been from the loss of Tim but thinking Brandt didn't want him. Maybe there could be something between them.

"Sure. How about a beer? I have to get a shower first. Meet me at the Wooden Nickel at five thirty?"

Gabe drew in a shaky breath, the excitement tingling across his skin. For the first time in his life, he felt free to move ahead. "I'll be there."

AT FIVE fifteen, Gabe stepped into the Wooden Nickel. Scanning the room, he saw only a few people at the bar, but it was Tuesday, which tended to be slow. Convincing Brandt he was worth the effort required talking, so they needed to be somewhere quiet. Gabe hoped Brandt thought he was worth the effort. Gabe couldn't shake the sense memories of their explosive session behind the bar, leaving him in a state of perpetual arousal. Even as he nursed his beer at the bar, he shifted uncomfortably as his semihard dick pushed against his zipper. Whenever the door opened, Gabe's heart leapt. It was after five thirty, and fear that Brandt wasn't going to show crept into his head. Gabe had no clue where Brandt lived, and Julia would never divulge that information. Maybe Gabe could find him online. Cyber stalking. How low would he go? Pretty low, he guessed.

"Hey."

That low, sultry voice never failed to hit hard. Gabe spun in his seat. "Damn, how do you sneak up on me like that?"

Brandt grinned. "I'm talented." He signaled the bartender, then placed his order.

Gabe smirked, thinking of just how talented he was after the parking lot incident.

When the bartender placed a Samuel Adams before Brandt, Gabe suggested they get a table. Brandt gave one of his economical nods and followed Gabe to the back of the room, away from the people and the jukebox. Gabe pulled off his coat and draped it over the back of the chair. Brandt did the same, and Gabe tried not to choke on his tongue as Brandt displayed a tight blue Army shirt with bulges in all the right places. What did a man like him even see in someone like Gabe? Gabe's confidence took a nosedive.

"Quiet here tonight." Brandt scanned the room.

"Usually is on a Tuesday. Thanks for coming." Every word was an innuendo that Gabe tried to avoid. He felt like a sex-crazed pervert.

"I'm glad you asked." Brandt's dark eyes left Gabe's nerves buzzing.

Gabe nodded and scraped up the courage to continue. Licking at his lips, he leaned his elbows on the table and scratched at his beer label with a thumbnail. "In my head, I had so much to say, but now, you have to know I'm really not good at this." He gestured with his hand between them.

Brandt cocked his head, and the corner of his lips lifted. "I could tell."

Gabe snorted. "I'm sure you could. I'm definitely not smooth or self-confident. Truthfully, I'm fumbling along in the dark."

Brandt leaned forward, his relaxed expression taking on a more serious edge. "I get it. Meeting people, getting to know them, trying relationships.... I was in the military for seventeen years. That's hard enough on straight relationships, but being gay, it's nearly impossible. Even with the repeal of DADT."

Gabe realized he wasn't the only gay man who was looking for a relationship and coming up empty-handed. "I couldn't imagine how hard being gay and in the military would be."

Brandt laughed. "Not hard because of a lack of sex. There were even straight guys who'd fuck me just to get off."

"Seriously?"

Brandt shrugged a shoulder. "Not many, but enough that if the rumor got around that someone was gay, they'd come nosing around. Tons of one-night stands or some longtime flings but nothing serious. I found the same thing when I started to look for a serious relationship. I have met guys who wanted the relationship, but we didn't click."

Gabe had had his share of those offers. "I tried a few dating sites, since there aren't a huge number of gay men in Westport or the surrounding area.... Well, those that are out, that is."

Brandt sat back. "Hey, I don't begrudge anyone the lifestyle they want to live. If you want to have multiple partners, Gabe, go ahead. I just wanted to let you know I can't do that. I'm getting older, and I'm looking for a relationship."

Gabe rubbed at his forehead. "I'm not looking for multiple partners. Far from it. I can't even get one partner." He huffed. "Hell, I was married to one person, one woman, for eighteen years. What you saw on Sunday was me saying good-bye to someone who wasn't relationship material. He, Tim, was the first person I fell in love with in high school. I mean, I loved him so much and never stopped loving him since, or so I thought."

"So you're saying you are looking for a monogamous relationship?"

Gabe shook his head and chuckled, wondering how he'd gotten to be the loose one in this thing between them.

He grinned wide. "Yes."

CHAPTER 12

THAT BROUGHT a satisfied grin to Brandt's face. "Good."

Gabe felt the relief of clearing that up right down to his toes.

"It sounds like you've had some of the same experiences I have in trying to date in the gay world."

Gabe snorted. "You have no idea. I can't get a relationship, but I can have sex every night of the week, make that day too, in as many freaky and weird ways you can think of. Makes you wonder."

Brandt leaned forward with a fire in his eyes. "I don't know why relationships are so off the table for so many gay men. Maybe have your cake… lots of different kinds of cake."

Gabe smirked at the cake analogy. "My friend Marty says most gay men aren't built that way. He's pretty campy and he's a player, but I think he uses that campy, flaming persona to catch a certain type of man, not just gay men. He even does drag every so often, and I swear the stories he can tell about so-called straight guys hitting on him even knowing what's in his pants are amazing."

Brandt's eyes widened. "I love drag. Man, I've seen some risqué shows around the world. Wherever I was stationed, I always checked out the shows."

"Well, maybe sometime we'll head over to Burlington and catch a show. They also have a yearly charity event called Winter is a Drag Ball. They always have a theme."

"I'd like that. So can I ask you something? It's personal, and you don't have to answer if you don't want."

"Sure."

"You were married to a woman, and you said that lasted for over eighteen years. Are you bi?"

Gabe exhaled. "I've asked myself that many times, but if being bi means being attracted to men and women, then no. I've never been attracted to women. I'm still not. I wasn't out as a teen. Tim asked me to come out because he was, but back then being gay wasn't as accepted as it is today. In this small town, much less. My mother and stepfather—

he's a retired Navy commander, just so you know—were very Catholic. Tim outed me right after graduation. I don't think he meant to, but they found out." He still wasn't sure it had been an accident.

"Bet the shit hit the fan with the commander." Brandt's concerned expression was touching.

"Oh, that's an understatement. Not just the commander, but my mother as well. I had to convince them what they heard was wrong. That I wasn't gay." Gabe closed his eyes, thinking of how he'd betrayed himself. Wishing he hadn't denied that he was gay wouldn't change the decision he'd made, but at least he would have been true to himself. "They really didn't believe me and were very cold after that. Didn't help that I'd never had a girlfriend in high school. Told them I was too focused on school and they bought it. Anyway, I was such a people pleaser that I set out to prove them wrong, to get back into their favor. When I got to college, the first girl who was interested, I snagged. That was my ex, Karen."

Brandt leaned forward and touched Gabe's hand. A shudder raced through him. Needing the touch, Gabe grasped Brandt's hand, uncaring who in the bar saw them.

"I can't imagine how hard that was for you. I mean, I never really came out to my family until I left the service, but I didn't have to pretend to be someone I wasn't. I was career military, no time for a wife and kids, and all my father knew was that he had a son serving his country, and he was proud. My mom passed away when I was in high school, so I'm not sure how she would have reacted, but I think she would have been okay with it."

"I'm sorry about your mom. Did you tell your dad?"

Brandt nodded. "He didn't say much of anything, actually changed the subject to the situation in the Middle East. I didn't push. It hasn't come up in the six months since I told him. I'm guessing he's either processing the fact that he has a gay ex-military macho son or is hoping it will go away. He lives in Massachusetts now, so I don't see him much. Wait until I bring someone home. Then I'll find out what he really thinks."

Gabe hoped that Brandt's father accepted him. Having a parent reject who you were was heartbreaking. "My stepdad passed away a couple of years ago, before Karen and I split. After the divorce, I told my mother. She calls on the holidays, talks my ear off about everyone else in the family. She blames me for ruining my marriage, even though Karen was the one who cheated. My mother says she wouldn't have cheated if I didn't like men, if I'd tried harder… if I'd been able to give her the children she so desperately wanted." Gabe felt the pain in his chest. "What she doesn't know is how I stayed in that marriage despite the lie I was living. I took my vows seriously. And how desperately I wanted kids too. Then she goes off and gets pregnant by someone else." Yeah, that part was what had been hardest on Gabe.

"I'm sorry, Gabe. I can see how much those kids mean to you."

He snorted. "I love them. I'm forty-three years old, in a broken-down aging body, and I latched on to the kids my ex had with another man. I let the man who I thought was the love of my life tear my heart to shreds, then realized I probably didn't really love him at all. I think I'd built him up in my fantasies over the years to survive living a life I didn't really want. And that realization I have you to thank for."

Brandt cocked his head. "How so?" There went that cocky, sexy eyebrow again, yanking at Gabe's gut.

Gabe rubbed his thumb over the back of Brandt's hand, the connection exciting and so new. "Because you noticed me. Seemed to be interested. I'm, well, you can see what I am. A formerly married fake-heterosexual guy with love handles and crow's-feet and possibly thinning hair. And then you come along and kiss me and"—Gabe leaned closer and whispered—"give me the most mind-blowing orgasm I've ever had. Scared the shit out of me because I believed there was no way it would ever happen again."

"That's why you ran." Brandt squeezed Gabe's hand, his hazel eyes intense.

"Yeah. Tim really did a number on me, but I did a lot of thinking over the weekend. And I realized Tim was an idea, a fantasy, and a player." Gabe snorted, and Brandt smiled. "He's been in so many relationships, can't keep one to save his life, and I was just another in a string of men. I didn't like how that felt. Then he showed up, and I knew I was over him. I told him so. He wanted a hug. Then he kissed me, but…." Gabe grinned. "While he was kissing me, I was thinking of you." That sent a flush of embarrassment and lust through Gabe.

"Oh yeah?" Brandt's voice was low, almost growly.

Gabe ventured to meet his gaze. "Yeah." He barely whispered the words, and right then he wanted to kiss Brandt again. Needed to kiss him, but that wasn't possible in a bar that was filling up quickly.

"Tim didn't look like he was ready to let go yet." Translation: What if he comes back?

"No. Even if he comes back and wants to start again, that part of my life is over. I was stuck in the past. I'd really like to go on that date if you don't think I'm some psycho, unstable person, which I'm not. I'm not sure how well I'll do, though, given that my last first date was in the nineties." Even with Patrick, they had bypassed that dating matrix and gone right to spending the weekend together.

While Brandt didn't release his hand, he silently surveyed Gabe. The silence was unnerving and scared him right down to his toes.

"So your last date was in the nineties?"

Gabe smirked shyly. "Yeah."

"And you said that you're forty-three?"

Gabe pursed his lips and nodded. "Yeah. Please don't tell me you were in kindergarten when I was dating or something like that."

Brandt actually chuckled, and the relaxing effect of that sound on Gabe was refreshing. "More like getting my driver's license."

"Phew. Robbing the cradle isn't my idea of fun." Gabe could feel his eyes growing wide. "I didn't mean to imply we were doing anything. I mean, I understand if you don't want anything more. I mean…." Shit.

Brandt leaned forward with a crooked grin. "You're kinda cute when you're all flustered."

Gabe snorted and then kind of hiccupped. *Suave, Gabe.* "Then I must be downright adorable most of the time, because it's my normal state."

"I wouldn't disagree with that—the adorable part, I mean. I'll need more research on the flustered part. There are so many ways I can think to fluster you."

Now Gabe's face was burning hot. His cock sat up and begged in his jeans with the memory of that sexy body giving him so much pleasure.

Down, boy.

"So," Gabe said, shifting in his seat. "Where do we go from here?"

Brandt's expression was unreadable for a moment. "I guess I need to make an honest man out of you and ask you out on a proper date." Brandt smirked, and his eyebrows rose. "Will you go out on a date with me, Gabe?"

Fuck, yes!

"Yes." He agreed before Brandt could retract the offer. Gabe knew he was grinning like the cat that swallowed the canary.

GABE HAD to wait until Saturday for his date. Work was busy and provided some distraction from his raging impatience. His excitement equaled going to the World Series and getting to meet the team after the game—in the locker room. Thursday he'd spent another afternoon at the park with the twins. Brandt had joined them for a short while, and they played save Princess Maddy from the dragon. Mikey was the knight who saved her. Brandt got to be the dragon, while Gabe had only a bit part as the king who sent Mikey out to save her. While the kids were energetic as always, they had been cranky and a bit unruly. Mikey especially had thrown a huge tantrum, thankfully after Brandt left, when they had to leave the park. So unlike him.

As he drove to Karen's from the park, he thought of Brandt and his ease with the twins. If the man didn't have dad material written all over him.... Gabe's biological clock was ticking, so to speak. Having kids this late in life, he'd be an old man when they graduated high school. He wondered if he should even think about having a baby with someone. Long ago, Betsy had agreed to be his surrogate with Karen when they had initially thought the issue was Karen and not Gabe. Would she still be willing? Would Brandt be willing? Could Gabe stop thinking about them as if they had a future before their first date?

He groaned and got out of the car. Randy's truck wasn't there again. Mikey had fallen asleep this time, and Maddy looked to be heading there. He carried them both to the door, but it was locked.

"What the...?" He rang the bell. "Why is the door locked?" Gabe said to no one in particular.

"Mommy 'fraid of woman," Maddy said.

"Did you say Mommy is afraid of a woman, so she locks the door?"

"Uh-huh." Maddy nodded. "I'm 'fraid too."

The door opened, and Karen reached for Mikey. "Bring her upstairs. They need a nap."

Gabe followed with Maddy, who had her head back on Gabe's shoulder. He laid Maddy on her bed and kissed her cheek. Her eyes were already closing. He covered her with her purple princess blanket. He kissed sleeping Mikey as well.

Karen told him she'd be right down. Gabe went into the kitchen. There were papers everywhere, drawers emptied, food pulled out of the cupboards. The mess was massive. When Karen entered the room, she didn't say a word about the state of the kitchen.

"Karen, what happened in here?"

She gazed around. "I'm looking for something. Don't worry. I'll clean it up."

"What're you looking for that you had to empty every drawer and cupboard?"

She shrugged. "Some papers I can't find. They weren't in the place they should be. Who knows where I put them?"

Yeah, he knew. For some reason this resembled something she'd do in a manic phase. He casually walked to the counter where her med box was located. He pulled a glass from the counter and took a quick look at the clear med box. All the pills up to that morning were gone. All that was left was her evening dose. He went to the sink, filled the glass with water, and took a drink. Karen sorted papers on the counter into piles.

"Why was the front door locked?"

Karen bit her bottom lip.

Gabe's annoyance grew when she remained quiet. "Maddy said you were afraid of a woman. She's afraid too. Are you having a problem with someone?"

Setting the papers down, Karen rubbed at her forehead. "I thought I saw someone lurking around the house a couple of times. Looking into windows. But when I went outside, no one was there."

Gabe stepped toward her, alarm bells ringing in his head. "Did you call the police?" *First she thinks Randy is having an affair, and then a woman is stalking around the house? Could she be dangerous?*

"No. I don't know what I saw. Maybe someone had the wrong house. I've been keeping the doors locked just in case. I didn't know Maddy knew what was happening. I'll tell her there's no woman."

"Do you think there's a woman?"

"I don't know, Gabe. I told you. I saw something, but then no one was there."

"Did you get a good look at her?"

"Short platinum blonde hair, blue eyes. Tall, I think. That was a week ago, and I haven't seen her again. So I overreacted. I thought maybe she was the woman Randy's been cheating with."

Gabe frowned. "Did you talk with Randy about what you think?"

She ran her fingertips over the counter, her eyes averted. "I did, and he said I was being ridiculous. But what was he going to do, admit to it?"

All Karen needed was a jealous mistress sneaking about. He was going to talk to Randy. He didn't care what Karen thought. Of course, he wasn't going to tell her either. "If you see anyone around the house, call the cops, okay?"

"I will. Thanks for talking with me the other night. I should believe that he's working late. I just get lonely."

"Being a full-time mom isn't easy. Are you getting out at all? Your entire life can't be in this house with the kids. You need a life too. I told you I can take the kids anytime after work or on the weekend. Well, except Saturday. I can take them Sunday. All day. Maybe you and Randy can spend some time together. Have some fun."

"What's happening Saturday?"

Gabe felt his cheeks flush. "I have a date. His name's Brandt, and he's a substitute gym teacher at the school."

Karen allowed a smile. "I'm happy for you, Gabe. You deserve to have someone in your life."

He couldn't agree more.

CHAPTER 13

GABE FUMBLED with the buttons of his dress shirt as he dressed for his date. Brandt's directions had been dressy but casual. He'd kept mum about their destination. Gabe's excitement over seeing Brandt grew by the second, having not been alone with him since that night at the bar. They'd talked on the phone since Thursday night, their calls lasting a couple of hours each. Nothing heavy or deep or long, just the weather, sports, and work, each reluctant to get off the line. Shortly his date would be there in person, and that made him want to dance and throw up at the same time. He'd come to like Brandt more than he should. When… no, if… it didn't work out, he was certainly going to crash.

Smoothing the front of his shirt and tucking it into his black dress pants, he turned in profile in front of the mirror. Sucking in his gut, he puffed out his chest. *Hold it. Hold it.* His muscles protesting, he released his stomach and turned from the mirror, planning to chuck the evil reflective surface. What if Brandt took a hard look at Gabe and came to his senses? The possibility was there, and Gabe's doubts surfaced once again.

"Think positive, Gabe."

He frowned when he heard the front door close. Only one person had a key to get in. Betsy.

"Gabe?"

Gabe exited the bedroom to see Betsy surveying the kitchen with a suspicious eye. He'd spent the entire day cleaning every inch of his rented house, because he'd neglected the dust elephants living under the furniture and in the corners. Truthfully, it had been more to dispel the nervous energy in anticipation of his date with Brandt. He hadn't put away the cleaning supplies yet.

"Hey, Bets."

Betsy looked up, her brow crinkling. "What's up, Cinderfella? Did you get all your chores done so you can go to the ball?"

"Ha, funny. Did some cleaning."

Betsy eyed him, as if any minute an alien was going to burst forth from his gut. "I had to come and see it for myself. Julia swore it was true, but I couldn't quite believe it without seeing for myself."

Gabe smirked. "And?"

"And you're either really high on some good shit or actually happy." She continued to assess him with a look of doubt.

"Well, happier. And after my date, I'm hoping that continues."

Betsy smiled, her eyes twinkling. "I've been so worried about you, Gabe. This is really good to see."

Gabe couldn't agree more.

As he fiddled with his shirt, Betsy sighed.

"What?"

She shook her head. "Well, I am kind of jealous."

"Why?"

"You have a date. I have leftovers and a movie on my DVR."

Gabe gave her a sorrowful look. "That sounds like every one of my Saturday nights for the past... well, forever. And I thought you weren't looking for a relationship." Her career had always been more important.

She crinkled her nose and pushed a lock of hair from her eyes. "Maybe I've been rethinking that decision lately. But I'm finding some men don't like strong women who have a black belt and a sidearm."

Gabe buttoned his cuffs. "There are men out there who like strong women."

She snorted. "Right. Most want a mommy."

The doorbell rang, and Gabe flinched.

Betsy's eyes widened, and she had an expression of curiosity. "Could that be your Prince Charming now?"

Gabe's heart rate kicked up. When he didn't move, Betsy waved her hand. "Get the door."

Gabe plastered on a nervous smile and opened the door. "Hi."

Brandt was a magnificent sight standing on his porch. His smile was dazzling. "Hi. You look nice."

"You too. Come in." Gabe stepped back and let Brandt enter. His gaze perused his wide shoulders and developed chest that filled out his dress shirt, which was light blue with subtle white pinstripes and a white collar. Blue chinos fit snuggly around his tapered waist and hugged his thick thighs. Freshly shaven, he'd gelled his hair, creating short spikes in the front.

"Brandt, this is my sister, Betsy."

Brandt extended his hand. "Betsy."

She shook his hand. "Brandt."

They both had that former-military-commander air about them.

Gabe was anxious to be alone with Brandt. "I'm ready."

Brandt nodded and turned to Gabe. "Okay. Let's go."

WALKING INTO the restaurant, Brandt's warm palm rested possessively on Gabe's back. Seeing the smug look on Brandt's face, Gabe almost imagined Brandt was proud to be with him. Of course, some women were appreciating the beauty of Brandt as they passed.

They were seated in a semiprivate corner. Gabe sat to the left of Brandt at the intimate square table. With the lights dimmed, the candles in the center of every table cast much of the light in the massive dining room. Large ficus trees and silk grapevines set off the red of the walls and carpet. The muted voices of the diners and the clink of silverware against china blended in with the soft sounds of melodic violin music playing from hidden speakers. The delicious smells of baking bread and marinara sauce filled the air. However, even that didn't prevent Gabe from catching whiffs of Brandt's aftershave. The spicy and musky smell was all Brandt. In the confines of Brandt's Mustang, the aroma had been concentrated and constantly assaulted Gabe's sense of smell—so very arousing and frustrating at once.

The waiter took their drink orders and left them. Glancing at his dining companion, Gabe opened his menu. "This is a great place. I love Italian." Actually, everything about the place was perfect. When thinking of possible date scenarios (and he'd thought up dozens of them), this wasn't one he would have equated with Brandt. He seemed more like the steakhouse-bar-dartboard-jukebox-pool table kind of date. This was suspiciously… romantic.

Brandt quirked the corner of his lips. "I know." Gabe waited for more of an explanation, but Brandt continued perusing his menu.

"You say that like you have some inside information."

Brandt glanced up from his menu, and his eyes widened. A slight blush colored his cheeks, increasing his attractiveness.

Licking at his lips, Brandt slowly lowered the menu to the table. "I may have done some research for tonight."

Gabe tried to stop the muscles in his mouth from betraying the seriousness he was feigning. Crossing his arms on the table, he leaned forward. "Would the source of your research use the code name Julia?"

Oh, the man was squirming like a kid caught breaking a rule. Raising a hand and coughing into his fist, Brandt nodded and exhaled. "Yes." At least he had the decency to look repentant.

"And Julia told you I liked Italian?"

Brandt pursed his lips, then shook his head. He was practically sweating over the fact he'd done some covert ops for the date. "Um, did I tell you I had already met your sister?"

"You met Betsy?" He was so going to kill her.

Brandt appeared to be reluctant to reveal any more of his deception, but answered. "Yes. I met Betsy. I called Julia to find out what would impress you. I didn't want you thinking I only eat beef and chug beers in a pool hall."

Gabe barked out a laugh that caught the attention of a few people dining around them, but he waved at Brandt to continue.

"Of course, Julia had to make a big production out of it. Made me go to her house, and when I got there, your sister was waiting. And while they gave me lists upon lists—" He let out an exasperated sigh. "—of what you like and don't like, I did the actual planning." He sat back, and his gaze went to the tablecloth. Gabe thought he looked hesitant to admit something. "You're not mad, are you?"

The earnestness of Brandt's expression, coupled with the fact he'd cared enough to endure Julia and his sister to make the perfect date, touched Gabe's heart. He choked up and swallowed hard. With a fond smile, he reached under the table and laid his hand on Brandt's leg. The muscle immediately relaxed under his palm.

Shaking his head, Gabe said, "It's the nicest, sweetest thing anyone has ever done for me. Thank you."

Brandt returned a tentative smile. "Your sister is quite a woman. Eight years in the military is a great accomplishment, and now a federal probation officer." Brandt gave him a quick once-over and furrowed his brow. "You sure you're related?"

Gabe snorted derisively. "Just what are you implying, Mr. Sawyer?"

Brandt's eyes widened, and he shook his head, but before he could answer, the waiter brought their drink order. Gabe sat back as the waiter set a wineglass before Gabe and filled it. Brandt received an Otter Creek beer and a glass, which he filled in lieu of drinking from the bottle. The waiter took their dinner order and left. Gabe swirled the house wine and took a drink of the fruity vintage. Not bad.

"I didn't mean to imply anything about you when I said that." Brandt fidgeted with his cloth napkin.

Gabe took a drink of wine. "I agree she is an amazing woman whom I admire greatly. And I do wish I could be more like her. She's actually my half sister. My dad died when I was ten, and a couple of years later, my mom married the commander after he'd retired. Betsy came soon after that."

"How did Betsy get out of going into the Navy with a retired commander for a father?"

Gabe shrugged. "Betsy has always been a master at getting what she wants. She's my baby sister, and I love her, but her ambition borders on the pathological," he quipped.

Brandt grinned. "Says the counselor."

"I can diagnose and treat them, but I can't save myself from, well, myself."

Brandt nodded in either agreement or acknowledgment. Gabe didn't ask which. They were silent for a few minutes and then filled some of their time waiting for their meal by talking baseball. Finally Gabe went for something more personal.

"Why did you join the military?" Gabe sipped his wine. It was going straight to his head.

"You know, join the Army and see the world. I lived in a small Vermont town in Addison County and was sick of the country. Plus, my family lost their dairy farm back in the nineties. It was rough going for a few years. The Army was a free ride out of nowhere." Gabe thought he spotted longing in Brandt's eyes.

"And the reason you stayed in so long?"

Brandt sat back as the waiter set a steaming dish of cheese-covered breaded ravioli before him. "Just a good fit. It made sense for me, and I was good at what I did."

Gabe nodded as his dish of chicken parmesan was placed before him. With that interruption, the personal portion of the conversation ended, but Gabe had learned valuable information about Brandt. He was an only child. He loved Chinese food, hated anything spicy, loved anything sci-fi, loved baseball and—Gabe couldn't believe it—golf. His favorite band was the Cure. His favorite movie of all time was John Carpenter's *The Thing*. Gabe loved sci-fi and baseball.

As they finished eating, Gabe had no clue if he should pay for his meal. Shit. Why hadn't he done his own research? Okay, so when he'd dated in his early twenties, the general rule had been the man always paid, but what happened when there were two men? And what if women even paid now? He was going to screw this up.

When the check came, Gabe took the safest route and reached for his wallet. Brandt snatched the folder and slid his credit card inside. "I invited you, so I pay."

So that's how it worked.

When they exited the restaurant, Brandt held out his hand for Gabe. With a slight smile and a flutter of his heart, Gabe twined his fingers with Brandt's as they strolled shoulder to shoulder. The restaurant was on the lake, and there were boat piers jutting out into the water. Gabe rejoiced in their intimate proximity to one another and unfettered touches.

They made their way to the walkway at the waterfront as the sun set behind the mountains. The calm surface of the lake reflected the waning oranges and pinks of the setting sun. They stood side by side and admired the view, hands still entwined. Boats of all sizes cruised on the lake. The evening had already received five stars for the perfect date. It couldn't get any better, or at least that's what Gabe thought until Brandt leaned back against the railing.

With a shy smile, he reached for Gabe and guided him between his large, beefy thighs. Strong hands pulled Gabe's hips tight against his. Luxuriating in the solid warmth and arousing aroma, Gabe wrapped his arms around Brandt's waist. Hands ghosted over Gabe's back, sending a tingle spreading over his skin. Gabe turned and laid his head against Brandt's chest, nuzzling into the soft skin of his neck. He felt as safe as a swaddled babe and like the luckiest man alive.

Brandt's chin rubbed gentle circles over Gabe's scalp. Then his moist lips ghosted over Gabe's forehead. Closing his eyes, Gabe lifted his head and began nibbling on Brandt's jaw. Moving forward, he kissed a trail over Brandt's chin, covered with recent stubble, and elicited a deep, satisfied groan. Excitement shot through Gabe. Reaching Brandt's mouth, he lingered and brushed their lips together. What looked to be chaste was in reality a highly erotic touch that finished with an almost ghostlike kiss.

Gabe pulled back, humbled and awestruck by Brandt's open and trusting gaze. He knew they'd just met, but he felt so comfortable with him.

"It's nice out here." The warmth of Brandt soaked through his clothes and into his body.

"Sure is."

Brandt ran his palm over Gabe's cheek, the light touch raising goose bumps on his skin. His body reacted to the closeness. "You know, for someone in their forties, you don't even come close to looking your age."

"Are you saying that I'm a hot older man?" Gabe tilted his cheek into Brandt's palm. He ran his hand up Brandt's back and his fingers over the nape of his neck. He felt the shudder run through Brandt. Gabe's cock stiffened in his dress pants, and he hoped Brandt didn't notice.

"Very hot." Another light kiss, which deepened, and soon they were breathing hard through their noses. Rising and falling with the kiss, Gabe was sure he'd never come down from the high. That was until his phone rang in his pocket. He pulled back and sighed. Only one person would be calling him. He really should ignore the call, but Karen could be calling about the twins. He rubbed at the bridge of his nose.

He pulled out the phone and confirmed Karen was calling. "It's my ex."

"Do you need to get that? It's okay."

"Thanks." As he lifted the phone to his ear, he turned away from Brandt. "Hey, Karen, is something wrong?"

"No, nothing's wrong. I'm good." Her high-pitched, upbeat tone was so out of character from how she'd been previously.

"Oh, good." Relieved, he smiled at Brandt and held up a finger. Brandt nodded. "What's up? I'm on my date."

"Oh. Shoot. Then why did you answer?"

Gabe looked over his shoulder to see Brandt smiling gently at him.

"Because I have a very understanding date." When Brandt tipped his head, Gabe only felt a little guilty for answering his phone. "Do you need something?"

"The other day you said that you'd take the kids if Randy and I wanted some time alone. Last night we talked, and he agreed." The words poured out of her mouth, and Gabe struggled to keep up. "You were right. We really need to take time to reconnect, you know?"

"Y-yeah, sure. I mean, yes."

"Tomorrow, Randy isn't working, and we need to reconnect, you know, get our marriage on track. And if you can take the kids for the day, we can go out and do something together. So can you take them?"

Taking a minute to process her speedy words, he said, "Of course. I said I would. Are you okay?"

She laughed. "I am. Taking my meds, seeing Dr. Nemer, and talking to Randy helped. Thank you, Gabe. Thanks for getting me back on the right track, again."

"You're welcome. How about I pick them up at eleven?"

"Sounds good. I'll have them ready."

He hung up and slid the phone back into his pocket. "Sorry about that. I told Karen I'd pick the kids up tomorrow for the day."

"Oh yeah?" Brandt smiled wide. "Where are we all going?"

CHAPTER 14

THE NEXT day, Maddy and Mikey sat between Gabe and Brandt at Centennial Field at the University of Vermont. The minor-league team, the Vermont Lake Monsters, were playing the Williamsport Cutters. Maddy and Mikey still hadn't come down from their excitement of taking the "big boat" that carried cars across the lake. Currently, they were both gorging on hot dogs, soda, and popcorn. Gabe knew they'd be bored sooner or later. Sitting for long stretches wasn't their thing, and even though he'd warned Brandt, the clueless-about-toddlers man insisted they come for a few innings. Gabe hadn't been able to turn him down.

Last night had fulfilled Gabe's mushy, romantic side. (Yes, he had one of those.) Today was fulfilling his need-for-baseball side. And in a surprising twist, Gabe found baseball fulfilling both sides since, in a somewhat romantic gesture, he and Brandt were sharing a plate of nachos with their beers, even if they did have two toddlers in between them.

"So how did you know I liked baseball?" Gabe pulled a particularly gooey cheese-covered nacho from the container and popped it into his mouth. "Wait. Forget I asked that."

Brandt grinned, totally lacking the repentance he'd shown last night over accosting Julia and Betsy for Gabe's info.

"If they divulged any of my take-to-the-grave secrets, I'll have no choice but to kill you," Gabe joked.

Brandt flashed a particularly malicious grin. "Do you mean the one where you climbed the tree to save that itty-bitty kitten, or how you cried when Leonardo DiCaprio died in *Titanic*?" A sardonic laugh followed Brandt's secret divulging.

Gabe groaned. "Triple homicide. Julia and Betsy are so dead. I will strangle them." He buried his face in his hands.

"Not nice, Unca Gabe," Maddy said.

Gabe looked down on her ketchup-covered face. "You're right, Maddy. I'll be nice from now on." He wiped her face with a napkin.

She smiled up from under the brim of her Monsters ball cap.

A hand touched Gabe's shoulder. Brandt had reached across the seats. "Hey, I'll never tell," he whispered.

Gabe eyed Brandt's sultry kiss-me lips. How he wanted to taste those lips, all salty and cheesy, and bitter from his beer. The roar of the crowd broke the moment, and with another pat, Brandt returned his attention to the field. However, Gabe couldn't rid his mind of images from their date the night before. The intimate touches, quiet stolen moments, public affection, laughter. The entire night had morphed into one homoerotic vision of what Gabe wished for his future. Pulling back on the reins had been so hard. Going home alone had been even harder.

Focusing back on the game, Gabe forced himself to stay in the moment and enjoy his time with Brandt and the kids. They both took turns "harassing" the umpire and other team, but they had to shout "nice" things, because Mikey and Maddy had joined in. Soon everyone was calling out the nice things and roaring, "Nice call, ump," "I like the pitcher's outfit," and Maddy's jumbled sentence that equated to "I hope your mommy doesn't get mad at you for getting your pants dirty!"

To Gabe's surprise, shy Maddy had then climbed into Brandt's lap. "Look, there's Champ." Brandt hoisted her on his shoulders to get a better look at the mascot for the Monsters.

"Champ! Lake." Mikey pointed, jumping up and down.

"Yup, Champ lives in Lake Champlain, but he comes for the games." Gabe ruffled his hair.

"Up!" Mikey lifted his hands to Gabe, who hoisted him onto his shoulders.

Gabe balanced Mikey and managed to get his phone from his pocket. He opened the camera app and took a shot of Brandt holding Maddy. When Brandt didn't notice, Gabe focused on his profile and snapped a pic. Brandt turned his head, his eyebrow raised in amusement.

"Taking my picture? That's gonna cost ya."

Brandt moved closer to Gabe, who shrugged, feeling embarrassed. "Smart a—um, I mean, smarty-pants."

"Good catch. Okay, Maddy and Mikey, on the count of three we're all going to say Champ. Ready?"

Gabe held his camera out and got them all in the frame. "Okay, one, two, three…"

"Champ!"

The kids then took turns seeing the picture and the next fifteen minutes taking pictures with Gabe's phone. When Maddy yawned and wanted Gabe, he sat and she crawled into his lap. Mikey stood at the end of the aisle, watching the field. Brandt sat next to Gabe and put his arm around his shoulders. Gabe was sure his face would freeze with the smile he wore.

Brandt ran his hand over Maddy's hair. "You having fun, sweetie?" She nodded, and Gabe knew that she'd either be asleep soon or catch her second wind.

"Do you ever think about having kids?" Immediately, Gabe wanted to bite his tongue off for asking. Might seem like he was sizing up a future prospect.

Brandt's smile faded, and he looked out over the field. Gabe hoped he hadn't ruined the mood. "More than I did when I was in the military. There, the life I was living was wrapped up in what the Army wanted me to be. What I did day to day, where I would live, what part of the world I would ship out to. I didn't want to have a kid that I'd only see for short stretches of time and who would grow up only knowing his father from pictures or on video. I want to be hands-on, be there for everything. Now that I'm out of the service...." Brandt looked to Gabe; his expression held hope. "Maybe I'll find someone who wants a relationship and wants to have a kid or two."

Gabe tried to appear nonchalant, as if they were discussing something as mildly important as the weather, but inside he was crushing big-time on Brandt.

"What about you?"

Gabe huffed. "I'm so old now that if I find someone to be in a relationship with, then find a surrogate, try to get her pregnant, and wait another nine months for the birth, well, let's just say I may need that kid to change *my* diapers sooner rather than later. I was thinking about adoption, you know, maybe an older kid, or even someone who's gay or a lesbian, even bi or transgender. Someone who might not get adopted otherwise."

Gabe knew that had to be a deal breaker. Most men to whom he'd mentioned adopting an older kid had balked, asking why he'd want to take on their baggage. At least a baby wouldn't have issues, which totally wasn't true.

"I think adopting an older kid is a great idea."

He could definitely say he was surprised. Actually he was blown away. Most men wanted an offspring to carry their DNA. Brandt leaned forward and kissed Gabe over Maddy's head.

There was a crack, and the crowd roared, bringing their attention to the field.

"A home run for the Monsters!" the announcer shouted.

The crowd went wild. Gabe and Brandt laughed as Mikey looked around and then raised his hands and cheered.

"Yeah, monstas," Maddy whispered. Gabe and Brandt both smiled at her, and Gabe kissed her forehead.

By the third inning, the Monsters were ahead by one and Gabe's back teeth were floating. Maddy had fallen asleep, and Gabe handed her off to Brandt. He took Mikey with him in search of the bathroom. Luckily the line was short, and he sighed with relief as his bladder emptied. He changed Mikey's Pull-Up as he talked nonstop.

Holding Mikey's hand and heading back to their section, he heard his name called. Gabe turned to see his long-lost friend Marty.

"Oh shit, Marty." Gabe engulfed him in a bear hug. After Marty's move to Vermont last fall, Gabe had seen far too little of his friend who— as Marty put it—had tried unsuccessfully to "gay" Gabe up.

"Jesus, Mary, and Joseph!" Marty planted a huge kiss on Gabe's cheek. "I've missed you, mountain man. Whatever are you doing on my side of the pond?"

"Duh, I'm at a game." He chuckled at Marty's attire. Every single item of clothing—including his ball cap and scarf—were in the blue and green colors of the team and had the Lake Monsters' logo. Marty never did anything halfway.

"And you didn't call me? Break my heart." Marty pushed out his lower lip in a super pout only Marty could achieve.

Marty and Gabe had spent many afternoons sitting at the ballpark, enjoying the game and commiserating over their love lives. If they'd been even remotely attracted to one another, it would have been a match made in heaven.

"Would it break your heart to hear I'm on a date?"

Marty looked down on Mikey. "He's a little young, don'tcha think?"

"Ugh, Marty, that's not even funny. We have Karen's kids with us."

Marty's expression was one of horror. He was so not a kid person. To him they were needy little animals. Marty turned around, as if trying to get a good look at his own ass. "Nope, there're no monkeys flying out of my butt, so you can't be on a date."

Gabe grunted, then smiled. "Always the fu—I mean, clown."

Marty rubbed his hands together. "So you found a gay man who came on a date when you had two kids in tow. Are you sure he's not a straight man thinking you're a single mom?"

"Jesus, Marty. They're just kids."

Mikey pulled on Gabe's hand. "Unca Gabe, go back."

Marty frowned at him. "Kids are the gay man's repellent. Well, except that small portion of gay men with breeder dreams like you. So spill about the date? Thinking of your type, he's some large alpha male with a soft side."

Gabe chuckled. "Ex-military."

"GI Joe? Ooooh, I always loved playing with my GI Joe *action* figure. I must check him out. Lead the way."

Gabe put up his hand. "Uhh, soon, okay. This is only our second date. Wouldn't want to scare him off so quickly." And Marty with his interrogation techniques could send a trained soldier running. He should have worked for the FBI instead of an accounting firm. If he combined those talents, he'd be the perfect IRS agent.

"Good idea. Call me." Marty gave him a parting hug. The man had never feared public displays of affection.

Returning to Brandt, Gabe collapsed into his seat with Mikey, who he'd had to carry the rest of the way. "Long line at the bathroom?"

"No. I ran into an old friend from Westport. I told you about Marty."

"The drag queen?"

"Yeah. He loves baseball and comes to these games all the time."

"You should have brought him down and introduced us. I'd like to meet your friends."

A shudder of fear ran through Gabe. "Oh, believe me, if you stick around, you'll meet him. I'll warn you, though. He's scary. He'd make a Gestapo interrogation look like a tea party."

"What do you mean *if* I stay around?" Brandt smiled and shifted Maddy to his other shoulder so he could take Gabe's hand. The sincerity in his expression couldn't be missed. "I'm not going anywhere. I'm in this for the duration of the mission, see where this goes, if you're in."

That comment twisted his stomach and curled his toes. Gabe rested his head against Brandt's shoulder. "I'm definitely in."

Brandt kissed his head. Gabe was content to lean against his man until his arm started to go numb from Mikey sleeping on him. He had to shift him.

"We probably should head out." Brandt stood with Maddy.

"Right. We have to get them home."

THE KIDS slept most of the trip, even missing when they pulled onto the large boat. Brandt reached over and held Gabe's hand while they were parked on the ferry. "You're quiet. What're you thinking about?"

"Sorry. Just thinking about Karen. I hope her date day with Randy went okay. They've been having problems."

"That's too bad."

Gabe mulled over just what to tell Brandt about Karen. Since he'd hinted he wasn't going anywhere soon, he knew telling him about her illness was necessary, given her ups and downs.

"Karen has bipolar depression and was diagnosed after we were married."

Brandt's expression showed his sympathy. "I've known a few men and women in the Army who had bipolar depression. I've seen how rough it can be on a person. Most of them were eventually given medical discharges. The stress of combat, even the Army's high standards, made them worse."

Gabe turned toward Brandt in his seat. "Take the stress of having twins when you're over forty after cheating on your closeted gay husband who could never show you the love and affection you needed or give you the family you wanted and add bipolar depression."

"Damn."

"In all the time we were together, Karen did pretty well. She went to therapy and took her meds even when she was doing okay. I think I was so diligent about making sure she did what she needed to do to stay healthy, she was able to stay well. If she didn't take her meds, I brought them to her. If she missed a therapy appointment, I made her call and reschedule. Made her eat regularly, exercise. What I really became was a built-in support system that she doesn't have now."

"What about her husband?"

Just thinking of Randy raised his anger but also sympathy. "I don't know. He's a good guy. Doesn't like me much, but I think he loves Karen and the kids. She thought he was cheating, but maybe they're going to patch things up today. If they do, then maybe he will be there more for her. Mental illness is rough on relationships, which are hard enough all around."

They were silent for a moment, and then Brandt said, "I used to have the wrong idea about people with a mental illness. If they just tried harder, worked harder, wanted to be better, then they would." His face hardened and his brow furrowed. "I had this one guy in my platoon. Sam. He was nineteen and as green as they come. He was a go-getter, a bit gangly, couldn't seem to get out of his own way, but a team player from the start.

"He never would have been accepted into the military if he had a diagnosed mental illness. He never would have made it past the entrance physical. Over time this spunky kid changed, became moodier, less social, sadder. Many of the guys get homesick, have a hard time adjusting. As instructors we're supposed to push them past that. It can be... a bit brutal, but we are training soldiers, you know? There were times this kid had the energy of ten men. First in line with a forty-pound pack. Other times, dragging behind everyone, barely able to run. I pushed him, yelled at him." Brandt paused. "One day he didn't show for training. Of course, me, I'm heading for his barracks, steaming mad, thinking of how I can punish this kid."

Gabe placed his hand on Brandt's arm, hoping this wasn't going where he feared it was.

"Found him sitting on his bunk, rifle over his lap, and he was running a rag over it, just really slow. Other than that he was still. I don't even think he heard me come in, and when I got a look at his face, his eyes.... I've seen that haunted look before, and it rarely ended well."

"What did you do?"

"I sat across from him and took the rifle. Checked the chamber. It was loaded, against regulations. For the first time in a long time, I was scared about what that meant. I sat with him for a long time without talking. I knew this wasn't a case of someone who thought they'd made a mistake by enlisting and wanted out. He wasn't homesick. Everything I'd seen since he'd stepped foot on the base hit me hard. It painted a different picture than what I'd believed was going on. Of course in my head I made it about me, wondering if I was the reason that he'd gotten to this place."

"But you weren't."

"I figured that out later, but at the time I wasn't sure what to think. Anyways, that was early in my career, and after that, I became more attentive to things like that. Of course, over my seventeen years, there were more soldiers with issues new and old, some with mental illness, some with PTSD. So I know some about mental illness even though I'm only a trained military monkey."

Gabe smiled gently. "You're *my* trained military monkey."

Brandt leaned over the console. "That I am, Mr. Reynolds. Actually, pretty much from the minute you walked into that gym."

"What?"

Brandt pursed his lips, and Gabe swore his cheeks reddened.

"But you hated me."

That brought a hearty laugh from Brandt. "Try instant attraction. And that threw me. I went right into hardass mode to stop myself from making a fool out of myself. Besides, you were so pissed at me."

"And thinking about how gorgeous you were." Gabe grinned.

Brandt shook his head. "We're a couple of saps, eh?"

"Yup, but I think I like it." Gabe's fear of rejection reared its ugly head, but Brandt wasn't Tim. If their relationship didn't work out, the reason wouldn't be because one of them ran away—he hoped.

"You know what? Me too."

CHAPTER 15

WHEN THEY got to the house, Randy wasn't home, having run out for milk, so when Gabe and Brandt dropped off the twins, he could only introduce Brandt to Karen. When Gabe asked how the day went, Karen plastered on a huge smile and said perfect. Gabe hoped that fake smile really meant okay.

Brandt was roped into playing tea party with Maddy and thoroughly charmed Karen. After they left, she texted Gabe to say she was happy for him. He was happy, ridiculously happy, and ready to take their relationship to that next level. He invited Brandt to his house, where they ate dinner and had a beer. Now that part of the evening had come where they turned into nervous and shy teens wanting to get into each other's pants.

Gabe's hands itched to touch Brandt, his bare skin, kiss and lick and suck and… everything. When Brandt wandered into the living room and perused the pictures on his mantel, Gabe switched on some smooth jazz. Brandt turned and gave him that cocky grin. Gabe returned a flirtatious smile as he dimmed the lights.

Brandt's brow rose. "Hmm, if I didn't know any better, I might think you're trying to seduce me." Brandt remained by the fireplace.

Gabe flipped a switch on the wall and the gas fireplace ignited. Brandt gave him a coy look.

"Is it working?"

"Maybe."

Gabe's heart rate picked up as his proximity to Brandt increased. His hazel eyes appeared to glow with the firelight. The shadows played off the angles of his face. Gabe thought he looked like a superhero. Too bad Gabe was the comic sidekick.

"What if I asked you to dance?" The question had been a joke, one where Gabe had expected a laugh but a decline, but when Brandt raised his hands in position, Gabe swallowed hard.

"Shall I lead?" That low, growly voice was so sexy.

Gabe nodded, and when their bodies touched, he shuddered. Closing his eyes, he allowed Brandt to lead him in a slow circle. Their cheeks brushed, the stubble on Brandt's cheek rubbing over his skin.

Betsy's voice popped into his head. *Cinderfella found his Prince Charming.* Too soon to tell, but Gabe's heart had definitely jumped on board for the ride.

The sounds of the saxophone and the swaying of their bodies lulled Gabe into a semihypnotic state. The rubbing of their chests, the occasional bumping of their hips and groins, the light circles Brandt traced over his back heated his libido.

"I do believe I'm the one being seduced," Gabe whispered into Brandt's ear.

Brandt exhaled sharply. "Good, because my intent is to totally lure you in, make you all mine."

Gabe swore his heart skipped a beat. He pulled his head back and gazed directly into Brandt's eyes. What he saw there was a burning need to match his own. "Mission accomplished."

Brandt huffed, then placed his hand on the nape of Gabe's neck. For a moment, he was still. Then he attacked Gabe's lips with a fervor. Gabe clutched him tight, needing their bodies to touch, wanting to climb inside of the man. The kiss continued, their chests heaving against each other, and Gabe's cock fought against his jeans for release. When Brandt's bulge rubbed over his, Gabe gasped into Brandt's mouth, a warm rush radiating out and filling his body. That spurred him to rub harder and faster. Gabe feared this would end as it had at the bar.

Reluctantly, he pulled back from Brandt, panting. A cold sweat broke out over his skin. His lips tingled. "I just… I don't want to rush this."

Brandt nodded, his eyes heavy-lidded, his lips red and appearing swollen. Gabe thought he was the sexiest man he'd ever seen. "Yeah, slow."

"Come with me." Gabe took his hand and led him into the bedroom. Anticipating Brandt being there, he'd cleaned his room and made the bed that morning. Good call.

"Nice room," Brandt managed to say before he once again mauled Gabe.

As they kissed and stroked, Brandt walked Gabe backward to the bed. Gabe's groin was on fire, the need to feel Brandt on him and inside him greater than his need for air to breathe. Gabe grabbed the hem of Brandt's T-shirt, and they parted long enough to lift the shirt over his head. Brandt was back on Gabe's lips as he ran his palms over the rounded mounds of his pecs, his hard nipples. Gabe felt a patch of hair on the center of Brandt's chest and ran his fingers through the hair on Brandt's stomach that ran beneath his waistband. When his hand ran across Brandt's bulge, the man whimpered.

Gabe wanted to draw more whimpers from him. He was on his knees and opening Brandt's pants before he could even react.

"Gabe." His name was said on an exhale.

Gabe had Brandt's pants down around his knees and then took his cock into his hand, sliding a closed fist from base to tip and back again. His light touch barely grazed the skin of Brandt's shaft.

"Oh, shiiit," Brandt moaned. When Gabe ran his tongue over the cock head, he felt Brandt's thighs shake. "Been a while. Not going to last."

Gabe stroked, and Brandt panted. "Hold it in, soldier, and that's an order."

Brandt chuckled. "Yes, sir."

"You still have to fuck me."

Brandt's hips bucked with those words. "Jesus, Gabe."

Opening his mouth, Gabe closed his lips around the shaft and slowly made his way to the base of Brandt's wide cock, then languidly back up to the tip. He stopped, leaving just the head in his mouth, pushing his tongue into the slit. More moans, and Gabe's cock was hard as steel and leaking in his underwear. He unbuttoned his fly and fished his cock from his boxers as he bobbed faster over Brandt's shaft, tongue massaging the underside, lips squeezing, his throat relaxing, letting Brandt in farther until Brandt's light brown pubes tickled Gabe's nose. Another shudder and Brandt moaned loudly.

"So good, Gabe. My God…. Your mouth…. You have to stop, or I'm gonna come."

His hands grasped Gabe's head, trying to get him to stop. Gabe pulled off and licked at the head several times as he looked up into Brandt's blissed-out expression.

"Come up here."

Gabe stood, and Brandt ripped Gabe's shirt over his head. He grasped Gabe's cock as he licked and bit over Gabe's neck, causing Gabe's eyes to roll back into his head. Brandt's large palm stroked Gabe's shaft within his tight grip. Soon Gabe was thrusting into the snug heat. Brandt's mouth was attached to the skin on his shoulder. The suction and teeth scraping the skin pulled groans and whimpers from his throat. His hands clutched at the mounds of Brandt's perfectly formed asscheeks. He kneaded as the muscles flexed beneath his hands.

Brandt released his skin, which Gabe was sure had been marked. Licking at the shell of Gabe's ear, Brandt whispered, "You're sexy as fuck. I can't wait to make love to you. To drive you out of your mind. Watch you come while I'm thrusting inside of you."

The fire in Gabe's groin roared, and he was so ready to share that intimacy with Brandt. He stepped back and plopped down onto the bed, pulling Brandt on top of him. The weight on his body was as erotic as a hand on his cock.

"Lay on me. I want to feel you holding me down."

Brandt allowed his full weight to settle on Gabe's lower body while he kissed and licked at his chest. Gabe's back arched off the bed when Brandt bit on his nipple. "Feels so good, but I want you in me. Please. Lube and condoms in the drawer." He pointed to the nightstand.

Brandt kissed him breathless again, and Gabe wondered if a person could die from what he felt. His pulse pounded in his ears, in his groin. His heaving breaths made him feel light-headed. He closed his eyes and palmed his cock, the sensation almost too much. He stroked slowly, deliberately.

"Fuck, you look hot."

Gabe opened his eyes to see Brandt with a condom in one hand and lube in the other. He dropped them onto the bed, then removed his underwear, pants, and socks. His body was beautiful and firm. The hard angles of his tribal tattoo reached over his left shoulder and part of the way down his chest, making him only more desirable. Gabe wanted to lick every inch of that tattoo.

Brandt grabbed Gabe's pants and yanked them off, then did the same with his boxers and socks. Totally naked, he was generally embarrassed by his soft body, but the way Brandt looked at him, as if he wanted to devour Gabe, was heady. Gabe lifted his knees and opened his legs, giving Brandt total access to him.

Gabe actually thought he heard the man snarl then dive for his crotch. His hot tongue and breath coated Gabe's cock. The total number of blow jobs he'd had from men in his life could be counted on one hand. Over the years, he'd fantasized about looking down his body as a hot man made love to his cock with his mouth. Brandt doing so was a fantasy come true. He didn't want him to stop, but he was so wound up. He hadn't ever had really satisfying sex with a man, even Tim, and he feared that he would come too quick.

Gabe hissed as the cold lube hit his hole. Brandt's large finger pushed in as Gabe pushed out. The burn was minimal. He could get three of his own fingers in there no problem. He imagined that equaled two of Brandt's.

"More."

Another finger and then his cock was in Brandt's mouth. "Shit!"

Gabe bucked his hips as Brandt swallowed his shaft. The moans from Brandt vibrated over his skin. Gabe lifted his chin to the ceiling, his neck stretched, his ability to speak gone, his breath stolen. His hips were no longer under his control, pushing his cock into the moist heat and then the fingers into his hole. The pulsing grew, his entire groin one large source of pleasure.

"St-stop," he eked out.

Brandt was off him in a flash, the condom on and lubed. Gabe wanted to face him, feel the weight on top of him, and Brandt seemed to understand this. He climbed over him, their gazes locked as Brandt positioned his cock at Gabe's entrance. Not once did his eyes waver from Gabe's, the intimacy between them surrounding them like a bubble. Only they existed at that moment. As Brandt pushed forward, Gabe pushed out. The head popped in and made him catch his breath. Oh God, Brandt was inside of him.

"You okay?" The hushed tone was reverent within the sanctity of the room.

"Yes." Wrapping his legs around Brandt's hips, heels on his ass, Gabe pulled him in, the pressure steady, guiding Brandt's cock in farther, slowly, as the burn increased. "Don't stop."

Gabe bit his lip. His eyes fluttered as the fullness increased. Brandt lay on him, his weight restricting Gabe's breathing.

"Oh hell, baby, you feel so good around me."

"So good," Gabe gasped.

Brandt grunted, pulled out, and snapped his hips, ramming into Gabe, who clutched at Brandt's biceps. Brandt's face was inches from his. Gabe couldn't break away from Brandt's intense stare, couldn't believe how strong his feelings were for the man, how quickly he'd claimed his heart. He knew what he felt was lust and that love took time to develop, but he could definitely see himself loving Brandt.

Brandt set a slow and steady pace. The slide of the shaft through Gabe's muscle and the friction on Gabe's cock, stuck between them, pushed whimpers from his throat. Brandt stroked Gabe's forehead and his hair, leaving a tingling in his wake. Gabe released his grip on Brandt's biceps and placed his palm against Brandt's cheek. Their breaths were nearly in sync, and Gabe imagined their hearts beating out the same rhythm as well. Two men joined by pleasure and seemingly their hearts. With the enormity of the emotions attached to their lovemaking and how Brandt gazed lovingly upon him, Gabe's eyes burned, threatening to tear. He blinked repeatedly and swallowed hard. How lame would it be to cry during sex? Then he remembered that he'd cried after his orgasm at the bar that night. This, however, was for a different reason. Focusing on the pleasure, he lifted his hips to meet Brandt's thrusts.

"I've never felt like this before." Brandt's slow and languorous thrusts were gentle, almost loving. Gabe was content to lie with Brandt upon him, to feel the man inside of him, allowing the slow burn to build.

"Me neither, honey." Gabe pursed his lips from having used the endearment, but Brandt didn't seem to be upset by the word.

Brandt grunted, then delivered an unexpected thrust. Another hard thrust and Gabe clutched at his shoulders. Brandt's mouth thinned as his thrusts increased, the power behind them growing, reaching a punishing pace. The sound of skin slapping against skin filled the air. Brandt's body tensed, his breaths increasing. The intensity of his stare was mesmerizing. Gabe gasped as Brandt canted his hips just right and pegged his prostate.

"Brandt." He nearly sobbed as his balls became painfully tight. If Brandt kept up the torturous pace, Gabe was sure he'd come. "Don't… stop."

Gabe's vision tunneled onto Brandt's face. His head swam, and he could barely take in a breath with Brandt on his chest. God, he felt like he was flying. Brandt grunted deep in his throat, and Gabe could tell by his stuttering thrusts that he was close. Gabe bucked up harder, the rubbing of his dick between them like tingling fingers reaching into his balls. His stomach clenched, and for a moment he was suspended, his breath caught in his chest, his groin contracting, his vision blackening, his balls so tight they were painful. Right there he stayed… one… two… three. Then his balls let loose their load. He exhaled a whimpering grunt as Brandt still pounded away, his face buried in Gabe's neck.

Brandt's breath caught, and then he bucked hard, pushing in farther than he had been, his muscles taut, his jaw clenched tight. He released a breath and groaned, continuing to push into Gabe, who wrapped him up tight. His entire body throbbed with pleasure as Brandt began to relax in his arms. Gabe held him tight, keeping Brandt's cock inside, not ready to feel the emptiness. He rubbed over Brandt's sweaty back, reveling in being trapped beneath his lover.

When Brandt lifted his head and gazed down on Gabe, he looked shell-shocked.

The look was enough to raise Gabe's concern. "Are you okay?"

Brandt was still for a moment. His mouth opened, then closed and opened again. "I've never…. Nobody ever…." Again his body was still, which kind of scared Gabe.

Gabe ran a hand over Brandt's cheek. "Just tell me, honey."

Brandt's Adam's apple rose and fell repeatedly. He licked at his lips. "I've never made love to anyone before. It's always been fucking. I didn't know it could be like that."

Gabe smiled. "Same for me. Even with Tim, something was missing. I didn't know it until now."

Brandt shook his head, as if he still couldn't believe what he'd just experienced. When his gaze was back on Gabe, he whispered, "What was missing with Tim?"

Gabe sighed. "His heart."

Brandt grasped Gabe's hand and held it against his chest between them. Gabe couldn't have asked for more.

CHAPTER 16

GABE PULLED into the parking lot of Steele Heating and Plumbing. Randy's large red truck was parked beside the building. He stepped out of his car, still warring with himself over what he was about to do behind Karen's back. Brandt had gone home late the night before, and Gabe had been too wired to sleep. He couldn't help but focus on Karen and her fears that Randy was cheating on her. The seed had been planted in Gabe's head. The more he thought of Randy rarely being home anymore, his lack of interest in Karen and the kids, his lack of care in Karen's illness, that possibility solidified. What if Randy wanted out? Gabe wasn't sure Karen could handle that.

Inside he found Mrs. Steele behind the counter. She'd taken over the business when her husband had died over ten years ago. She smiled, her deep wrinkles gathering around her eyes and mouth. He guessed she had to be in her seventies by now.

"Gabe Reynolds. Well, aren't you a sight for sore eyes. Come over here and give me a hug."

When she rounded the counter, arms spread wide, Gabe accepted her hug and the kiss she planted on his cheek. When Gabe had come out as gay, she had been one of his biggest supporters, taking him aside and telling him God never turned his back on any kind of love.

"Hi, Mrs. Steele. Looking beautiful as always."

She snorted. "You young men are always trying to charm a tired old woman." Her deep blue eyes twinkled.

He laughed. "But none of us have caught you yet."

"And none of you will. I'm too sly for all of you." She winked at him, and he chuckled. He loved her sense of humor.

Going back behind the counter, she asked, "What can I do for you?"

Gabe stuffed his hands into his pockets. "I was hoping to speak with Randy."

Her smile faded slightly but didn't disappear. She cocked her head as if she had something to say but merely nodded. "He's in the back shop, working. He's always working, that one. Wish I had three of him."

Gabe pursed his lips. "Karen tells me he works a lot."

"He does. Old Barney can't work anymore, and then Cray broke his leg. I don't know what I'd do without him, although I tell him the work can wait and to head home early, but he insists on finishing."

"I'm glad you have the help. Is it okay if I go out and talk with him?"

"Of course. Maybe you can talk some sense into him. I know he has a family to support now, but a man can only work so long before his home life comes calling."

"I'll try. It was nice to see you again."

"Don't be a stranger, Gabe." She waved as he closed the door.

He rounded the building, headed to the shop out back. From what Mrs. Steele had said, cheating seemed to be off the table, since Randy was actually working long hours. How to get the man to pay more attention to Karen and work on his marriage was the issue at hand. Gabe had a premonition that what he was about to do was going to go so wrong. Still he trudged on.

The sound of metal banging against metal filled the air. Stepping into the shop, Gabe spotted Randy before a partially disassembled boiler, grunting as he tried to remove a pipe with a wrench. When the pipe didn't budge, he banged on it, swore, and threw down the wrench. Forget catching him in a good mood.

Gabe cleared his throat. "Randy?"

Randy turned his head, his dark eyes narrowing. His shaggy blond hair poked out from beneath the old, dirty ball cap he wore. His blue coveralls were grease- and oil-stained. He was only in his late thirties, but a lifetime of too much sun and smoking had aged his face.

"Gabe? What're you doing here?"

"I wanted to talk to you about Karen… and the twins."

Grabbing a once white rag off the table, Randy focused on wiping his hands in short, jerky motions. "You mean my wife and my kids."

Gabe drew in a deep breath and exhaled. Again with the territorial bullshit. "Yeah."

Throwing down the rag, Randy placed his hands on his hips. "What about them?"

Gabe rubbed at his temple, where a throbbing started. *You're a counselor, for God's sake. You talk to people all the time.* "I'm concerned about Karen and how she's been doing lately. I've talked to her a few times and been to the house. She's not doing well. Her depression is getting worse, and I'm afraid she's cycling quickly again. Have you noticed?"

"What're you trying to say? That I wouldn't notice what's going on with my own wife?" The scowl was as deep as whatever threat he thought Gabe was to his family, which Gabe didn't understand. Again, Karen had cheated on Gabe, and she had chosen Randy.

"I never said that. I'm asking because you're her husband. What have you seen lately? Is she having erratic moods, sleeping more, irritable, crying a lot, a lack of energy, seems to be sad all the time or too happy, talking fast…. You know, everything we saw after the twins were born." Gabe didn't know if the man was just that removed from his marriage, ignoring what was right in front of him, or if he truly didn't believe she was sick.

"What I've seen is Karen whining about having to stay home with two kids while I have to work my ass off to keep her in that house. You should know how expensive that house is to heat and what the upkeep costs. I don't care what queen that house is named after. It's drafty. There's no insulation in the walls. The electrical is probably as old as the house. The plumbing is a nightmare. None of it's up to code. And I'm working my ass off to keep it together. And she refuses to move. I'm sure you're here because she ran to you like she always does when she has a problem. 'Let's call Gabe. I bet he could help.' 'Gabe took the kids today to give me a break.' 'Gabe didn't have any problem keeping up the house.'"

And there was the reason Randy disliked him. But Gabe hadn't known how entrenched he'd become in their marriage. He wasn't sure how to stop Karen from turning to him with her problems and turn to her husband instead. Actually, he did know how, but could he turn his back on her? What if Randy didn't help her?

"That sounds frustrating."

Randy kicked a can on the floor, and it skittered over the concrete. "Frustrating? Whenever I try to help, she tells me that you never did it like that or tells me what you would do. I'm sorry, but I'm not you. And maybe I am working long hours, and maybe some of them are because I can't take it anymore. I feel like there's one too many people in this marriage, and one of us has got to go."

Gabe wiped at his mouth. He'd created Karen's dependence on him over the years. He was smack-dab in the middle of their marriage. "You're right."

That widened Randy's eyes.

"Karen needs a lot of support. Always has. And I gave her that support without question, most likely out of guilt, because I couldn't love her like she deserved." Without someone there every day to talk to her, remind her to take her pills, remember to eat, exercise when she didn't feel like it, keep her from doing something she'd regret during her manic phase, she'd started to fall apart. Damn, he'd been like her personal live-in counselor. "Do you believe she's sick? Because she thinks you don't."

"Of course I know she's sick. Some days are better than others. I've tried to help her, but I can't compete with the great Gabe. She's my wife, and I love her, but I can't live like this." His hard expression softened, and for the first time, Gabe saw his pain and indecision. "You know, when Karen and I first met, I remember thinking how beautiful she was and how sad she looked. Then she told me how lonely she was, and that you didn't really love her, and I thought I could do something about that. I felt sorry for her, but… I guess that's not a good foundation for a marriage, is it?"

Gabe wasn't sure what to say, given his marriage to Karen had been built on a lie itself.

Randy leaned against the metal table next to him and huffed. "She and I got into a fight last week. I told her something I never should have said, but I had to make her see how hard I was trying." Shame crossed Randy's face, and Gabe wondered what he could have said.

"What did you tell her?"

"I told her that I never wanted the twins. I mean, when she got pregnant, she was so happy. So fucking happy, and I was just wishing it had never happened. I never wanted kids, never understood them. Back after their birth when she was having such a hard time, I had to take the kids to my mom's because I didn't know what to do with them. I don't have that parenting instinct, I guess. They were crying, and I just wanted it to stop. I know you think that makes me some horrible person."

Gabe shook his head. "Not everyone wants to be a parent. There's nothing wrong with not wanting kids, but you have two kids now." Was Randy saying he didn't want them?

"I know, and if they hadn't been mine, I wouldn't have stuck around. But they are mine, and I love them. I try hard to be a good parent. I said that to Karen when she accused me of not caring." He rubbed at the nape of his neck. "I do care. On Sunday, I had planned to take them all to the petting zoo, spend some time together as a family. Karen knew that, but still she let you take them. Said she wanted to spend time alone. My only day off, and I had wanted to spend time with my family, only most of my family was with you."

"I didn't know." Karen hadn't told the truth when she'd said Randy had agreed to a day alone. "I love Mikey and Maddy too, but I never want to come between you and them." He was a roadblock to them being a family. His heart ached at the thought of not seeing them for a while, but he had to do it. "I'll step back from Karen and the kids." His throat tightened. "I just… I can't do that unless I know you're going to be there to make sure she's taking her pills and going to her appointments and well enough to take care of the kids. If she does what she should, then there's no reason she wouldn't be able to do that."

"I can do that." Randy looked Gabe right in the eye. "It's not forever either. I don't mind you spending time with the twins. They like to go with you, but I just need time to get my family back in order."

Gabe bit on the inside of his cheek. "They might not understand why I'm not coming to see them anymore. Maybe I could call them and talk once in a while. Just to say hi?"

He was clawing to find any way to keep in contact with them.

"Okay, but I'll be the one to call you and let them talk. I don't want to involve Karen right now."

Randy was stepping up, and Gabe needed to know he could make decisions, even though those decisions were ripping his heart out. "What do you want me to do if she calls?" Maybe being in control would spur him into action at home.

"Can you send her back to me for whatever she needs? Maybe don't solve her problems or give her advice? I'd like to be the one to help her."

Like a good husband should. Not an ex-husband.

"Okay."

Randy shifted his weight and stuffed his hands into his coverall pockets. "Thanks, Gabe. I do appreciate your help. I figured you'd tell me off if I even suggested any of that."

Gabe shook his head. "All I want for Karen and the kids is to be happy. To have a family." Gabe hadn't realized how much he'd felt like part of that family until right then.

Randy nodded, then turned back to his work. Gabe left, rushing to his car, dragging his heart behind him to start accepting his new role as a real ex-husband.

CHAPTER 17

DESPITE HAVING been pushed temporarily from the twins' lives, Gabe couldn't help feeling good throughout the next week. He attributed that to Brandt, who had done everything he could to improve Gabe's mood. The sex was amazing and had been repeated many, many times over, with the same breathtaking results. They'd spent time watching movies, going to a couple of baseball games, and had even rented a canoe and paddled around the lake. Brandt had yet to spend the night, a step Gabe saw as another level in their relationship that he was ready to take. He just wasn't sure where Brandt was in terms of moving forward. All indications were full speed ahead. However, Gabe didn't want to jump before he should. He'd never taken the time to let a relationship build and grow naturally. Sometimes he could be too impatient.

Karen had called several times over the week, and Gabe had dutifully redirected her to Randy for help with her issues, despite her reluctance. She did say that Randy was spending more time at home like he'd promised. The others in Gabe's life were doing better as well. Travis appeared happier in school, and most of Gabe's clients seemed to be seeing better days. Life was just better, or as Julia had said, maybe Gabe finally viewed the world through a different lens. Three weeks into dating Brandt, and Gabe allowed himself to be optimistic, even hopeful that things would work out.

Gabe pulled into the youth center parking lot for work. As he was getting out of the car, his phone rang. Without hesitation, Gabe pulled the phone out and grinned, seeing Brandt's smiling face on the screen.

"Hey, honey, what's up?" He leaned against his car.

"Nothing much. Getting ready to torture some teenagers. How about you?"

Gabe chuckled. "About to counsel some of those teenagers that you torture on a daily basis."

"Ha-ha. You're a funny one."

"Aren't I? I missed you last night." Actually he had bellyached, pined, and moped with Betsy, who'd chided rather than consoled Gabe, all because Brandt had needed to stay home and get some lesson plans done. Apparently Gabe was a distraction. Go figure.

"Missed you too, hot pants."

Gabe caught himself before he giggled like a girl.

"I was hoping to make it up to you tonight by cooking dinner for you at my place."

Gabe's brow rose. "Uh-huh. Didn't you describe your place as a one-room hovel that even a third-world insurgent wouldn't be caught dead in?"

Brandt huffed. "Well, yeah, but we won't be in my hovel above the garage. The Kramers are going to Europe for a few weeks and said I could stay in the house if I wanted. I'm going to be living in the lap of luxury." Brandt sounded pretty damned proud of himself.

"That's a beautiful house, and on the lake too. I may just have to accept your invitation." Gabe grinned, wishing the day weren't just beginning. Someday they were going to have to plan a nooner.

"Oh, you'll accept and be there with bells on."

Gabe snorted. "Oh really? And why is that?"

Gabe could practically hear Brandt smiling through the phone. "Because I'm irresistible."

The truth, but Gabe wasn't going to give him the satisfaction. "Hmmm, don't let that head get too big, Mr. Sawyer."

"Just remember that name, sweetie, because you'll be screaming it tonight."

A shiver ran from one end of Gabe's body to the other. He felt as if he couldn't breathe. He swallowed hard and managed to say, "Promises. Promises."

"Later, Mr. Reynolds."

Gabe hung up, his world shifting again just from talking to the man. He wondered if his aging heart could take the man six years younger than him. As he started inside, he wondered if all the sex they'd been having could be considered exercise. He smirked. If so, he had been training like an Olympian.

Once inside, he greeted their only volunteer, Vicki, at the reception desk, picked up his messages, and started his day. Around ten o'clock Karen called.

"Gabe, can you take the kids tonight?"

Guilt washed through him as he recalled his conversation with Randy. He couldn't break his promise, even if he ached to see the twins. "I wish I could, Karen, but I have plans."

"Could you change them?" She sounded a tad anxious.

He swiveled in his chair from the computer. "What's wrong? Are you okay?"

"I'm a…. Randy, he has to work late, and I really need to get some things done. Maddy was home today with an earache—"

"Is she okay? Does she need to see the doctor?" Why hadn't Karen called him? Then he scolded himself because that was Randy's territory.

"No. She's fine. The nurse at the preschool checked her yesterday afternoon. Her throat's a little red. It's been going around the school. I'm probably going to have to keep her home tomorrow too. I just need a couple of hours."

Gabe didn't like how she sounded. "I thought Randy wasn't working as much."

"He's not, but he has to do a couple of late nights a week."

Gabe rubbed at the bridge of his nose, his good mood fleeing fast. "I'm sorry Maddy doesn't feel good. But I can't change my plans. You should talk to Randy about this."

Karen sighed impatiently. He knew she was angry that he wasn't helping her. "I did, and he said I had to wait until he got home, but I have to do this tonight, Gabe."

He turned to his computer and pulled up his resource page. It couldn't hurt to give her a number, right? "What about Andrea's niece, Violet? She's graduating soon. You've used her in the past."

There was silence.

"Karen?"

"I don't trust other people with the kids. I only trust you. I can't have a stranger in the house."

"You used to have a couple of sitters when the kids were around six months old. It's good for them to spend time with other people, and it's good for you to have more than one person to depend on."

Another long sigh. "I know. Maybe I'll call her."

Gabe knew she wouldn't call, and that had to be her decision. "You sure everything's okay? Meds good? Seeing Dr. Nemer?"

"Yes!" she snapped. "I'm sorry. Maddy didn't sleep well last night."

Gabe's gut tried to get him to change his plans, but he needed to keep his promise to Randy and see Brandt. "Make sure you sleep when she naps, okay?"

"Yeah. She needs some juice. Bye."

He hung up the phone, reassuring himself that he'd done the right thing. When his cell phone vibrated, he swiped the screen and found a text message from Brandt.

Can't stop thinking about you.

Grinning like the kid who won the big game, he texted back. *Same here.*

Couple of saps, I tell ya. LOL

And you love it.

You bet I do. <3 <3

Gabe stared at the red hearts, and his good mood was back. When he realized he'd been sitting and gawking at his phone, he stuffed the distraction into his pocket. His next client was probably waiting for him.

He went to the reception desk and found his next client, Jana Holmes, sitting in the waiting area, furiously texting on her phone. The tenth grader came Mondays during her free period. Usually someone from the school drove her there and waited inside, but Gabe didn't see anyone.

"Hi, Jana."

She looked up. "Hi, Mr. R." She popped up from the chair and walked to him.

"Did someone from the school drop you off?"

"Yeah, Mr. Grant, but he got a call and said he had to run back to the school. I'm sure he'll be right back."

"All right. Come on in."

As he shut the door, she plopped onto his futon. Her phone beeped as they sat down. He gave her an expectant look. She shut off the ringer and handed him the phone, which he placed on his desk.

"So how was the weekend with your dad?"

"Good."

He raised his brow. "Care to elaborate?"

She shrugged a shoulder. "I don't know."

They did the same dance each week. He'd thought about sending her an agenda ahead of time. Maybe she'd come prepared to talk.

"Last week we talked about how you felt being ordered by the court to go to your father's house. You just had your first weekend there."

She nodded.

"We also talked about how you'd only seen your father once since he got out of jail six months ago, and felt as if you were being forced to stay with someone who was a stranger."

She pursed her lips, and her unaffected attitude faded. She clasped her hands in her lap and rubbed her thumbs together. Her breathing had accelerated. Finally, some feelings were heading to the surface.

There was a knock on the door. Gabe sighed. Bad timing.

He opened the door to see Vicki. "Ms. Messier's on the phone. She says there's an emergency at the school and needs to talk to you now. I can hear sirens," she whispered.

He remembered what Jana had said about Mr. Grant being called to the school. An icy cold ran over him. He picked up the phone on his desk as Vicki and Jana both watched with rapt attention.

"Julia, what's wrong?" The high-pitched wail of a siren drowned out her reply. "Is that an ambulance?"

"Gabe!" Even shouting, he could barely hear Julia over the commotion of voices and sirens. "There was an accident in the science lab. Some students… injured… well…." The phone cut out.

"Julia, I can't hear you. You're breaking up."

"Can you… hospital now?"

"You want me to meet you at the hospital?"

"Yes!"

Gabe hung up the phone.

"What's going on?" Jana asked.

"Something happened at the school. Jana, call your parents and wait here until someone picks you up. Vicki will be here with you."

Gabe grabbed his keys and school ID. He flew past Vicki, who yelled after him that she'd reschedule his appointments. His hands shook as he tried to insert the key into the ignition. He prayed no one was seriously hurt, but the calm-in-the-eye-of-the-storm Julia had sounded so freaked. If kids were hurt, Gabe might be able to calm them down and help contact parents.

Within twenty minutes, he was at the nearest hospital in Elizabethtown and barely recalled driving there. He'd called and sent several texts to Brandt, asking him what happened, but he didn't respond. If the building was evacuated, then he might have left his phone in his office. Gabe weaved around people in the emergency room—the sheer number of kids being triaged in the hallway was staggering. Gabe searched for anyone he knew, hoping to find Julia. A weak voice called out to Gabe. He spun around and spotted Travis huddled on a gurney, an oxygen mask covering his face.

Gabe rushed to his side. "Are you okay? What happened?" Gabe placed his hands on Travis's shoulders and surveyed him for injuries.

Travis removed his oxygen mask and immediately started hacking. Gabe placed the mask back over his mouth and nose. "Take some deep breaths."

Travis inhaled, then exhaled, and his coughing abated. He chanced to remove the mask again. Deep red blotches covered Travis's face and neck. Tears filled his wide, scared eyes. Gabe wrapped an arm around his shoulder as Travis shook against him.

"I'm okay." His throat sounded raw. He leaned into Gabe.

"Good. I know you're scared, but I'll stay with you."

Hospital staff rushed by them, trying to deal with the overwhelming number of patients.

"Are the others all right?" Travis's voice had the rasp of a whiskey-drinking, two-packs-a-day seventy-year-old.

"I don't know." Gabe squatted down to Travis's level. "Can you tell me what happened?"

Travis coughed, then drew in a stuttering breath. "I was making up a lab with Mr. Smyth and a couple of other students. He was doing a demonstration under that hood thing with the clear sides. He was mixing chemicals. And there… there was an explosion. And…." Travis paused for another round of dry, chest-aching coughs. His eyes misted over. "The sides of the hood blew out." A sob escaped. "Mr. Smyth's shirt caught on fire and smoke filled the room. It burned to breathe, and… I… I fell down… couldn't catch my breath." His sobs were interspersed with hacking coughs as Gabe took his hand.

"It's okay. You're going to be okay. You're safe."

He shook his head. "Mr. Sawyer…." Travis hiccupped and shuddered.

Tight bands squeezed around Gabe's chest at hearing the name, and all the blood seemed to drain from his head. "Mr. Sawyer?"

CHAPTER 18

TRAVIS FLEW into another coughing fit, and Gabe forced the mask back onto his face, then urged him to lie back onto the gurney. "Rest, Travis. I'm going to find Ms. Messier and see if everyone is okay."

Travis grabbed Gabe's wrist, and his eyes widened with a moment of terror. "Gregg."

Gabe frowned. "What about Gregg? Was he in class with you?"

Travis nodded with a look of desperation. "He was sitting next to me. Please, find out if he's okay." Travis tried to sit up again, but Gabe held him back.

"I'll go find Gregg right now, and then I'll come back and tell you what's going on. Okay? But you have to stay here and keep the mask on."

Travis surveyed Gabe's face, then nodded.

"Did someone call your dad?"

Travis shrugged and closed his eyes as a nurse came up to the gurney.

"Travis, I need to take you for a chest X-ray." She unlocked the wheels on the gurney. "Are you his father?"

Gabe shook his head. "I'm his...." Gabe wondered if he should identify himself as Travis's counselor.

"He's my counselor."

Just as Gabe was going to ask the nurse about Travis's dad, the man came through the crowd. "Travis, are you okay?" His father's voice was unsteady, and he was pale.

Travis's eyes filled as he wrapped his arms around his father. Gabe stepped back as the nurse filled him in on his son's condition. Gabe waved as they moved toward X-ray, promising to find Travis later.

Running a shaky hand through his hair, Gabe went in search of Gregg and Julia and, God help him, Brandt. Was he hurt? How bad? Gabe could barely breathe as the bands around his chest tightened more. Gabe fought his way to the counter, where an overwhelmed receptionist scurried about. As he tried to flag her down, an arm grabbed him.

He turned, and Julia engulfed him. "Thanks for coming."

Gabe wrapped his arms around her. "I saw Travis. He said there was an explosion in the lab. Dan and Gregg… are they all right?" He couldn't get the words out to ask about Brandt.

Julia pulled back, wiping a tear from her cheek. "I just got here. The fume hood that should have contained the explosion failed. Flames burned Dan's arms and stomach. Travis and Gregg and another student in class inhaled the fumes. The smoke filled some of the other classrooms too. We had to evacuate the entire building. It's a mess." Julia wrapped her arms around herself. "Is Travis okay?"

Gabe ran his hands over his face. "I don't know. He can't stop coughing. They took him for X-rays when his father arrived. Travis wanted me to check on Gregg."

Julia's eyebrows disappeared under her fringy bangs.

Gabe shook his head. "I know. His biggest nemesis and he wants to make sure he's okay." Gabe could only shrug.

Julia bit at her lower lip and avoided looking at Gabe. Gabe closed his eyes, gathering his courage. "Travis said something about Brandt." The lump in Gabe's throat grew as Julia shook her head.

Please no….

"He saved them. You know the science lab is across the hall from the gym. The kids in his gym class said they heard the explosion, and Brandt ran into the science room. The classroom door was closed, so the fumes were strong. I'm not sure what chemicals Dan was using. Brandt carried Dan and the students out one by one." Julia's anguish cut right through Gabe. "Brandt collapsed in the hall, and when the ambulance took him, he was still unconscious. I haven't heard anything else."

Gabe took in a deep breath. The shaking started in his hands, partially from relief that Brandt wasn't dead, but also from the knowledge he'd been hurt and he didn't know how badly.

So help me, if I cry here….

He wasn't sure what to do. He wasn't family. Really, in terms of getting medical information, he wasn't anybody, and that roiled his gut. "I sh-should find out about Gregg. Can you find anything out about Brandt, please?"

Julia nodded. Gabe squeezed her arm, then moved toward the receptionist. The hallway was slowly clearing. Gabe prayed those students had gone home and were unharmed.

The receptionist said she would find out what she could about Gregg. After another hour of pacing and hand-wringing, Gabe was able to see Gregg and then Travis. Both boys, including the third boy in the room, David Ware, were under observation due to chemical burns in their lungs. Barring any complications, a full recovery was expected. Gregg and Travis had both been relieved to hear the other was okay. Something funny was going on there, but Gabe didn't push it—yet.

Dan Smyth hadn't been so lucky. Second-degree burns covered his forearms. Luckily, the fireproof gloves and goggles had protected his hands and eyes. His stomach had third-degree burns and would require skin grafts. He was being shipped to the burn unit at the University of Vermont Medical Center in Burlington. And Brandt—the big strong man who'd manhandled Gabe into unadulterated bliss and carried four people out of danger—the ex-soldier, was struggling to breathe, his already scarred lungs unable to get in enough oxygen. They feared he might eventually require a breathing tube. Currently, he was being prepped for transport to Champlain Valley Physicians Hospital in Plattsburgh. When Gabe had asked what "already scarred" meant, Julia hadn't known.

Since Gabe couldn't claim family status, or even partner status, because really he wasn't sure, he'd been shut out. In fact, he had no clue if Brandt's parents had even been contacted. Julia's only statement to Gabe was that the emergency contact in Brandt's employee record had been called. Gabe was nobody to Brandt at that moment. What if he needed Gabe? Would they come and get him?

After thirty minutes of Gabe checking on the few students left, finding out when their parents would arrive, and pacing, anything to keep his mind from the worst scenario, they were informed that Brandt was in the ambulance and heading out. That information had Gabe sprinting to his car for the forty-minute drive to Plattsburgh. Forty minutes alone in the car, forty minutes to think and catastrophize. And man, could he take a situation and bring it to the worst conclusion ever.

Gabe sat in the partially padded waiting room chair at CVPH, legs stretched out and crossed at the ankles, arms folded over his stomach, and head tilted back. Three hours and he'd heard nothing. The ER nurse said when Brandt was stable they'd tell him that Gabe was there for him. That did no good for Gabe's nerves.

His phone rang. Julia. "Hi."

"Any word on Brandt?"

He rubbed his face. "Nothing. They keep telling me they'll let him know I'm here when he's stable. I don't even know what that means. How're things there?"

"A mess. I'm back at the school to oversee the cleanup. The rest of the students have gone home. Travis, Gregg, and David should be out tomorrow, barring complications. School will be closed for a couple of days."

"How's Dan?"

He heard her huff. "I spoke with his wife. Carrie said he's resting, and a burn specialist is coming in to discuss treatment soon. He was lucky his hands and face were protected."

"Yeah."

They were both silent, neither seeming to know what to say.

"Do you need me to come there? Hang out with you?" She would if he needed her.

"No. No sense in both of us sitting here doing nothing." He just wanted to zone out and wait.

"Okay. Call me when you know how he is."

"I will. Talk to you later."

Gabe clutched his phone. He wasn't leaving the hospital until he saw Brandt. Just that morning they had been laughing and joking, planning another evening together. He opened his text app and scrolled through the dozens of text messages they'd shared over the last week. Truthfully, that only served to remind him of what a short amount of time he'd been with Brandt, even if they'd spent nearly all their time in the last three weeks together. He sighed and leaned back to wait.

Dozing lightly, his head filled with images of Brandt with that adorable smirk, those hazel eyes twinkling as he gazed at Gabe, his husky voice whispering in Gabe's ear. Damn, he felt totally lost and alone. When the emergency doors slid open, Gabe looked in that direction. A tall man in a rumpled uniform—with a white shirt sporting several rows of colorful service bars, blue pants, and shiny black shoes—pulled the cap off his shorn head. The man walked confidently to the receptionist. Tall with broad shoulders, trim waist, graying temples, strong jaw, and light blue eyes, the soldier commanded attention.

"I was called and told Brandt Sawyer was brought here." The deep Southern drawl was surprising.

The receptionist clicked away on the keyboard. "And you are?"

"Lieutenant Colonel Lucas Gage, ma'am." He had that same authoritative tone, the same confident air as Brandt.

The receptionist nodded. "You're listed as his emergency contact. Mr. Sawyer was moved to a room not too long ago. If you follow this hallway and take the first set of elevators to the third floor, the nurses there can direct you."

The stoic man's shoulders rounded a bit. "Is he okay?"

The receptionist gave the soldier a sympathetic look. "The nurses can fill you in."

He nodded and turned toward the elevators.

Gabe rushed after him. "Excuse me. Lieutenant Colonel Gage?"

The officer snapped around, stopping Gabe in his tracks. "Yes?"

Gabe wiped his hands on his trousers, then held one out. "I'm Gabe Reynolds. A friend of Brandt's."

He eyed Gabe's hand in much the same way Brandt had at their first meeting. Gabe waited. Finally the man took Gabe's hand into a firm grip. "Call me Lucas."

He nodded and felt like prey as Lucas's eyes assessed every inch of him. His face gave nothing away. Lucas stuck his hand into his pocket and pulled out a cell phone. Gabe wasn't sure what he was doing as he clicked away at the screen. When he looked to Gabe and back to the phone and then repeated the pattern, Gabe wanted to shake him. Couldn't he see how freaked out he was?

"Ahh, that's you." Lucas turned the phone and showed Gabe the selfie he'd taken at the baseball game with Brandt and the twins.

Gabe worked hard to suppress the swelling pressure behind his eyes.

"Brandt sent me that picture a couple of weeks ago. Said he'd met someone who, and I quote, 'sucker punched him in the gut.' I have to say the man's never been, well, sucker punched before."

Gabe tried to smile, but his body was going to explode at any moment. "I need to know he's okay."

"Come with me and we'll see how he's doing."

Gabe swallowed repeatedly, pushing that lump down. Feeling as if he finally had control of his raging emotions, Gabe looked up and nodded, wishing he could release the tension overwhelming his body.

As they headed toward the elevators, Lucas asked, "Do you know what happened?"

Lucas pressed the Up button, and as they waited, Gabe filled him in on what Julia had told him about the explosion. When the doors opened, Gabe stepped in after Lucas.

"That's Sawyer. Always charging into danger. We've been friends since we were stationed together at Fort Benning about a hundred years ago." He chuckled and shook his head. "The man doesn't have an ounce of fear in that thick head of his." He scowled. "Fucking hero."

Gabe remained silent since he didn't know anything about Brandt's past. When the doors opened, they proceeded to the nurses' station. Gabe hung back as Lucas gave his name to the male nurse manning the station. A loud crash echoed through the hall. Gabe and Lucas both turned. A distraught red-haired nurse ran out of the room with a frown. She walked quickly down the hallway and stopped at the nurses' station. Her bright hair clashed with her lilac scrubs.

"If he doesn't calm down, I'm going to tie his ass to the bed."

The male nurse Lucas had been speaking with curled his lips into a smile. "The cavalry has arrived. Meet Lieutenant Colonel Lucas Gage." He pointed to the soldier.

"Excuse me?" Lucas frowned.

The red-haired nurse came around the counter, hands on her ample hips. "You're here for Brandt Sawyer?"

Lucas shifted uneasily. "Yes, ma'am."

"I know he used to be in the military. Do you outrank him?"

Lucas's eyebrows rose. "He's not in the military anymore, ma'am."

"*Did* you outrank him?" The impatience practically dripped from the words.

"Yes, I did. But I'm not sure what that has to do with now. Is he all right?"

She huffed. "I have a feeling he's never been all right. That has to be the most stubborn and downright prickly man I've ever met. I thought maybe you could order him to shut up and follow orders or something."

Gabe closed his eyes and thanked God. Brandt had to be okay if he was giving the nurses such a hard time.

Lucas covered his mouth, feigning a cough, but Gabe could see the corners of his mouth twitch. "Not sure he'll listen to me."

"We also need to find someone named Gabe before the nurses revolt and he finds himself on the wrong end of an enema."

Gabe raised his hand and rushed to the desk. "Me. I'm Gabe."

She gave Gabe a sympathetic look. "He says you're his partner. You must have the patience of a frickin' saint."

"Is he okay? Can I see him?" He just needed to see him with his own eyes. See he was all right.

"He's been given breathing treatments for the chemical burns in his lungs, which is complicated by a fair amount of old scarring, and with the burns, the amount of oxygen he's absorbing is low. But he still has enough energy to keep trying to get out of bed and leave."

Lucas chuckled. "He's a horrible patient."

"Can I see him?" Gabe was so close, and this nurse stood in his way.

"Be my guest. Don't forget your chair and your whip." She left, grumbling something under her breath.

CHAPTER 19

LUCAS TURNED to the other nurse. "What room, sir?"

"Second door to your right. Just follow the crashing sounds." The man chuckled and went back to his chart.

As they neared the room, Gabe heard Brandt trying to shout. "Get away." Pause. "Enough blood." Pause. "I want out of… here." His voice sounded weak and gravelly.

Lucas placed a hand on the partially opened door and rolled his eyes. In an instant, he hardened his face and pushed the door open.

Brandt reclined on the bed, his arms pulled tight to his naked chest. A nasal cannula delivered oxygen. A sheet covered his lap, and his chest was bare. His menacing scowl was directed at a young man in blue scrubs. A wild look of confusion and fear in his eyes, the man cowered a safe distance away from the bed.

"Stand down, Major!" Lucas's voice boomed through the room, and Gabe felt the vibrations through his own chest and froze in his tracks. The man in the blue scrubs spun around.

Brandt immediately looked to Lucas and pretty much stood at attention (as much as one could when in bed). His chest rose and fell in exaggerated movements.

"Major, you will sit still, shut up, and allow this man to draw your blood. Is that understood?"

Brandt's jaw tightened as he appeared to struggle not to glower at the officer who outranked him—or used to outrank him. "Yes, sir." He dropped his arms.

Lucas nodded to the frightened phlebotomist. "Go ahead, sir. He won't give you any more trouble."

The man's head snapped between Brandt and Lucas. Tentatively, he moved toward the bed. Quickly spreading out the supplies from the kit on the nightstand, the man prepped Brandt's arm, then ripped open a package containing the needle. Brandt sighed heavily and turned his head away from the needle-wielding man. That gave the scared man some confidence, and he quickly drew the blood. Took all of thirty seconds, and then he fled the room.

"Your antics are becoming legend around here, and you've been here for what? A whole three hours? The nurses are already plotting their revenge." Lucas moved closer to the bed.

Brandt continued to stare off at the wall. "Luke... you know how much... I hate being here... I want to go home." His voice cracked, and he appeared to pout. His frame deflated as the stiffness left his body. The grayish, pallid tone of his skin was unsettling.

Lucas laid a hand on Brandt's shoulder. The touch seemed to relax Brandt further. "I know, but you've got to let them take care of this. Don't make it worse, or you'll be stuck in here longer." The quiet softness in Lucas's voice belied his imposing exterior. "But I brought someone to see you, and you need to keep making that good impression on him."

Gabe stepped farther into the room, arms wrapped tight around his middle. Brandt's gaze locked with his, and Gabe fought the lump in his throat.

"Finally. Come here."

Gabe rushed to the bed and then stopped, afraid to touch him. "Are you hurt?"

Brandt raised his arms in reply. Gabe bent, and Brandt pulled him down until he sat on the edge of the bed. Brandt squeezed him so tightly that he himself had trouble breathing. He didn't care.

"Are you okay? I was so scared." Gabe forced the unsteadiness from his voice.

"You're shaking.... I'm going to... be okay."

Gabe let his fear go. Brandt was safe. He pulled back and cupped Brandt's pale cheeks. His breaths were so shallow and fast. "If you ever scare me like that again...."

Brandt raised a brow.

"Well, it won't be pleasant."

"I promise." Brandt took Gabe's hand and kissed his palm. "Do you know if Dan... and the kids are okay?"

"Travis, Gregg, and David are in the hospital but will be okay. Dan's at UVM in the burn unit. He's going to need skin grafts, but he's alive. They're all alive because of you."

Brandt started to cough, and Gabe held his hand as the hacking reddened his face and brought tears to his eyes. He sighed. "Fuck. Hurts."

"Do you need anything?" Lucas asked.

Brandt pointed to the gray plastic jug on his bedside table. "Water."

Lucas poured the cold water into a cup and dropped in a straw. Gabe held the cup while Brandt drank, then set the cup on the table.

Gabe rubbed Brandt's chest in soothing circles. "The nurse said you have old scars in your lungs. I don't understand."

The scowl wasn't unexpected, and neither was Brandt looking away from him.

"I'm sorry. You really shouldn't be talking." Gabe didn't want to upset Brandt and start another coughing fit. "Have you seen the doctor lately?"

He shook his head no. When he looked to Gabe, the anguish in his eyes was like a knife in Gabe's chest. "I can't be here… please, get me out."

Gabe squeezed his hand. "How about me and Lucas go find your doctor and see what's going on? Okay?"

Brandt gave an economical nod. Gabe smiled, but Brandt only sighed. Kissing Brandt on the forehead, Gabe stood and then followed Lucas out of the room. In the hallway, Lucas did an about-face and stopped in his tracks, surprising Gabe.

His jaw was clenched, his brow heavy over his eyes. Gabe suddenly felt as if he'd done something wrong. Maybe he wasn't what Lucas thought Brandt needed. Gabe stiffened his spine, ready for something awful. When Lucas seemed to collapse against the wall, Gabe was confused.

"Are you okay?"

Lucas swiped his hand over his face. He looked exhausted. "When the principal called and told me what had happened in the lab, I knew his lungs had already been compromised before. Then I had to catch a flight and drive here. Luckily, I was in the States. But I had about four hours to think the worst, you know?"

"Yeah, I've been sitting here waiting, so I get it." Gabe chewed on his lip. "He was injured in the service. That's why he left?"

"Medical discharge. I can't tell you what happened. It's up to him to share what he went through with you or anyone else. I will tell you that he was in Walter Reed hospital for over a month and then spent another three months living in Tranquility Hall for rehab. Most of that time, he was alone. His family only visited when they could. I imagine he's terrified that will happen again."

"Shit." He had to be reliving the worst of those memories now. "He's coming home with me. No questions asked."

Gabe braced for an argument, but Lucas merely nodded. "I was hoping you'd say that. Let's go find ourselves a doctor and get the sitrep on what's going on."

Gabe nodded and followed Lucas to the nurses' station, already planning what needed to be done to make Brandt comfortable at his place. "Wait."

Lucas stopped and turned to face him. "What if Brandt says no? I mean, about coming to stay with me." What if that was going too fast?

Lucas shrugged his shoulder. "He won't have a choice. There's no way the doctor is going to let him go home alone. I'll make sure of that." Lucas winked.

Gabe was glad to have an ally.

Two hours later, as Gabe waited for the doctor to check in, he reclined in a chair next to Brandt asleep in the bed. The nurse had given him a mild sedative, and with the extra help, he appeared to be resting peacefully, despite his accelerated rate of breathing. Lucas had gone to buy clothes and toiletries, since he'd jumped on a plane with only his wallet.

In the quiet of the hospital room, Gabe pulled out his phone. There was a voice message from Karen and several texts, including a couple from Julia and Betsy. He rubbed at his forehead, trying to think of what he needed to do. First he had to let Andrea know he was taking at least a week off. They were short-staffed, so he e-mailed the names of those who would definitely need a check-in and those who could wait. He couldn't remember the last time he'd taken more than a couple of days off, so he was due.

Once that e-mail was sent, he opened his text messages. He sent Julia an update and also texted Betsy to let her know what was happening. She immediately replied, hoping Brandt was okay, and asked him to call when he could. He sent back his thanks.

Last, he looked at Karen's texts.

"Fuck," he groaned.

Over ten texts ranted on about how angry she was about Gabe speaking with Randy behind her back. She was pissed about Gabe's "macho, chest-pounding, caveman decision" without her input and his deceit, which she wasn't sure she could forgive. None of the blame mentioned Randy, which was a good thing since he was now her main support. What had he told her? That was something Gabe should have discussed with Randy before leaving the shop. Sounded as if he'd told his wife everything they'd discussed. Gabe had expected backlash from their decision, but not until she realized Gabe was distancing himself. Randy probably shouldn't have told her about their plan of Gabe's removal. He was about to text a response to Karen when Brandt shifted and groaned, his eyes fluttering open. Gabe stood, and when Brandt saw him, he appeared relieved.

"Hey. Do you need anything?"

Brandt licked his lips. "Water, please."

Gabe poured a fresh cup of ice water. Brandt's hands shook, so Gabe held it steady as Brandt took a drink.

"Thanks."

Gabe set the cup down and took Brandt's hand in his. With his fear waning and adrenaline crashing, he had time to think of what losing Brandt would have meant. His stomach had that funny feeling like he got on certain rides. He had to admit he was falling hard and couldn't stop that speeding train even if he had to. Brandt had captured his heart and could do what he wanted to the fragile organ. If Brandt decided that Gabe wasn't the one for him, Gabe was sure he'd only manage to survive but never love again.

Ha, you thought that with Tim as well, and that wasn't true.

But what he felt for Brandt was a kind of love that he'd never experienced before. And he both loved and hated that at the same time.

"What's wrong?" Brandt's concern showed in his beautiful hazel eyes.

Gabe smiled. "Nothing. I'm just really glad you're going to be okay." Gabe rubbed his thumb over the back of Brandt's hand. He admired the strength in those hands, loved to feel them on his body. A shiver raced over his skin.

Brandt cocked his head and narrowed his eyes, appearing to doubt what Gabe had said. He gave a closemouthed smile, and his eyes softened, crinkling at the corners. "I'm really glad… you're here. Thanks." Brandt lifted his chin, and Gabe covered the distance to bring their lips together. Brandt's warm, rapid breaths puffed over his face. That funny feeling in his gut increased tenfold.

"Get a room."

Gabe jumped back and turned to see Lucas sauntering into the room. Out of uniform, he wore a sweatshirt and jeans. He wasn't bad-looking for an older man. Then Gabe realized Lucas had to be younger than he was.

"Got one." Brandt grinned suggestively.

"You're looking better." Lucas patted Brandt's shoulder. "I ran into the doctor in the hallway. He'll be in shortly to deliver your sentence."

Brandt frowned deeply but remained silent.

On cue, the door opened and the doctor walked in, holding a binder. "Hello, Mr. Sawyer." He looked at Brandt, then to Gabe expectantly.

Gabe held out his hand. "Gabe Reynolds." He didn't qualify who he was. He wasn't sure what to say. The doctor fixed that.

"Ah, the partner. Good. I was hoping they'd track you down. I'm Dr. Robert Collins. I'm a pulmonologist." He set down the chart and moved to the side of the bed. Lucas stepped back to give him room. Dr. Collins placed the ends of the stethoscope in his ears. "Let's take a listen. Your O2 stats are already improving with the oxygen." The doctor checked several places on Brandt's chest, stopping to listen, then moving on. "Okay, deep breath."

Brandt complied.

The doctor moved the stethoscope. "Another." He then had Brandt sit forward and moved to his back. "Another deep breath." By the time he'd finished, Brandt was panting.

The doctor pulled the stethoscope from his ears and flipped it over his head, resting it around his neck. "I'm not hearing any signs of pneumonia or fluid in the lungs, which is good. There is some crackling, but that's expected." As the doctor spoke, he poked around Brandt's abdomen. "That doesn't mean it isn't a possibility, given the injury you've sustained. A respiratory therapist will be meeting with you with exercises to strengthen your lungs and avoid the fluid buildup. Don't skip them, or you'll be right back here and in serious danger."

Brandt raised his hand. "I know. I've done them before."

"Right. I contacted Walter Reed for your records once I learned of your former lung injury. Given the sustained amount of smoke you had inhaled with the first injury and the level of scarring, I'm surprised you're as healthy as you are. That definitely helped you in this situation."

"When can I go home?"

Dr. Collins surveyed the chart. "I want two more blood gases at least twelve hours apart. Depending on those results, you may be able to go home tomorrow."

Gabe could see Brandt's entire body relax.

"You will need to be on continuous O2 until you can sustain an oxygen saturation above 98 percent. Use it when you sleep, *even* if you feel you can go without it. If you don't, you will stress your heart by making it work harder to get oxygen to your body. You must avoid anything strenuous until cleared medically. For a few days, I don't even want you walking to the bathroom, so you'll need a commode chair. No stairs for at least two weeks, or longer, and you can't stay alone. If your lungs start to fill with fluid, you'll need to call an ambulance to get you to the hospital." He looked to Gabe. "Don't drive him no matter how fast you feel you can get him there. If anything happens to delay your trip, he could suffocate."

Gabe's fear socked him in the gut, and icy panic washed over him. "Are you sure he should even go home?" Even with the scowl Brandt gave him, he didn't back down. "Brandt, we'll be forty minutes from this hospital. Wouldn't you feel better staying here?"

Brandt didn't hesitate to shake his head. "No. I need to… go."

Gabe bit his lips to keep from arguing. Maybe he wouldn't be able to leave once the doctor saw his blood gas results.

Brandt huffed out a breath. "My apartment has stairs."

"You'll stay with me." Before Brandt could argue, Gabe said, "I took the week off, and I can take longer if you need me to."

"Good. I'll be back in the morning to check in. Let the nurses know if you become very short of breath or start coughing up anything different than you have been." The doctor left, and the silence was thick, nearly stifling.

"I don't want you to have to… take care of me." Brandt had crossed his arms, and he refused to look at Gabe. The air took on an icy chill.

"You want to leave the hospital, then you have one option. Stay with Gabe or stay here. I have three days of emergency leave. Then I head back. It's your choice." Lucas's tone was steady, almost harsh, but in reality those were Brandt's only options.

Brandt stared off as he no doubt contemplated his options. Finally, he nodded tersely and said, "Okay."

Lucas left the room. Gabe patted Brandt's shoulder, and while he didn't pull away, he didn't respond. He merely closed his eyes, an expression of dissatisfaction remaining until he fell asleep. Was he angry that Gabe was his only choice? Maybe giving him that option wasn't a good idea and was indicative of how Brandt really felt about Gabe. However, he'd told everyone that Gabe was his partner. That meant he was serious, right?

Gabe decided to believe the latter and chalk this up to Brandt being a cranky patient. And Lucas had mentioned he hated hospitals. Hopefully, this time tomorrow, Brandt would be free and his mood would improve.

CHAPTER 20

GABE GRITTED his teeth as Brandt, once again, refused to eat the soup Gabe had made for him. Being released from the hospital hadn't made Brandt any more cheery or cooperative. Gabe hadn't slept much since they'd returned to his house. The doctor had advised Brandt to sleep practically sitting up. Hard for a guy who slept on his stomach the entire night. To keep him upright and on his back, Gabe had piled a wall of pillows around Brandt, leaving little room for Gabe. And since the spare room had gone to Lucas, who had finagled a few extra days of leave, Gabe slept on the couch.

That had been three days ago, and even that amount of time out of the hospital, Brandt was still a downright growly bear.

"Brandt, you need to eat. You only had half a sandwich for lunch. If you get weak, you'll get sicker."

Brandt frowned. "I'm not hungry."

Gabe sighed. "Just take a couple of spoonfuls."

"No."

"I can make you something else."

"Not hungry."

"How does your chest feel? Any pain when you're breathing?"

"No."

"Coughing up anything?"

"No."

"Do you need anything more?"

"I'm good."

Great conversation.

Brandt's breathing had slowly been improving, and he no longer had to gasp for air to speak. He had been cooperating with completing his breathing exercises. Other than that, he appeared to be moping, and Gabe had no clue what to do. Frustration mounting, Gabe wasn't sure how much longer he could keep his mouth shut. Why had he suggested Brandt come there? The coldness had appeared after he'd practically forced him to stay. Their relationship was going to be ruined before they could even make a good go of it.

"I'm going to leave it here. Please, try to eat." Gabe bent and kissed his forehead, but Brandt didn't speak or even move.

Gabe left the room, stomped right out the back door to the deck, lifted his head to the sky, and screamed.

Hearing a chuckle, he turned to see Lucas, beer in hand, sitting in one of the Adirondack chairs. "Sawyer tends to elicit that reaction in most people. Beer?" Lucas pointed to the six-pack minus one on the deck beside him.

"Yes." Gabe grabbed a beer, screwed off the top, and sucked down the cool liquid. He plopped into a chair and let his head fall back. "Has he always been this stubborn?"

"Yup."

"I get that he's grumpy because he's hurt, but this is above and beyond the call of duty." Gabe refrained from mentioning how terrified he was that Brandt was done with him.

"You ain't seen nothing. This is mild compared to Walter Reed. But I know Sawyer. He's a black-and-white fellow. It's either this or that. Nothing in between, nothing gray." Lucas took a drink. "That type of thinking shuts down a lot of options, you know?"

"I'm not sure what you're trying to say."

Lucas shifted in his chair, turning toward Gabe. "He's a strong individual molded to think with an Army brain. He's only as useful as his body is. When his body wasn't up to par, the Army discharged him. To Brandt, who'd considered the Army his family for so long, that was devastating. You're either in or you're out. That's why being at Walter Reed was so hard for him. The reminder of the fact that bodies could be broken was everywhere."

"Jesus, is this about some petty idea that because his body is damaged that he's either in or out with me?"

"To you it sounds petty, but I think this incident reminded Brandt that he's more fragile than he wants to be. I think he's scared about what that means for his future, not only for himself, but with you."

Gabe swallowed. "But he'll get better."

Lucas rolled the beer bottle between his hands and sighed heavily, his gaze on Gabe's backyard. "After his first injury, the doctors told him that over time the ability of his lungs to oxygenate his blood will decrease. They were weakened, and eventually he'll develop emphysema and more than likely need a lung transplant."

Gabe squeezed his eyes tight, needing to control any overreaction. His chest squeezed, and the pressure stole his breath. "How soon?"

"When this first happened, maybe fifteen or twenty years. Now with this injury.... Shoot. I was hoping he'd come around and tell you this himself, but he's a stubborn jackass. When he was discharged, Dr. Collins told Brandt that he needed to see his doctors back at Walter Reed for another assessment. His feeling is that original time frame would change, possibly be drastically sooner."

Gabe needed to process the information. Truthfully, he didn't give a crap about how damaged Brandt was. He loved his body but also his mind, healthy or sick. He just loved him.

He huffed. "Jesus Christ, I don't give a rat's ass about any of that. Being scared that you can't be who you've always been, that your ideal self has changed, I get that. That it takes time to work through the grief. But to think I wouldn't want him if he wasn't that perfect man?"

"It has nothing to do with you or anyone else not wanting him. It's how he envisions himself in his own head. When he thinks of you and him together, he's seeing a certain version of himself, who he was when you met. Now he has to change the version of himself he sees, and he doesn't like it. No matter what role he's in, that version of himself needs to change. Partner or son or a teacher or a friend."

Gabe understood that. Many times, the barrier for some wasn't being accepted by others, but rather the acceptance of who they themselves had become.

Lucas sighed. "I'm guessing Brandt saw himself as some kind of strong, capable protector who can surmount any physical problem. Being in the military, like I said, the condition of your body is who you are."

Gabe was out of his league with that issue. "You know him best. What can I do to break him out of this? I feel like he's slipping further away from me. I don't want to lose him."

"Why don't you bring those cute kids over? Maybe that would soften him up."

"I wish I could, but I promised my ex's husband I'd back off for a while. It's a long story. But just know that isn't possible." A great idea, though, that had Gabe itching to call Karen. Although she wouldn't talk with him. He'd texted her, saying he was sorry for going to Randy, but there had been no reply. Randy hadn't returned his messages either. He couldn't worry about them right now.

"Give him some time. Let him process all of this. I'll talk to him tomorrow. I'm heading out the day after, so he might want to stop being a jackass and lighten up."

Gabe's beer was empty, and he'd relaxed as much as he could. "I'm going to check my e-mail. Maybe do some mindless Internet surfing."

"I recommend porn."

Gabe snorted. "That's something I do alone in a dark room."

He put his beer bottle into the recycling bin. Inside, he sat on the couch and powered up his laptop. Clicking on the web browser, he was going to open his e-mail. Instead, he went to Facebook. Talk of the twins had started that ache in his chest again. Going to Karen's page, he clicked on the photo icon and was immediately hit in the face with Mikey's and Maddy's cuteness. There was no lack of pictures. Gabe opened each one and studied them closely. He laughed at the one of Mikey stuck in a bucket he'd wedged his butt into. The one of Maddy in her yellow princess dress warmed his heart. Her blonde hair glowed in the sunlight. Light blonde hair and bright blue eyes and dimples in their chins. Just like Randy.

He clicked through more pictures, wondering how they'd become so important to him, how someone else's children felt as close as his own. Maybe that's what he'd been hoping for all along. Maybe that was the reason he'd remained close to Karen since their split. Those kids were supposed to be his, were supposed to be a part of him. Instead another man had stolen what he'd yearned to have for so long. A family. Didn't he deserve a family?

His lip quivered. He had to see Maddy and Mikey.

THE NEXT day Gabe stepped into Bright Minds Preschool at lunchtime. The school had an open invitation for family to join them each day for lunch. Gabe had grabbed a sandwich on the way there. His biggest fear was running into Karen or Randy. Didn't matter, the twins would narc on him. At their age, secrets weren't their forte.

Walking into the main area of the school, he was hit by the squeals and shouts and laughs of a room filled with toddlers. Immediately, he spotted Maddy playing with the large dollhouse with another boy and girl. Mikey ran in circles with what looked to be a superhero action figure, possibly Captain America, in his hand. The relief of being there with them was immense, and any stress he had fled.

"Gabe. Welcome." Mrs. Dunning, the owner of the preschool, made her way around the toys strewn on the floor. She was shorter than average, with long black hair reaching her waist. Her denim jumper with the apples on the bodice, red-and-blue striped socks, and clogs screamed "teacher of small children."

"I stopped by for lunch, if that's okay."

Her surprised expression seemed exaggerated, which he imagined had been honed by interacting with kids for years. "Certainly. Free time is about to end, and then we eat. Give me a second to bring this motley crew to order."

Turning, she went to the counter and grabbed a bell. Ringing it once, she waited, and several children stopped what they were doing, including Maddy, while others continued their play. Ringing it twice, she waited again. Those kids who'd heard poked at those who hadn't. Mikey was in that group. Probably 75 percent of the kids were now standing still and looking at her. Another ring of the bell and she had the entire room's attention. Gabe was astonished.

"Wonderful, children. What does three bells mean?"

In a loud chorus, the children answered, "Three bells mean we're doing swell!"

"That's right. Now I want you all to quietly put your toys away, then get your lunches. How will we pick up?"

Another chorus. "Quietly." The soft words made Gabe believe this woman was the kid whisperer.

Mikey caught sight of Gabe and charged for him. "Unca Gabe!"

That caught Maddy's attention. In a flash, both kids were in his arms.

"Where you go?" Maddy cupped his cheeks.

Gabe beamed. "I've been working, sweetie."

"You miss truck. Big truck." Mikey's eyes widened, and his arms stretched out.

"A big truck, really? Wow. Let's sit down. I'm going to eat lunch with both of you."

They settled at a really low table with short chairs. Gabe passed on the chair and sat on the floor.

Maddy touched his hand as if to say, "Finally you came," while Mikey kept on about the truck. Gabe nodded as his words melded together because he was talking so fast.

"So you saw a really big red truck."

"Uh-huh. My house."

Gabe didn't think he was referring to Randy's truck.

Maddy appeared frightened. "Fire."

Gabe froze, his sandwich halfway to his mouth. Big red truck. Fire. Fear clenched his heart in an iron fist. "Did you have a fire at your house?"

Maddy nodded, then took a bite of her cheese sandwich.

"Big fire." Mikey raised his arms above his head.

Gabe set his sandwich down. "Did firemen come to your house?"

Mikey gave an exaggerated nod, those blue eyes as wide as ever. "In big truck. Spray water."

"Where was the fire?" Gabe feared something Karen had done or failed to do was the cause.

"On stove." Maddy frowned.

"Are Mommy and Daddy okay?"

"Mommy hurt." Maddy's eyes grew glassy. Gabe could see her fear growing and decided to change the subject.

"Hey, guys, remember the baseball game?"

That got their minds off the fire. Gabe spent the remainder of lunch talking about the big boat and Champ. When it was time to say good-bye, Gabe hugged them both tight, kissed them, and promised to see them soon. He asked them to keep his visit a secret but knew that was a fat chance.

When he got to his car, he pulled out his phone, debating who to call. Karen had been hurt by a fire, according to the kids, but she wouldn't answer his calls. Randy would probably slug him for breaking their deal.

He dialed Charles.

"Gabe. How're you?" Charles sounded hesitant.

"I'm good. I was—"

"Wait. Before you say anything or ask me anything, I have to tell you that Karen rescinded her release for me to talk to you."

Gabe opened his mouth. Why had he expected different? "Shoot."

"She was quite irate that you spoke with Randy without her permission. She said you'd agreed not to."

Gabe clutched the phone. "I had to. She wasn't telling me the whole truth. And I found out from Randy that I'm near the top of the list of issues they have. I agreed to stay away from Karen and the kids, but I don't know if I should. I wanted to see how she is. I was just with the kids, and Mikey said something about a fire at their house."

Charles was silent for a moment. "Didn't you just say you agreed to stay away from the kids?"

Shit. "Yes, but… I had to see them to check in, and I was right. Something happened."

"Gabe, stop and listen to yourself for a minute."

Taken aback, Gabe stayed silent. What was Charles getting at?

"Since your divorce you've been right there, still fulfilling to some extent your role with Karen as her caretaker. A role her husband should have taken over."

"But he didn't. He couldn't do it!"

Gabe wasn't sure where the anger came from, but its ugly head was poking out.

"How do you know? Did you always know how to help her? Was it easy at first?"

No, it hadn't been easy. They'd been married after they received their bachelor's degrees. Gabe had only just begun grad school when she was diagnosed. "No. I made tons of mistakes. I didn't understand." How easy it had been to forget the beginning. "And there were times I couldn't take it." Particularly during her first manic episode. He'd found her up in the middle of the night painting the walls of their student housing apartment a bright purple color. Her elation, her over-the-top enthusiasm, had scared him so much he'd left her there alone and didn't return for a good twelve hours. If not for Karen's best friend, Ann, Gabe might not have made it through.

"But I did have help. I accepted help from Ann." God, he wished she were there to help, but she'd passed away from cervical cancer when she was thirty-six. Another time in Karen's life her illness had gotten away from her.

"Have you given Randy any time to find his own supports with his family or his friends?"

"Jesus, Charles, what do you want from me?" Gabe floundered as he felt blame was being placed on him, and that illogical thinking was so unlike him.

"What do you think I want from you?"

Gabe wanted to scream at Charles not to pull that therapy crap on him, but he bit his tongue. He rested his head against the steering wheel. He knew Charles would wait as long as he had to for Gabe to answer. But his throat tightened, and he wasn't sure if he attempted to speak that he would be able to make a sound. How had everything gone so wrong in such a short period of time?

"Let me put this another way. What are you getting out of your continued relationship with Karen?"

What was he getting? Wasn't Karen the one getting, the one he was trying to save, keep from hurting herself, because if anything happened to her, those kids would.... He squeezed his eyes shut, his gut clenched and his brow furrowed deeply. If he'd eaten much at lunch, he might have thrown up.

"If anything happened to Karen, the twins would be taken away from me." He whispered the words with an innuendo of guilt. His greatest fear, besides being alone for the rest of his life. He did care for Karen, loved her as a friend, and didn't want to see her hurt, ever. But would he have been so involved in her life if the twins hadn't been born?

He heard Charles sigh. Gabe felt drained and so confused. Was what he'd said true?

"You should take some time to think about that. Where do you fit, and what will your continued participation in that family's lives do to them?"

In other words, why Gabe should be involved at all. How could he do that if he couldn't even go a couple of days without seeing Mikey and Maddy?

"Yeah. I will. Thanks, Charles."

"Listen, Gabe. You can call me anytime. I'm not just here to talk about Karen."

Gabe clenched his jaw. "Thanks. Talk to you later." He chucked the phone onto the passenger seat, needing to go home. Home where Brandt sulked and lay in that bed day after day. He might not be able to help Karen or see the kids, but he could try to help Brandt. He also needed a distraction. Getting through to Brandt required drastic measures if Gabe had any chance of pulling him out of his funk—if that was at all possible. He picked up his phone, searched his contacts, and hit Send.

"Hi, Marty. I have a huge favor to ask."

CHAPTER 21

ON HIS way to the grocery store, Gabe passed Travis's house. He thought he should just check in on him, see how he was healing after the explosion, and let him know that if he needed anything while Gabe was out that he could call him directly. Of all his clients, Travis was the one whose internal state could change without notice. Pulling into the driveway, Gabe parked behind the few cars already there. He hoped he'd find him home.

Travis's father opened the door. "Mr. Reynolds. Come in. Nice to see you."

Gabe stepped into the foyer of the small house. "You as well. And again, call me Gabe."

Travis's father looked relaxed, even happy, given his usual state was the opposite when Travis was having issues. "Okay, then call me Phil. Is Travis expecting you?"

"No. I was driving by and thought I'd stop and see how he was doing with his recovery. I'm taking a couple of weeks off from work and wanted to check in."

The happiness faded from Phil's face, and Gabe knew his concern.

"I'm available anytime for him to talk. And I will check in weekly otherwise. I had a friend who was hurt in that explosion, and he needs my help."

"A teacher?"

Gabe hadn't planned on telling anyone about Brandt, but he did. "Mr. Sawyer, the gym teacher."

Phil's lips curled in, and he looked to the floor. His hand fisted on his thigh. When he looked up, the sorrow was immense. "You tell that man thank you for me. If he hadn't done what he did and got Travis out of there, he might not be here. I'm not sure what I'd do without him, even if he's a pain in my ass."

Gabe lifted the corner of his mouth. "I'll tell him."

He pointed to a doorway. "The boys are in the back room playing games. Go on in. I've got some food cooking on the stove."

With that he disappeared. Gabe was hesitant. If Travis had friends over, he might not want everyone to know that Gabe was his counselor. After another moment he decided he was there and he'd peek in and maybe could get Travis's attention.

What he found when he peered into the room made him catch his breath, and his jaw practically hit the floor. On the couch, Travis was locked in an embrace with Gregg…. Gregg Nolan. His biggest nemesis. His bully. The kid who'd made Travis's life a living hell for over two years. Two years ago, when Travis had first known he was gay, he imagined Gregg had come to the same realization. The bullying and name-calling had apparently been a smoke screen to hide his attraction to boys—and to Travis. Jesus Christ.

And there was no doubt about what was going on. The intimacy between them was apparent, hands traveling over each other's bodies. Travis was not only tolerating touching another person, but the touch was intimate. Gregg's face was visible to Gabe, and he was awed over the loving gaze and gentle smile. When they began to kiss, Gabe cleared his throat. The pair jumped apart as if jolted by electricity. Both boys immediately colored red from the neck up.

"M-Mr. R-Reynolds. What are you doing here?" Travis's eyes were wide with fear. Gregg looked as if he were in the headlights of an oncoming car.

Gabe didn't want to scare either of them, but he had to make sure Travis knew what he was doing. "Something you want to tell me, Travis?"

"Umm… well, I think this kind of explains it all." He waved a hand toward Gregg.

Gabe sat on the chair across from them. "I see what's happening. Last I knew, you both hated one another. And you"—he looked to Gregg, who sank back farther into the couch—"you were constantly beating on Travis. Forgive me if I find this disturbing."

"I did beat on him, and I hated myself for it. I hated that I was attracted to guys, that I was a fa—"

Travis raised his brows at Gregg.

"That I was gay. If my parents knew…." He swallowed hard. "I thought if I just wanted to be straight hard enough, showed everyone that I was strong, a jock, then I would be." He lowered his eyes.

Travis reached for his hand, and Gregg looked at him. The vulnerability in his expression wasn't anything Gabe thought he'd ever see.

Gabe looked to Travis, who hardened his expression, no doubt ready to defend his decision. Gabe rubbed at his forehead, not sure what to say. Was this really the time to open up a counseling session? Probably not.

"You're comfortable with this relationship?" God, what he wanted to ask was how he could trust someone who had pretty much terrorized him.

Travis nodded, his smile kind of dreamy and dopy when he looked at Gregg. "Yeah. I know what I'm doing. There are things only Gregg and I know that might explain this better, but no one else needs to hear them."

Gabe was intrigued but let that go. "I'm concerned about…. If you two…. Have you been more intimate than this?"

Gregg's face reddened even more. He definitely wasn't used to talking about his feelings or anything so private.

"What I mean is, we've talked about your difficulty with others being close." Gabe was close to revealing personal information Travis had told him in confidence, and had to tread lightly. But he felt as if he had to assess if Travis was in any danger of falling back into those memories of his mother's abuse. That could undo years of healing.

"I don't know why, but Gregg touching me doesn't bother me. I trust him, as weird as that is to say. I'm not sure if I could let anyone else get as close. I need you to trust that I know what I'm doing here. I think… I think Gregg is good for me."

They both smiled shyly. God, young love, how naïve and blind… and exciting.

"Does your father know about this?"

Travis frowned slightly. "He does, and you know he doesn't care that I'm gay, and he's even okay with me having a boyfriend but…. He is not as happy that it's Gregg. He said he'd be watching us carefully."

Gabe dropped his hands into his lap. Travis was good for now. He'd counseled him for over eight years and cared greatly for the kid's well-being and happiness. He knew life and how it liked to kick people around. He had to allow Travis to live those trials and tribulations of being a teen, because relationships forged in the teen years rarely lasted.

"Okay. As long as your dad is keeping an eye on you both, I'm going to head out. I'm taking a couple of weeks off from work, but you can call my cell if you need anything. Anytime. Okay?"

Travis nodded. Gabe looked to Gregg, who froze. "That goes for you as well." Gregg nodded slightly.

"I'll see you boys later."

Before he could exit the room, Travis said, "Tell Mr. Sawyer we said hi and thanks for helping us."

Gabe looked back, ready to ask why Travis thought he would see Brandt, but they were both chuckling, grinning wide, and he knew they wouldn't buy anything he said to the contrary.

"Yeah, okay."

When he got to the front door, he heard them explode into fits of laughter. He couldn't help but chuckle himself at their behavior. Gabe didn't care how they'd found out or who knew. He loved Brandt Sawyer, and he planned on telling him so.

AFTER HITTING the grocery store, Gabe entered the kitchen, loaded down with bags. Lucas grabbed those that were tipping and in danger of falling to the floor.

"Did you leave anything at the store?"

"I have more in the car."

"Planning for the apocalypse?"

"Nope. A small gathering of people."

"A party?" Lucas looked at Gabe as if he'd lost his mind.

"Not a party, a few friends over to hang out, watch some movies, you know, a gathering."

Gabe might have appeared to have lost his mind, but he was going to do anything to get Brandt out of bed. Even if it was to yell at him. Brandt could get up and move around; he just had to bring his oxygen tank with him.

Lucas pursed his lips. "Are you thinking that this is going to do Brandt any good? Because I'm thinking just the opposite."

He shrugged a shoulder. "It's not for him. It's for you. He just happens to be stuck here while it's happening."

Lucas lifted his chin and looked down his nose at Gabe. "Me? What are you talking about?"

"You're leaving tomorrow. I'm giving you a going-away party."

"Have fun without me. I won't be your pawn in whatever twisted game you're playing. No, sir."

Gabe grunted. "You're afraid of Brandt."

Lucas narrowed his eyes. "Am not."

"Are too."

"Am not."

"Uh-huh."

"Listen here, the day I'm afraid of that stubborn jackass is the day I grow purple wings."

Gabe lifted the corner of his lips. "Your wings are showing."

"Ugh!" Lucas raised his hands and dropped them dramatically.

Gabe knew he'd won. "Can you get the rest of the groceries? I'm going to rouse Sir Cranky."

"It's your funeral," Lucas muttered as he went out the door.

Gabe went to the bedroom. He found Brandt in bed as usual, staring at the TV. Was he watching *The Price is Right*? Things were worse than he thought.

"Hey, honey." Gabe sat on the side of the bed, right in line of the TV. Brandt had no choice but to look at him.

"Hey," Brandt muttered.

Gabe rubbed his fingers lightly over Brandt's arm and swore he shivered. "How're you feeling?"

Brandt shrugged. "Crappy. Just want to rest, maybe sleep."

Or lie there all depressed and hopeless like.

"I bet being in this bed for so long has really stiffened you up." Gabe started to massage Brandt's upper arm, working his palm into the hard muscle. Brandt's eyes closed for a moment, his face growing slack. Gabe suppressed a smile.

Gabe worked down his forearm, over his palm, his fingers, then back up. He'd missed the feel of Brandt beneath his hands. And seeing Brandt's calm expression, the limpness of his body, he seemed to have missed the feeling as well.

Gabe worked his shoulder and his left pec. "Roll over and I'll get your back."

Brandt hesitated and opened his mouth but closed it quick. He rolled onto his stomach, and Gabe straddled his thighs. Methodically, he worked the muscles until they were putty in his hands. Gabe swore he heard Brandt groan as he kneaded the knots out of his lower back.

His hands were cramping, but Brandt was totally pliant beneath him. Gabe bent down, placing his mouth next to Brandt's ear. Brandt's breaths were slow and steady. "I've missed touching you. Your skin, your muscles beneath my hands. Nothing feels better. No one I've ever touched compares to how you feel. How you make me feel. I'm never going to get tired of touching you or feeling your hands on me."

Gabe climbed off Brandt and stood next to the bed, then raised his hand and slapped Brandt on the ass. Brandt gasped and turned to face Gabe. The shocked expression was priceless.

"Now get up and shower. We have company coming."

JULIA, DAVE number two, and Betsy sat on the couch talking with one another. Lucas occupied the chair next to them, waiting for the dreaded Brandt shoe to drop. Gabe went into the bedroom and nearly fell over, seeing Brandt dressed in a T-shirt and jeans and sitting on the edge of the bed. He'd thought getting him to leave the bedroom would be an act of war.

"Hey, honey. Now that you're up, we can change the sheets before the vermin show up." Gabe stood before Brandt, who gazed up at him. Gabe picked up his oxygen tank. "Hmm, maybe we should camo this thing, butch it up a bit." That brought a hint of amusement to Brandt's eyes. "Come with me. We have some guests."

Gabe was sure Brandt would resist, but he stood. His skin no longer had that ashy gray, and his breathing was steady and slow. Gabe took his hand, and Brandt let him.

"I must say, Mr. Sawyer. Looking as hot as always."

When Gabe attempted to move forward, Brandt stopped walking. Gabe gave him a questioning look. Brandt shifted, then licked at his lips. When he ran his hand over Gabe's cheek and then rested his forehead against Gabe's, he let out a long, drawn-out sigh.

"I know this has been so hard on you. I promise no matter how long it takes, I'm here. Okay?"

Brandt nodded.

"No matter what, you are the best thing that's ever happened to me."

Brandt's eyes opened. He rested his hand on Gabe's neck and huffed. Whatever he wanted to say wasn't coming for him. But he managed to say, "Me too, baby." Gabe was good with that.

"Thanks for trying for me. Come on." Gabe led him into the living room, and silence filled the room. Brandt settled into the chair, then looked at everyone.

"This is it? I thought you said there was some kind of party going on out here." Brandt gave the room a speculative once-over.

"Couldn't start without you, sunshine." Lucas gave Brandt a knowing look and nodded sharply. Brandt nodded back.

Gabe knelt on one knee before Brandt and rubbed his thigh. "Want something to drink or eat? We have pigs in a blanket." Gabe's singsong voice brought a smirk to Brandt's face, not quite back to his old self but a start.

"Sounds good."

"How about a soda?" Gabe sighed and went into the kitchen to grab a can from the fridge. The knock on the door heralded the arrival of his surprise guest.

Opening the door, Gabe shook his head, grinning. "I must say, Ms. Maybelline Couture, you look fabulous." Gabe had only seen Marty in drag once, and oh, man, he dolled up really nice. Towering dark brown wig, dark smoky eyes, red pouty lips, a rack that definitely wasn't homegrown, waist cinched tight, and wide flared hips in a low-cut, high-slit purple sequined dress. He had that Judy Garland slash Liza thing happening.

"Darling, I always look fabulous." Maybelline threw her purple boa dramatically over her shoulder. "Now, where's that hunk of beef of yours? Momma's hungry."

Maybelline pushed past Gabe, who chuckled. Then he thought of the Southern lieutenant colonel seeing Maybelline for the first time, and he rushed to stop her.

"Hold it. I have to introduce you, right?"

"I guess I put my big old cart before the horse. Announce away, sweetie." Maybelline adjusted her ample bosom.

Gabe grabbed the soda, biting on his lips to keep from smiling too wide as he entered the living room. Betsy and Lucas were deep in conversation, probably something about the military. Gabe hadn't thought, but maybe he could kill two birds with one stone. They were both single and had that service thing in common. Julia and Dave number two were talking to Brandt, who appeared to be more relaxed.

Gabe handed him the soda, and Brandt took the can, then grabbed Gabe's hand. The expression on his face appeared to be one of gratitude. "Thank you."

Gabe had a feeling he was thanking him for more than the can of soda. Gabe bent down. "You're very welcome." Gabe kissed him lightly, the touch of their lips sparking and zinging through him. It had been so long since they'd been intimate, too long. Brandt must have thought so as well. Jesus, Gabe wanted him.

A throat clearing caught their attention. Gabe sighed and turned to see the whole room staring at them.

Betsy snorted. "Would you like us to leave you two alone?"

With a grin, Gabe flipped her off, and she gave him a less than convincing look of contempt.

"I'm waiting, and Ms. Maybelline Couture never waits!"

That raised some brows and caused some chuckles among the crowd.

Brandt's surprised expression told Gabe he'd hit the mark "Is that who I think it is?"

"Sure is, honey. Enjoy."

"Oh Lord," Julia groaned. "You didn't."

"Oh yes I did. As I said earlier, I have a special surprise for you all. She's traveled across the lake, all the way from Burlington, Vermont, for one show only. May I introduce Ms. Maybelline Couture!"

CHAPTER 22

IN TRUE Maybelline style, she burst into the room to applause, arms stretched wide, red lips puckered. When Gabe looked to Lucas for his reaction, he appeared to be pinned to his seat, his hands in a death grip on the chair, eyes wide with something akin to horror or fear, as if a speeding train were about to smash him into itty-bitty bits.

"Oh, my lovelies, thank you, thank you so—" Maybelline halted upon seeing Lucas, only for a moment. The surprise on her face fled quickly, and then she was sashaying again. Perhaps she'd seen his reaction. Damn, Maybelline was even feistier than Marty and would kick the ass of anyone who crossed her.

Gabe looked to Brandt, who shrugged. Lucas averted his eyes, which darted around, his knee bouncing, his jaw clenching. Did he hate drag queens?

"Thank you so much, all of you. Oh, is it hot in here or what?" Fanning herself, she walked toward Brandt, hips snapping from side to side. "Well, well, well. I do believe I've found the source of the heat in this room. Just look at this hunky, gorgeous alpha male here. Mhm, mhm, mhm. You're a big one, aren't ya? All over, I'm sure. And ex-military to boot, I hear."

Brandt's face flushed red despite his kid-in-a-candy-shop grin.

"Gabe, honey, when you said you'd found a man, you didn't tell me you'd brought home GI Joe. Damn, sweetie, I bet you know how to handle a loaded weapon, if you know what I mean."

Brandt laughed along with everyone… well, everyone except Lucas.

"Let's get to the entertainment portion of the evening. I'm going to sing you one song, and then I'm getting out of this dress, because these babies"—she jacked up her breasts—"are sweating like a virgin on prom night. Gabe, darling, my music, if you would, please."

Gabe hit the Play button, and Maybelline gave them an entertaining, over-the-top, dramatic rendition of Gloria Gaynor's "I Will Survive." Brandt beamed, thoroughly enjoying the show, clapping and even feeling up Maybelline's breast when she bent to wrap her boa around his neck. Gabe noticed Lucas had even started watching, definitely trying to school his expression. Given he barely knew the man, he wasn't going to ask what was wrong.

A roaring round of applause and Ms. Maybelline Couture bowed graciously, waving as she exited to the kitchen.

"I just love Maybelline." Betsy looked to Lucas. He forced a smile and nodded.

Brandt rubbed Gabe's arm. "Thanks, baby. I needed that."

"I know you did. Just know we are all here to help you with whatever you need. You aren't alone."

Brandt nodded, looking down. Maybelline returned, duffle bag in hand. "Can I use your little girl's room?"

"You know where it is." Gabe stood. "There's food in the kitchen, so everybody eat."

GABE SHUT off the bathroom light and joined Brandt, who was already in bed, reclining against a pillow. His chest was bare, the blanket covering his lower half. No matter what his body looked like or how poor his health became, Gabe couldn't imagine not wanting him anymore.

He noticed the nose cannula was missing. "Should you take off the oxygen?"

"I'll be okay for a while."

Gabe nodded. "It was a fun night, wasn't it?"

"Yeah, it was. Marty is one of the best drag queens I've seen. He doesn't do it professionally?"

"No. He does around six shows a year in Burlington. I think when he was younger, he was more into doing the shows, but we never really talked about that."

What had stuck in Gabe's mind about the entire night had been Lucas's reaction to Maybelline and even Marty. After Maybelline had removed her makeup and wig and Marty had returned to the party, Gabe couldn't help but notice Lucas keeping his distance, even after their introduction. Only when Gabe had walked in on them in the kitchen had he seen them that close. Even then there had been an air of opposition, maybe even hostility on Lucas's part. When Lucas noticed Gabe, he'd excused himself and left the room. Questioned by Gabe, Marty had admitted he had no idea what was wrong with the lieutenant colonel.

Well, nothing that pulling that stick out of his ass wouldn't cure. Gabe had asked if Marty knew Lucas, but he'd denied ever meeting him. Gabe wondered if Marty had picked up on something from Lucas and attempted to exploit whatever that was. He often did that if he thought someone didn't quite agree with his chosen hobby.

"You okay?" Brandt gave him a puzzled expression.

He was probably overreacting. Brandt smiled as Gabe climbed onto the bed. He sat cross-legged next to Brandt's thigh and rubbed the warm skin of Brandt's belly. He'd missed him so much.

"I'm sorry for being such a jerk. God, I was such a total asshole, and you were just trying to take care of me. I'm surprised you didn't deck me." Brandt took Gabe's hand and ran his fingers over his palm, eliciting a shudder from Gabe.

"You were really hurt, and I imagine scared and angry and reminded of something that you probably wanted to forget."

Brandt pursed his lips and furrowed his brow. "You know what happened?"

"I only know that whatever happened damaged your lungs, and your recovery was long and hard and lonely." Gabe checked Brandt's expression to see if he had been right. When Brandt took both of Gabe's hands into his, Gabe took that as a confirmation.

Brandt looked down at their clasped hands. "I was forced to leave the military because of my injury, and it was as if someone had cracked my chest open and ripped out who I was. If I'd chosen to leave, prepared to become a civilian, that would have been different, but one day I'm fighting a war, and the next I'm in a German hospital on a ventilator."

Gabe, seeing his unease, said, "You don't have to tell me anything you don't want to. Sometimes it's best to leave shit in the past."

Brandt raised a brow. "Is that a counseling technique?"

Gabe rolled his eyes and smacked his chest.

"Owww." Brandt covered his chest with his palm where Gabe had hit him.

Gabe's stomach flipped. "Oh my God, did I hurt you?"

Brandt's expression of pain morphed into one of amusement. "As if you could."

Gabe clenched his teeth and smacked him again. It was nice to joke around.

"I want to tell you what happened because, well, I think you should know."

"Okay."

"My team was in the Paktia Province in Afghanistan. We were under orders to retrieve several suspected members of a group believed to have bombed a local village. Intel placed enemy insurgents in several abandoned buildings, so I had my team set up around the perimeter. On my command, several members of the team infiltrated the largest building just before it blew. I ran into that building without thinking. The heat and the smoke were intense and burned my lungs. I went in three times and got two of the three men who'd gone inside out. The third one had been too close to the bomb to survive." He wiped a hand across his mouth. "After two weeks in Germany, I was flown back to the States and spent another month at Walter Reed and three in rehab regaining my strength and increasing my lung capacity. I was medically discharged after that."

Brandt rubbed at his chest, and Gabe wondered if a physical ache lingered or if painful memories were the cause.

"I'm sorry. You had your entire world ripped away from you. That couldn't have been easy."

He huffed. "I did three tours in war zones, and I have to say, I'd take them any day over those four and a half months."

Nothing like a reminder of those times. "What have you been thinking about when you were in bed?" Gabe wondered if he was in control or if his past was.

"So much crap that sometimes it's easier to just stare at the wall and let those two events play in my head. They're just too similar to each other. The explosion, the screams, and the smoke. So much smoke. And I was on autopilot. Running in with only one thought—don't let them die. They have families, friends, years ahead of them."

"Which time?"

He grimaced, and his chest hitched. "Both." Brandt's emotions, the fear, the hopelessness, the mourning, the pain of his losses had to come to the surface before they could ever be set to rest. Given Brandt's reaction after the explosion at the school, Gabe was pretty sure that he'd never properly dealt with the aftermath of the first explosion.

Gabe ran his hand over Brandt's biceps, tracing the sharp angles and straight black lines of his tattoo. "Tell me what was different this time."

Brandt cocked his head. "What do you mean?"

"You told me how the two events were similar. Tell me how they differed."

He huffed with disgust. "Well, my lungs are worse this time. I probably decreased their already shortened life by ten years or more."

Gabe ignored the implicit connotations of that statement. Brandt had gone to the negative, where most people tended to go. He needed to dig deeper, past the injuries to his body, since healthy and strong were where his self-worth currently lay.

"That's not different, just worse. Same injuries with the same results. What happened in one event and not the other?"

Brandt swallowed. His rate of breathing visibly increased, and his hands twitched involuntarily against Gabe's. As Brandt searched his memories, Gabe continued tracing the tattoo over and over, loving the feel of Brandt's skin beneath his fingers.

"I didn't get everyone out in Paktia."

Gabe gave him an expectant look, prompting him to go further, but Brandt seemed to be too stuck in what hadn't happened.

"That's what didn't happen. What did happen?"

Brandt was so close. Not that anything he discovered with Gabe's help would make a huge difference, but this was a start.

His confused expression brightened slightly, not much. "I… I got everyone out this time."

"You did. What about after? Your recovery. Anything else different?"

More silence, then he nodded. "I'm not in the hospital."

Gabe smiled gently, hoping to prod him without needing to ask.

Brandt looked right into Gabe's eyes, his hazel eyes as beautiful as ever. "I'm not alone this time." He exhaled noisily. "Shit, I was acting as if I was. I was right back there at Walter Reed in my room alone for hours just wishing… well, wondering how I'd gotten to be so alone in my life."

Gabe rested his hand on the side of Brandt's neck. "You aren't alone at all. I'm here. Lucas is here, well, until tomorrow, and Betsy and Julia are here as well. We're here and aren't going anywhere."

The tension escaped Brandt, his shoulders falling, his jaw unclenching. "Kind of dumb, right? I let the past take over. Man, it was so easy, or is so easy to fall back into that frame of mind. What if it happens again? No. I can't let that happen. How do I do that?" Brandt appeared to be afraid.

"If you want, I can give you some cognitive-behavioral exercises that deal with ingrained reactions and thoughts. Of course, as a professional, I suggest a counselor who isn't me, because we're in a relationship. Usually just me suggesting counseling has people running." Gabe figured Brandt would run, but that would be his decision.

"You know, the first time around, I saw the required psych people, played by their rules, but didn't really participate. I thought I was strong, unaffected, didn't need help with anything." He growled deeply. "Macho."

Gabe laughed.

"Maybe now… I don't know." He shook his head and raised his hands. "Maybe I could use some of that help."

Gabe ran his palm down Brandt's cheek. "There's nothing wrong with needing help, and you know that, because you're all about teamwork."

"That's different. You're not admitting to weakness by working on a team. It's the size of the mission that depends on how many people need to be involved."

"Okay. Then let's say this is a minimum of a two-person mission, maybe three."

Brandt smirked. "A mission, huh?" He grasped Gabe's wrist, then lifted Gabe's hand to his lips and placed a light kiss on his palm.

The intimacy of the act tightened Gabe's throat, and he swallowed. "I missed talking to you, missed touching you."

"Me too. Can you ever forgive me?"

"Always."

Gabe bit his lower lip as they stared at one another. He wanted to kiss Brandt but wasn't sure if….

Brandt solved Gabe's dilemma by leaning in. The kiss was tentative, hesitant, but then increased in heat. Gabe needed Brandt in the worst way. He broke away and climbed off Brandt and stood next to the bed. Gabe pulled off his shirt as Brandt watched. Carefully, Gabe removed his sweats over his erection, and Brandt's eyes immediately focused on his cock.

Gabe ghosted his hand over Brandt's stomach, and the muscles twitched. Venturing farther, he hooked the sheet with his finger, pulling it down, revealing Brandt's cock. He was naked. Gabe raised an eyebrow. Brandt grinned confidently.

"I see you were hopeful."

"I was. Come here."

Gabe straddled Brandt's lap, his ass settling on Brandt's shaft. Gabe shimmied his hips. Brandt moaned and grabbed him by the waist. "Tease."

Another shake of his hips and Brandt lightly slapped Gabe's ass.

"Oh yeah." Gabe groaned.

Brandt chuckled. "So it's like that, is it?"

Gabe nodded.

"You're so hot." Brandt ran his hand over Gabe's hip and across his thigh, eyes intent on his body.

When Brandt looked up, Gabe's doubtful expression must have told him something, because he said, "You're gorgeous. Your face, your neck, your shoulders, your chest, your stomach."

Gabe snorted and poked his stomach. "I jiggle. I bet no one in the Army jiggles."

"Oh, the Army jiggles the higher up you get. And you don't jiggle. You're sexy. Thought so the first moment I saw you." Brandt's eyes moved over his body slowly, deliberately, as if worshipping him, and the action trapped Gabe's breath in his throat.

Brandt's entire body, his mind, his soul was everything Gabe wanted and needed. He'd never, in his entire life, been so sure of anything. He felt as if the entire world had opened up to him.

Brandt's gaze locked with his, a single moment frozen and expanding through time. Brandt cupped his cheek, his palm warm, reassuring. Beautiful hazel eyes were Gabe's sole focus. Brandt's thumb caressed his cheek. "I love you."

CHAPTER 23

GABE'S CHEST seized. He sucked in a deep breath, and his release was shaky. The pressure in his chest increased as his heart swelled. How could three words mean everything, truly mean happily ever after?

Gabe grasped the hand against his cheek, time moving once again, that single moment forever in their memories. "I love you too."

Brandt's smile was bright as he wrapped his arms around Gabe. When their lips met, the kiss was overwhelming and deep. Easily, Brandt flipped Gabe onto his back. He grabbed Gabe's wrists, bringing them above his head and pinning both with his wide hand. Another kiss and Gabe tried to catch his breath as Brandt writhed on him, kissed and bit his skin. He drove Gabe absolutely wild. Gabe's cock leaked wetness over Brandt's stomach, and his balls felt large and heavy between his legs. Every nip and bite on his neck clenched Gabe's hole. He wanted—fucking needed—Brandt to fill him up until he was screaming for release.

Moans and pants and whimpers filled the air as Gabe fought to form even a sentence. "Brandt… fuck, yeah… please…."

"You're so fucking hot when I hold you down and you beg." Brandt bit Gabe's earlobe. The sting zinged right to Gabe's hole, and he bucked harder. "That night at the bar. I fucking came in my pants," he confessed. "But not this time." Brandt pushed his hard-as-a-rock shaft into Gabe's groin. Gabe's breath stuttered as he imagined being impaled ruthlessly on that hardness. "This time I'm coming in your tight ass."

"Please. Please," Gabe sobbed, then whimpered as the solid mass lifted from him.

Gabe's hands automatically sought contact with Brandt. Gabe sat up and hungrily attached his mouth to a copper-colored nipple. He sucked, then bit at the nub.

"Ah, fuck!" Brandt wrapped his large hands around Gabe's head, holding him in place. The hands then guided Gabe to the other nipple. Gabe immediately clamped his teeth and worried that nub until it throbbed against his tongue. Releasing it, Gabe soothed it with his tongue and blew a shot of cool air against the heated skin.

Brandt pushed him back onto the mattress. Above him, Brandt's chest heaved, and a fevered flush crept up his chest and into his face. Hooded eyes surveyed Gabe wildly. Brandt looked as if he were going to eat Gabe alive. Brandt's rough hands ran the length of Gabe's stomach and chest and he plucked Gabe's nipples. He hissed and arched his spine.

"You're so responsive. Like a cat in heat. You move with every touch."

"Only your touch," Gabe whispered.

A low growl filled the air as Brandt grasped Gabe's cock in a tight grip. Gabe gasped, combusting from the inside out. Organs liquefying, cells imploding, nerves ablaze. Any moment, Gabe imagined the fiery lust would render him a pile of ash.

"Say it again."

Gabe fought to gain the words.

"O-only your touch, Brandt."

In one motion, he engulfed Gabe's cock, quickly bottoming out. Gabe cried out. He could feel Brandt's nose buried in his pubic hair. Fuck, he wasn't even gagging. The oversensitized skin on Gabe's prick along with the tight grip on his balls threatened to send him over the edge.

"No." He grabbed at Brandt's head. "Stop."

Brandt released his cock with an erotic pop but maintained his grip on Gabe's aching balls. Leaning over with a wicked grin, Brandt ran his hot tongue from base to tip of Gabe's weeping cock. Gabe moaned and tried to wiggle away, but Brandt planted his hands on Gabe's hips and pinned him down. With one swipe of his tongue, Brandt cleared the precum from the tip of Gabe's shaft, then dove up and shared the sweet liquid with Gabe. Gabe sucked on the invading tongue as if it were a cock. The action elicited another moan, cut short as Gabe gripped Brandt's thick shaft tightly and pulled from base to tip.

Breaking the kiss, Brandt moaned louder. "Fuck, your hand feels good."

Gabe increased the rhythm, giving the head a hard squeeze and a twist. Brandt's head fell forward, his chin practically touching his chest, which heaved with each gasp for air. With a sharp snarl, Brandt pushed Gabe's hand from his prick. Diving forward, he once again attached himself to Gabe's lips, sucking, biting, and effectively owning the orifice. Without stopping the assault, Brandt reached out, fumbling with the nightstand. There was a snick of a cap, and within moments, a wet, slick finger probed Gabe's pucker, massaging and then gaining entrance. A crook of a finger and Gabe arched off the bed as nerve endings tingled through his groin and balls.

"Shit!" A load of precum leaked onto his belly from the enflamed purple head.

If he were a prisoner of war and Brandt was interrogating him with his hands, Gabe would spill every national secret, including his own pin numbers, bank accounts—everything. Brandt had reduced him to a pile of blubbering putty.

Foil ripped open and another snick of the cap. Hands grasped his hip and shoulder and, in one motion, flipped Gabe with ease, trapping his sensitive cock between the mattress and his stomach. Brandt pried Gabe's asscheeks apart and started suckling on his hole. With a yelp, Gabe pushed back as Brandt's teeth grazed and nipped. How much torture could he endure before he exploded into a million pieces? Wave after wave of blazing need washed over Gabe, pulsing, throbbing, expanding, until it felt too big, too large. Gabe kept pushing back against the probing tongue until his ass was high in the air, shoulders pinned to the bed.

The heavy weight of Brandt draped over him, and he licked the shell of Gabe's ear, sending a shiver racing down his spine.

"I'm going to hold you down."

Gabe couldn't suppress the whimper.

Brandt rose above Gabe and then pushed the spongy tip of his condom-clad dick at his opening. Greedily Gabe bore down and all but sucked the hard tip in. Mind-numbingly slow, Brandt pushed in, stretching Gabe's hungry hole with a delicious burn. He placed a hand on Gabe's shoulder, forcing him into the mattress while Brandt guided his dick into Gabe. When his hips were against Gabe's ass, Brandt lay flat, effectively crushing Gabe between the hardness of his body and the softness of the mattress.

"So full." Gabe gasped as Brandt laced their hands together and tucked them beneath Gabe's chest.

"I can't believe how I feel inside of you." Brandt pulled out at a torturously slow pace, then back in as leisurely. The slide of the hot, hard skin along his hole produced a radiating tingle. Each thrust forced

Gabe's excruciatingly hard cock into the mattress and his stomach. Sweat formed between his flesh and Brandt's chest as it slid over his back. Brandt set Gabe's skin afire as he licked and sucked along the nape of his neck, over his shoulders, at the sides of his neck, panting in his ear. Gabe began a steady chorus of moans and whimpers.

"Love the sounds you make. Love you."

Brandt punctuated the statement with a snap of his hips, forcing a huff from Gabe's lungs. And the thrusts intensified. Sounds of slapping skin echoed in the room. That weightless, floating sensation filled Gabe's body, signaling his encroaching orgasm. He was getting ready to explode.

"I-I'm going to come."

The words brought a frenzy of hard and fast strokes from Brandt. Gabe clutched Brandt's hands tighter. He wanted to crawl inside of Brandt and never leave.

The grunting, stroking in and out of his ass, the musky smell of sex and sweat, the weight bearing down on him, brought the perfect storm as Gabe's cock swelled and forced the cum out onto his belly. Screaming Brandt's name, Gabe soared as his ass pulsated around the rock-hard shaft pounding his hole.

Brandt's arms tightened around Gabe as his thrusts increased. With two sharp breaths and a grunt, Brandt's cock throbbed as he filled the condom. Gabe reveled in the aftershocks of his release. Heavy breathing filled the room, and Gabe felt the loss when Brandt rolled to the side. Gabe reached over and grabbed the cannula from the nightstand, and Brandt put it back into place.

"Thanks." Brandt adjusted the tubing as Gabe opened the valve.

Gabe was concerned over Brandt's rapid breaths. But he didn't have time to say anything before Brandt rolled Gabe over his body and settled him against his sweat-soaked chest. He then threw a leg over Gabe's hip. They entwined their fingers on Brandt's chest, totally and utterly sated for the moment.

"You do realize we have to wash these sheets, since you came all over them," Brandt whispered.

Gabe let out a chuckle. "Twice I've come from you fucking me."

"Does that mean it was good?"

"I think the earth moved."

"The earth always moves when I'm with you."

"Dork," Gabe muttered before being drawn into a slow, lazy kiss.

Brandt brushed Gabe's hair from his forehead. "Mmm. You're in love with a dork."

"That I am."

THE NEXT morning Gabe entered the kitchen to find Lucas standing at the sink, mug in hand, staring far off past the kitchen window. Something in his expression was off.

"Good morning."

Lucas turned, and his smile was halfhearted. "Morning. There's coffee."

"Thanks. I could use some." Gabe grabbed a cup and poured himself some. Staring into the dark liquid, he thought of his insecurity about his body, his lack of confidence before Brandt had barreled into his life and confessed to love him for who he was, jiggly gut and all.

After opening the fridge, he pulled out his hazelnut creamer and dosed the caffeine-laden liquid until it turned light tan.

"Sawyer still sleeping?" Lucas had moved to the table.

Gabe joined him. "Yeah, he's out like a light."

"From what I heard last night, I'm not surprised." Lucas's smirk wasn't quite hidden behind his mug. "I'm thinking all is well."

"A man doesn't kiss and tell." Gabe turned his nose up.

Lucas barked out a laugh. "There was more than kissing going on, but to save your virtue, this conversation will go no further than us."

Gabe shook his head. "What time are you heading out?"

"Plane leaves at two o'clock, so I should leave by twelve thirty. Still have a few hours to lounge around civilian life." Lucas's smile faded. He appeared to be distracted, even agitated.

"Everything okay?"

Lucas furrowed his brow, eyes on his coffee. He shifted in his seat. His dark hair was mussed on the top, and Gabe imagined by the time he left he'd be Army ready. "Yeah. I've been thinking lately about when to retire. Somehow I thought I'd be in the Army as long as it would have me, but I'm getting older. Got my twenty. Maybe it's time to do something else."

Gabe studied him for a moment, knowing he wasn't discussing what he really had on his mind, but Gabe played along. "That's a big decision."

Lucas emptied his mug. "Don't I know it. I feel restless, unsettled, and I've never felt like that before. As if something's missing."

"What do you think that is?"

He shrugged. "Hell if I know."

"Where's the coffee?" Brandt walked into the kitchen, scratching at his belly. The black bag containing his oxygen was slung over his shoulder.

"Well, good morning to you too, sunshine." Lucas went to the sink and rinsed his cup.

Brandt grunted.

"Such a large vocabulary this early in the morning."

Gabe chuckled as Brandt growled at his friend. There was a knock on the front door. Lucas and Brandt both looked to Gabe.

"Probably Betsy or Julia."

He entered the living room and opened the door to see Randy. A very red-faced, pissed-off Randy. He looked different without his coveralls and not covered in grease.

"Randy… um…. Hey."

"I thought we had a deal, Reynolds." Hands clenched into fists at his sides.

Fuck. "We do. I… I didn't mean… I did see the twins yesterday, and I know I said I wouldn't but—"

"But what? You just happened to run into them at their preschool?" He narrowed his eyes further.

"No I… I had to see them. I had a shitty day and wasn't really thinking." Just being a selfish prick.

"Gabe, is everything okay?" Brandt stood behind him, body tense and ready. Behind him, Lucas had his flank.

Gabe tried to smile, downplay the situation, but he could tell they didn't buy it. "Yeah. Just give me a minute."

Both of them had their eyes focused on Randy, no doubt having pegged him as a threat.

Randy, while still visibly angry, lost some of his ire. "You just couldn't leave well enough alone. I was trying to keep my family together, trying to do what's right, and you were there at every turn. Karen won't talk to me because she thinks I made you go away and deceived her. And she's accusing me of cheating again, following me when I'm at work, checking my phone, my e-mail, saying there's some blonde lady creeping around the house. There's no one there!" He grasped his hair in his fists with a look of utter frustration and defeat. "I've been trying so hard, doing everything and anything to please her, but she's irrational. She's up all night rearranging crap and cleaning and wanting to talk. The fire department had to come because she'd lit a bunch of stinky candles she says were for protection and then started rearranging the furniture and knocked over the bookcase. The candles lit the curtains on fire. She tried to pull them down and burned her hand. What if she'd burned down the house? What if… what if the twins…." He shook his head. "I just can't do it anymore."

"Randy, it sounds like she's manic, maybe even delusional. Has she been taking her meds? She might need—"

He slammed his fists against his thighs. "I don't know! She won't talk to me about that stuff. She wants you to do it for her. She asked me to call you and tell you that she wasn't taking her meds so you'd have to come over. I told her you and I agreed that you'd back off and give us some room. Then the twins told me they saw you yesterday at school. And Karen was glad. Do you want to know what she said?"

Randy looked out into the driveway and waved for someone to join him. Was Karen there? Was he going to drop her off at his door? Jesus Christ, his baggage from his past was being spilled out for Brandt and Lucas to see. Randy's chest hitched, and his anger quickly dissipated. Before him, Gabe saw that same wounded man he'd seen at the shop. When Randy spoke again, his tone was less confrontational, more controlled, measured, unsteady. He seemed to be trying to hold himself together, keep from breaking down.

A hand rested on Gabe's shoulder. Gabe looked back to see Brandt right behind him, possibly with the thought that Randy had brought backup.

Randy stepped back from the door. "Karen…. She said she was glad you saw the kids, because they shouldn't be kept away from their real father."

CHAPTER 24

GABE'S BRAIN picked that moment to stop working. Their real father? The twins bolted onto the porch, laughing and squealing, and wrapped themselves around Gabe's legs.

"Karen's checking herself into the hospital today, and she wants…." Randy pursed his lips. "She wants them to stay with their father until she's better. So here they are. They're all yours, just like you wanted."

Their real father.

"What do you mean 'real father'?" At least Brandt was functioning. Gabe looked helplessly to his partner.

Randy scowled. "You're the boyfriend, right?"

Brandt didn't hesitate to scowl back. "That's right."

"It means Gabe is their biological father. Apparently I was a convenient way for her to get out of her crappy marriage." He appeared as if he had more to say, but he clamped his lips tightly together.

"Wait, how is that possible? Gabe? Hey?" Brandt touched his cheek, but Gabe wasn't even sure what to say.

Watching as if everything was in slow motion, Randy knelt and opened his arms, asking the twins to hug him good-bye. Until Mommy was better, they would be staying with Gabe.

He had to say something, had to stop Randy. He had questions, so many questions.

"No… wait," he managed.

Randy kissed Mikey and then Maddy on the forehead and stood, his chin quivering. "I'm done fighting for something that was never mine to begin with." He took in a couple of deep breaths, blinking rapidly. "I love you guys with all my heart. Be good." He stalked off the porch.

Gabe turned helplessly to Brandt, then back to Randy walking to his truck. Gabe managed to get by the kids and ran into the driveway. "Randy! Stop!"

But the man fired up his truck and spun his tires, fleeing the house. Gabe watched as the red truck disappeared through the trees.

"Oh shit." Gabe wiped at his mouth. When he turned, Lucas and Brandt were on the porch with the twins. He then noticed the two suitcases off to the side.

Their real father?

Looking to the twins, who were attempting to climb Brandt, Gabe didn't know if he should laugh or cry.

GABE RUBBED at the back of his neck, a knot of pain lodged beneath his skull. After calming the overexcited kids and feeding them lunch, they'd settled into the living room to watch a DVD Gabe had found in Maddy's bag. Some strange movie with talking dogs and cats and a plot to take over the world. The kids were on beds of blankets and pillows, with Brandt sandwiched in between them, in hopes they'd fall asleep. Gabe needed them to nap, give him time to breathe, to even comprehend what had happened. And find out where Karen was. What was she doing? Sending their world spinning off into the cosmos, that's what she was doing.

He scrunched his brow together and massaged his temples, trying to make a plan. He'd tried to call Karen with no answer, left messages and texted. Next step, call and see if she'd checked into the psych ward at CVPH. But who would take her there? Not Randy. Well, he hadn't said if he was or wasn't taking her. Gabe hoped she didn't drive herself.

Randy also wasn't answering his calls. Gabe had called about a dozen times, leaving messages until the voice mail was full. Then he'd started texting. The man had been devastated, and Gabe was concerned about Randy as well. What if he did something rash? Losing his marriage and his kids and dealing with the lies. Maybe he'd gone to his mother's. Gabe would call there too if he could find the number.

A hand on his leg startled him. Brandt knelt on one knee before him. "Hey."

"Hey."

Brandt gathered him in his arms, and Gabe rested his head on his shoulder as Brandt rubbed circles over his back.

"Kids are asleep. How about we go into the kitchen?"

Gabe nodded. When Brandt stood, Gabe dragged his exhausted body up from the couch. His mind was running on high, and he needed the swirling thoughts to kick into a lower gear.

"Want something to drink? A shot?"

Gabe huffed. "I'd need the whole bottle." He leaned his elbows on the counter and scrubbed at his face.

Brandt rubbed his hand over Gabe's back. "Do you think what Karen said was true?"

Gabe bit down on his tongue until the pain surged. "I need to find out where she is. And Randy too. He was so upset. Maybe I should go out and look for him. What if he does something stupid?"

"You have the kids here, and while they're comfortable with me, I'm not quite comfortable being alone with them."

He sighed. "You're right. It's just… I'm responsible for this entire mess, and I have to fix it."

"While you may have seen the kids when you said you wouldn't, you aren't responsible for Karen's lying, her mental illness, or her mess of a marriage. You've tried to help. Maybe you should have stayed away from the beginning. I don't know. That's hindsight now." He lightly gripped the nape of Gabe's neck and gave him a slight shake. "You're a good person."

If Brandt knew what he was thinking of doing at that moment, he might not believe that. Self-centered and selfish would fit.

"I was in the middle of their marriage, apparently."

"You were trying to help Karen. And you're a big part of those kids' lives, and you deserve to see them. If I'd known you were going to agree to stay away from them, I would've stopped you."

"Actually, that was my idea."

"Then I would have saved you from yourself."

Lucas came out of his bedroom with his bag. Gabe had forgotten he had to leave soon.

"Heading out?" Brandt asked.

Lucas nodded, pulling the keys to his rental car from his pocket. "Yeah, I'm sorry I have to leave with everything going on."

"It's okay. Not much you can do anyway."

Lucas gave him a doubtful look, then gave Brandt a back-slapping hug.

Gabe knew Brandt was sad to see him go. "Keep in touch, and don't let the brass work you too hard."

"You got it. I'll call you in a few days. Gabe, it was nice to meet you. Keep this one in line. He requires a firm hand."

Gabe shook his hand. "Will do."

Lucas saluted and headed out the door.

Gabe closed his eyes. He had to focus. "Okay, I need to call the hospital and see if Karen has checked in. From what Randy described, she's manic and delusional, believing things that aren't true and showing signs of paranoia."

"Is that part of having bipolar depression?"

"Psychosis can be, and she needs to be hospitalized immediately. She could be in danger of hurting herself. She's already tried to commit suicide once, which puts her at greater risk. I hope what Randy said was true and she checked into the hospital. I'm going to call her doctor. If he doesn't answer, I will call a few contacts I have at the hospital. Karen's been there more than a few times since she became ill. You need to get some rest. Bit too much excitement for you."

The corners of Brandt's lips curled. "Yes, dear."

Gabe snorted and went to get his phone. He paused as he passed Mikey and Maddy, still fast asleep. Maddy was curled around her pink unicorn with the rainbow horn and Mikey was flat on his back, arms stretched wide, taking up as much space as possible. His love for them could fill the ocean.

Their real father.

He pushed that aside. Couldn't deal with the implications, the lies right then. He had to find their mother and make sure she was safe. The ball of anger he had to contain wasn't going to help anyone.

When he retrieved his phone from the coffee table, Gabe noticed he had three missed calls from Betsy. If there had only been one, he might have waited to return her call later. But three? Opening the phone app, he chose her number from the list of recent calls. As he waited for her to answer, he powered up his laptop to check his e-mail. Her voice mail picked up.

"Hey, Bets. Just returning your call. Call me back."

Brandt came in from the kitchen carrying two cups of coffee and sat next to Gabe on the couch.

"Damn, I love you." He reached for a cup, and when he saw the light tan color indicating his creamer, his smile was even more grateful. "Did I say I love you?"

"Not nearly enough." Brandt pecked Gabe on the lips. "Anything yet?"

"I was just looking for the number. Just so you know, I may have to lie a bit to get that information."

"A little subterfuge is often necessary to reach your objective."

A knock on the kitchen door interrupted them. Gabe rose and was going to answer it when the door opened. Betsy stepped inside.

"I was just trying to call you. What's going on?"

The furrow in her brow, the tight thin line of her lips, her determined expression cut right through Gabe. "I have to show you something. Where's your laptop?"

"In the living room. What is it?" Gabe followed Betsy. Brandt stood with a smile when she entered, but that quickly faded upon seeing their faces.

Betsy halted abruptly, her gaze on the sleeping kids. "Why're the twins here?"

Gabe rubbed at his forehead. "Randy dropped them off. It's a long story."

"Shit." She knelt and turned the laptop to face her. "Is Randy with Karen?"

Gabe wasn't sure where she was going with this as she worked on his computer.

"Is Randy with her?" Betsy's barking tone sent a jolt through Gabe as she repeated her question.

"I don't think so. They got into a huge fight, and he dropped the kids off here. Karen told him she was checking into the hospital and wanted me to watch the kids. Betsy, what the hell is wrong?" His fear was clawing up his chest and growing.

"Do you think she's in danger?" Brandt asked.

"I don't know. Gabe, look at this." He looked over her shoulder as she pulled Karen's Facebook page up. "She posted this around eleven this morning. I happened to get on here, and I immediately started to call you when I read this. You read it and tell me if I'm just overreacting."

Gabe knelt and turned the computer to face him as Betsy and Brandt looked on.

To all of my family and friends on Facebook. What wonderful people you are, so bright and shiny each day. You all make my days a little better just knowing you're here. Thank you. There comes a time in life when people need a change, something isn't working right, hasn't worked right for such a long time that there's nothing more to do in the current situation. I've decided to change my situation and move forward where I am free to make my own bright light. I'm heading out and will miss you all, especially my little lumpkins. So long.

Gabe could scarcely breathe as his hands gripped the sides of the coffee table.

"Do you think she means she's going into the hospital?"

Gabe tried to shake his head.

"Fuck!" Gabe scrambled to his feet. "I have to go to the house. I need… my keys…." He twisted and turned, searching every surface, his pockets…. Where the fuck were his keys?

Maddy popped upright in her bed, bleary-eyed and confused. Mikey stirred but didn't wake.

"I'll drive you." Betsy headed for the door.

"No. Brandt can't be alone with the kids. I need you to stay."

"Just go with Betsy. You shouldn't be driving. Call 911 on the way. Better to be wrong than…." Brandt let those words hang.

Better to be wrong than right.

"We'll be good here until you get back. Go!" Brandt waved his hand at them, and they bolted out of the house and into the car.

As Betsy backed out of the driveway, Gabe slammed his fist into the dash. "Fuck, I forgot my phone."

"Here." Betsy handed over hers, and Gabe dialed 911. His leg bounced up and down as he waited.

"This is 911. What's your emergency?" the man asked.

"This is Gabe Reynolds. I'm a mental health counselor in Westport. I have reason to believe that my ex-wife, Karen, might hurt herself, if she already hasn't."

"Sir, are you with her now?"

"No. I live outside of town. I'm going there now."

"Did she say she was going to hurt herself?"

"Not directly, no. She has bipolar depression and hasn't been doing well. She tried to commit suicide a few years ago." Gabe ran his hand over his head, stopping to pull the strands. Betsy rounded a corner and nearly tipped her small car up on two wheels. Gabe grabbed the oh-shit bar as the car rocked.

"What is her location, sir?"

"Three-two-five Robin Lane in Westport. It's a large red house with white trim."

"I'm entering that address in now. Does she have access to guns in the house?"

Shit, she did. "Her husband has hunting rifles." But she wouldn't use one. Would she?

"Sir, ambulance and police are already at that location at a call for an unresponsive woman in her forties."

Gabe dropped the phone and buried his face in his hands. What had he done?

CHAPTER 25

TIME DOESN'T stop for anyone or anything, but there were times in Gabe's life when he'd been sure time had slowed when he wasn't paying attention. At that moment, he was convinced time had stopped altogether. He might have believed it really had, if not for the quiet whispers and sniffs of those standing around him, the light breeze rustling the leaves of the towering trees, the flutter of the flowers draped over the coffin.

Karen's coffin.

Closing his eyes, Gabe concentrated on Brandt's strong arm wrapped around his shoulder. He focused on the heat of Brandt's body next to his side, the warmth across his back and on his shoulder, the only parts of his body that were warm. When Gabe had kissed Karen good-bye at the funeral home, her skin had been so cold. That chill had gone straight from his lips and had settled deep inside of him. He shivered slightly, thinking he'd never be warm again despite the sun being high in the sky. A beautiful June day.

The minister droned on, reading prayers meant to comfort the living. Across from Gabe on the other side of the coffin, Randy stood, shoulders hunched, eyes never straying from the casket. His mother stood next to him, her hand on his arm. Karen's stepbrother, who had flown in from San Diego, was on the other side of Randy. Karen had never been particularly close to him, but Gabe was glad he'd come. Betsy stood beside Gabe, Julia beside her. Dave number two had accompanied her. He was looking more and more like a keeper. Charles was there, and even Travis and Gregg had come.

So many people who'd known Karen, many her entire life, were there to say good-bye, to mourn her tragic passing. Gabe knew what some people thought of her suicide. If they only knew how she had actually been strong to survive as long as she did until that last fatal dose of pills ended her suffering.

"Now Karen's husband, Randy, would like to say something." The minister stepped aside, and Randy took his spot at the head of the casket. For a moment, he stared wide-eyed, as if the coffin had just appeared out of nowhere. Then he opened the piece of paper in his hand and cleared his throat.

"Karen was my wife. But first and foremost, she loved being a mother to Maddy and Mikey. They were everything to her. Her sun and moon she called them because, despite being twins, they are as different as night and day. She loved them with every part of her being, with her soul. She knew they were a gift, a precious gift that she'd had to wait far too long to get. Sometimes I'd catch her watching them play, and she'd have this beautiful expression filled with wonder and awe and love." He wiped at his nose and exhaled.

"I tell you all of this because some of you might not understand why someone who had two beautiful children who meant the world to her would choose to leave them." Tears spilled and streamed down his face, but he didn't bother to wipe them away. "You may think what Karen did was selfish. You may think, how could she have taken the momma of those children away?" His voice cracked as he shook his head, and his chin trembled. "Karen was never selfish or cruel. You see, Karen was sick for a long time. And despite all the treatments and all of the people helping and supporting her, despite her trying to get better, she didn't. I'm guilty of not being there all of the times she might have needed me, and for that I can only apologize and hope that she forgives me. She tried so hard, so hard every day. And none of us can doubt that because, unless we've experienced what she did firsthand, we can't say any different. I want to thank Karen for trying so hard for her kids and for me." Randy looked up, his bloodshot eyes full of sadness. "And for Gabe."

Gabe choked on a sob. Brandt squeezed his shoulder and took his hand into his own.

"Good-bye, Karen. I hope you found your light."

Randy touched the casket and then walked to his mother, where he collapsed into her arms, sobs wracking his frame. No one was left unaffected by his words. Gabe fought to hold himself together. He just had to make it to the car. Maddy and Mikey were at home with a sitter, so Gabe had to get it together before they arrived home.

"Gabe. It's time to leave."

Gabe looked up. People were moving to their cars. Brandt raised a brow in question.

"Just a minute." Gabe stepped forward and laid his hand on the casket, the deep mahogany wood warm to the touch from the sun. The dozens of flower arrangements surrounding the burial site perfumed the air with that too-much-of-a-good-thing flower smell. He ran his fingertips over the wood. He wondered how to apologize for not being there.

All he could say was, "I'm sorry." Then he left Karen behind.

Brandt took his arm and led him to the car. Before Gabe even hit the passenger seat, the tears flowed. By the time Brandt slid into that car, Gabe was sobbing.

"So sorry, baby." Brandt pulled Gabe to his chest as the wretched sobs took over his entire body.

AS HE sat on the deck, Gabe clutched the paper he'd received earlier. The sun was setting on the day of Karen's funeral. He'd come out to get some air and a break from the twins. He couldn't imagine their confusion. Mommy was in someplace called heaven, and she was stuck there. Daddy wasn't there for them. And they weren't in their home. The afternoon had been rough, with temper tantrums and sour faces and tons of tears. Thank God for Betsy, Brandt, and Julia. Gabe wasn't sure what he would have done without them.

He sipped his wine, wishing the wine was whiskey or something equally as numbing, and wondering how people recovered from such a tragic loss. As a counselor, he knew how to help people process their grief, but helping was so different from living the reality firsthand. He'd never known the depths of despair and heartache one could endure and still have their heart beat. As Karen's husband, his greatest fear had been finding her dead. As a counselor, his greatest fear had been not being able to save someone from the ravages of mental illness, to lose them to the disease so sinister yet at times invisible to those closest to the person.

Gabe thought of Randy, probably home, hopefully with his mom and family. He'd lost so much through no fault of his own. Karen, through her misguided efforts to get what she so desperately needed, had turned to deception. Randy hadn't even wanted the children. Maybe that's what had spurred her to say what she had.

Many kids Gabe counseled shouldn't ever be with their sperm donors. Some were abusive, drug addicts, gamblers, workaholics. Not all were bad. Many were good people without parenting skills…. Like Randy. But people could be taught to parent. Gabe didn't need to be taught and was ready for the job without hesitation.

So why did he feel so guilty? Why had a hard ball of guilt shoved itself under his ribs? Gabe's yearning for kids of his own had dug deep into the pit of his gut long ago. He recalled so many times, waiting with Karen for some stupid stick to reveal two lines and grant him his wish. The heart-crushing ache when only one line continually appeared had been etched forever into his memory. He deserved two lines. He deserved what those other dads had with their sons and daughters. The laughter, the tears, the challenge of raising them to be good people. Watching parents, he'd smiled tremulously as they pushed their children on the swings and taught them to hit a ball, held their hands when they crossed the street, loving them for all they were worth.

Gabe wanted that.

He couldn't help but feel deceived. Karen had wanted the kids to be somewhere that they were wanted. But Randy had been the daddy in their eyes since birth, and that was special, right? God, he wanted that special feeling, the feeling that, hey, these are my kids, and that makes me the luckiest man on earth.

His breath caught in his chest, and he exhaled. Looking at the paper in his hand, he believed himself to be a good person, a good man who'd finally been gifted with everything he'd ever wanted. A loving partner and two beautiful kids. Would he still be a good person now that he had everything? People knew that you were a good person by your actions, what they could see. It's what they couldn't see that mattered as well, and you had to judge for yourself if your motives were selfish or altruistic.

Gabe furrowed his brow. Maddy and Mikey were his kids. His kids, and he would give them everything they needed and wanted. A good life with him and Brandt. That's what Karen had wanted for them, and that's what he would do.

Draining his glass, he stood and stretched, the day fading into evening. Inside, he placed his glass in the dishwasher. As he entered the living room, Maddy shouted, "Daddy!"

Skipping a beat, his heart stuttered, then shifted into overdrive. He clutched at his chest, eyes darting to where Maddy was playing with her stuffed dogs, her babbling mostly incoherent, but clearly there was a mommy and a daddy dog.

Brandt looked up from where he was reading the paper in the chair. "You okay?"

Gabe's gaze went from Brandt to Maddy, then to Mikey, who jumped on a minitrampoline Julia had brought over so he could contain his nuclear-like energy to one spot. "Unca Gabe! Jumping. Tramoline."

"Awesome." Unca Gabe. That's who he'd always been to them. Their uncle. Brandt looked at him expectantly. "No. I'm not okay. I have to something I need to do. Can you stay with the kids? I won't be gone long."

Brandt stood. "Of course, but where're you going?"

Gabe held up the paper that he hadn't set down for hours. Earlier, he'd shown Brandt the document that further solidified his role as dad. "I have to deal with this now." If he didn't, he wasn't sure he would sleep.

Brandt glanced to the paper in Gabe's hand, then back.

"I want you to be careful. A grieving man isn't a rational man. He might not hear what you're saying."

Gabe smiled and chuckled. "Giving the counselor advice?"

"No. I'm giving my partner, who I love, advice."

"Love you too." And Gabe had to be grateful for what he had, even if he feared losing it all someday.

THE HOUSE was dark. Getting out of his car, Gabe frowned, seeing Randy's truck in the driveway. Maybe he'd gone with his mother, which would be good for Randy, not so good for Gabe. He had to return the letter to Randy that handed over parental rights to Gabe. Everything Gabe had yearned for in one piece of paper.

Ringing the bell, Gabe listened intently for any noise to indicate Randy was home. Nothing. Another ring. Nothing again. Right then, even if Randy wasn't home, he wanted to go in. He'd lived there with Karen for so many years. Their house. Legally so since the house was still in both of their names. In their divorce, he'd agreed to sign the house over five years after the ink had dried on their divorce papers. He hadn't really known Randy and feared him taking advantage of Karen or, during a manic phase, Karen using the equity of the lien-free house. A wound from his past. Her extravagant spending spree during her first manic phase so many years ago had nearly wiped them out. But they'd gotten through that.

Gabe tried the door, but it was locked. He circled around to the garage and tried that door. Open. He stepped inside the darkened space and went up the stairs. He tried the kitchen door and again was granted entry. Flicking on the light, he looked around the large kitchen with eating area. He'd become accustomed to thinking of this as Karen's house, yet when he'd received the letter from Randy declaring him a father, he'd envisioned living there with Brandt and the twins. Meals around the kitchen table, family games in the living room, bath time in the huge antique tub upstairs, bedtime stories in the room Maddy and Mikey now shared, then later having separate rooms decorated to fit their personalities, and holidays, birthdays, graduations, and grandchildren. Gabe had envisioned their entire lives, and it had been wonderful.

Wandering through the foyer, he stopped at the doorway to the living room. Sprawled in the rocking chair next to the fireplace was Randy, chin to his chest, eyes closed, funeral suit rumpled, blond hair mussed, bottle of Jack Daniel's dangling from his fingers. The bottle was nearly full, so maybe he wasn't dead drunk. Or maybe he was on his second one.

"What the fuck are you doing here, Gabe?" Randy hadn't opened his eyes, hadn't moved. His words weren't slurred, so possibly he was sober enough to talk.

"What are you doing sitting here alone? Where's your family?"

Randy raised his head. His eyes shone bright in the light from the kitchen. "Told them to go home."

"Why'd you do that? You shouldn't be alone."

"Why not? Might as well get used to it, right?" Randy raised the bottle to his lips and swallowed several large gulps, then gasped and coughed. With a strained voice, he asked again, "Why're you here?"

Gabe lifted his hand, holding the paper. "I have your letter."

Randy grunted. "Couldn't even give me one day, could ya? Figures. You've wanted those kids since the day they were born. Now you got 'em." He lifted the bottle and took another drink.

Gabe went back into the kitchen, grabbed two glasses, then returned to Randy. Without asking, he took the bottle. Randy merely narrowed his eyes. After pouring them both a generous amount, he handed Randy a glass. He accepted the offering and didn't throw the liquid into Gabe's face. That was a start.

Gabe settled onto the couch and sipped the alcohol. The burn felt so right for such a terrible day.

Randy laid his head back on the chair. "So, now I have to sit here and drink with you as well. What the hell? Kind of like drinking with the enemy, isn't it?"

"Is that what you think I am, Randy, the enemy?"

He merely shrugged.

"I'm not taking anything from you that you didn't freely give to me."

"They're your kids. Always have been, even if they called me daddy. Karen was always yours too, even though you didn't love her. Turns out I was the one-too-many-people in our marriage."

Gabe wasn't sure that was entirely true, but he let it go. He could admit that he'd been too entwined in Karen's and the twins' lives. He'd own that.

"I loved her with all my heart, and it sucks not to be enough, you know? I mean, at first I was, before the twins were born, and then everything fell apart."

Gabe narrowed his eyes. "Is that why you don't want them? Because they changed what was between you and Karen, because they're just kids and—"

"Stop!" Randy sat forward, a fire in his eyes, liquor sloshing in his glass. "I'd never blame those kids. I love them with everything that I am. I would do anything for them."

Gabe clenched his jaw. "Then why didn't you fight for them, Randy? Why did you sign your parental rights over to me when you damn well know that you're their biological father?"

CHAPTER 26

RANDY WAS silent, his eyes closed, brow furrowed.

"Tell me, Randy. Why would you give them away like that?"

Randy stood, face twisted with anger and grief. "Because that's what she wanted. She wanted them to be with you. Why else would she have lied to me? Why else would she tell me those babies are yours and not mine?" He slung the glass of Jack into the fireplace, and glass and liquid exploded, coating the brick walls.

His shoulders sagged, chest heaving, grief his only remaining expression. Slowly, he sat back in the chair and his head fell back. Tears wet his cheeks and glistened in the light from the kitchen.

Gabe let the silence surround them for a few minutes. Randy stared off into nothing, not moving except for the steady rise and fall of his chest.

"She wasn't thinking straight. You know that. She couldn't rationalize what you said about not wanting the kids. All she heard was the father of her babies didn't want them, and she knew someone who did."

Randy huffed. "I told her what I meant when I said that. At first I didn't want them, and being a parent wasn't something that came natural to me. But I tried hard and learned, and there were so many good times. I don't want you to think there weren't. You know, times when I thought she was finally on the road to recovery, and then…. She could be so up and down, but I don't blame her. But part of me wants to be angry with her."

"It's normal to be angry with someone who decided to take their life and leave you behind. I'm angry with her for what she put us all through, for putting us in this situation. Anger is a part of grief, and it all sucks no matter what you feel."

Randy looked up at the mantel beside him. His gaze was on a picture of his family on the beach. Gabe knew that had been taken on Cape Cod. A family vacation. Randy's family.

Gabe lifted the letter he held between his fingers. His moment of truth. His chance at happily ever after. Only that was a myth. Life was hard. Life was unfair. Life was a son of a bitch that gave and took. The measure of happiness was within a person. Each person had to define their level of happiness by their expectations, wants, and greatest desires. He'd been so wrapped up in wanting what he didn't have, he thought he couldn't be happy without it. Time to redefine his definition of happy.

He stood, going to Randy, determined to finish the task he'd come to do. The man looked up, face still wet, all hope leached from his eyes. Gabe opened the letter and held it so that Randy would see that Gabe had signed the declaration. Randy's eyes went straight to the signature, and Gabe thought he saw his breath hitch.

"I came here to give you a choice. I do love the twins. So much that I want to do what's right for them. I'm not their father." Gabe's grief surged, his eyes burning. "You are. We both know that. If you weren't, I wouldn't be here. I'd be filing this with my lawyer and the court. But I know you'll be good to them. You're a good father. That can't be taught. Parenting skills can." Gabe took in a deep breath.

"You have a choice. Accept this paper and I move in here with Mikey and Maddy. You can still see them, spend time with them, be a part of their lives. Or tear up this paper and the twins come home to live with you, here in this house. I'll place the house in trust for them. It'll be their house. Not mine."

Randy eyed Gabe with suspicion. "Why would you do all that?"

"It was really Karen's house, and they should—"

"No. Why would you give me that choice? You got what you've wanted. You'll be a better father than me anyway." He waved his hand toward Gabe. "Apparently you're like God or something."

Jesus, what had Karen done to make Randy feel that way about Gabe? "Not sure where you heard that. I've made a lot of mistakes." So many, and the guilt of Karen's death now weighed heavily on his shoulders. He couldn't help but feel responsible. Maybe no one was responsible. Or everyone was. Or Karen was. So many people to blame.

"Karen didn't think so." Randy wiped the wetness from his face with the back of his hand.

"Doesn't matter now, does it? Karen's gone. We're the ones left behind to make the decisions, no matter what Karen said or thought she wanted."

"You're saying she was wrong?"

"Yes, I'm saying she was wrong. We're the ones who need to decide what's best. You and me."

Randy looked to the paper held out before him. He reached up and grasped that paper with his forefinger and thumb, his eyes on Gabe as if he wasn't sure he'd truly release the document.

Gabe allowed the paper to slip from his fingers. His muscles relaxed, his gut settled, and his jaw unclenched. He didn't realize how wound up he'd been over that decision, that responsibility. Randy studied the paper intently, his jaw tensing and relaxing, his brows twitching almost imperceptibly. He had to decide if he wanted to be a single father of twins. Gabe actually found himself rooting for him, hoping he'd take the challenge.

Randy looked to Gabe. "I can do some of the things they need, like get them meals and give baths and even braid Maddy's hair. But they need to know so much… and what if they get sick and I don't know it? What if I mess them up and they start to hate me?"

Gabe chuckled. "You know what you sound like?"

Randy furrowed his brow. "What?"

"Someone about to become a father."

Randy's confusion morphed into an expression of comprehension. "So you're saying every parent has those fears?"

Gabe snorted. "Yeah, even me, and I don't have kids." That was a monumental moment for Gabe. He didn't have kids, and that was okay. He still had time, still could adopt, hopefully still be involved in the twins' life, still be Unca Gabe.

Eyes on the paper, Randy's face vacillated between determination and doubt. One deep breath and he ripped the only thing standing between him and his children.

Gabe smiled wanly, feeling a touch of sorrow. He'd done the right thing. If he hadn't, that truth would have eaten at him for the rest of his life.

He patted Randy on the shoulder. "Since you've been drinking, I won't bring the kids over tonight. But tomorrow they'll be glad to get home."

Gabe grabbed the bottle of Jack with the intention of putting the liquor away. On his way through the foyer, Randy said his name. Gabe stopped and turned.

Randy had stood, and his gaze was anywhere but on Gabe. He shifted from foot to foot. "Um… I'm… I'm gonna need help… with Maddy and Mikey."

"What about your mom or other family? Or you could hire someone." Gabe wondered how far to go and hoped he wouldn't get shot down. "Or I could help."

Randy's eyes met Gabe's, and he gave a sharp nod. "I wouldn't turn down help, but my momma drives me a little nuts. And my family isn't too close. There's not really anyone who can come here." More shifting and unease.

"And you don't trust me or like me." Part of Gabe understood, and part of him was pissed that Randy wasn't accepting his generous offer. Randy looked down. "How about this? You think about it. We can talk tomorrow when I bring the kids home." What Gabe really wanted to say was he'd come calling as soon as there were two toddlers terrorizing the house. His lips curled slightly at that vision. He wasn't as altruistic as he'd like to be.

Randy nodded but was silent.

"I'm heading home and getting some sleep. I suggest you do the same. Tomorrow your kids come home."

Gabe continued to the kitchen, not bothering to drop the bottle of Jack on his way out. He might need it sooner or later.

BY THE time he arrived home, it was after ten and the house was dark. He thought everyone was asleep until he saw the light on in the bedroom. He found Brandt reclining in bed, laptop on his legs. Gabe took a moment to take in his gorgeous man. He'd come tearing into Gabe's life, flipped it upside down. Gabe had been captivated by his good looks and love of kids. But there was so much more to Brandt Sawyer. The warmth in Gabe's once cold heart, the hope that had filled that dark pit where he had none left, was amazing. Gabe had failed at love, at relationships, and he couldn't say that he didn't fear losing this one.

Brandt raised his brow as he looked at the screen. "Planning on lurking outside the door all night?"

Gabe huffed, entered the room, and climbed onto the bed. Brandt set the laptop on the floor. Gabe caught a glimpse of the web page he'd been looking at.

"What were you doing online?"

Gabe settled in next to Brandt on top of the covers, reclining against the headboard.

"I contacted my old case manager at Walter Reed to schedule an appointment to see the pulmonary specialist who treated me after I returned stateside."

Gabe turned toward Brandt. "Are you okay? You aren't getting worse, are you?" Had the stress of the last few days harmed him?

Brandt raised his hand. "Slow down. I'm fine. I'm healing. Breathing easier. Getting more stamina. Ready to take on the world. Well, as long as the world doesn't have any stairs and isn't farther away than the kitchen." Brandt snorted and then exhaled, gaze shifting downward. "When they told me that I might need a lung transplant someday, I had decided that I wouldn't take that option. I had an uncle who had a heart transplant about twenty years ago when he was in his forties." Brandt shook his head. "The toll the surgery took on him and the side effects of the antirejection meds... I wondered why he'd even bothered, you know?"

Gabe chewed on his lip. "Did you ever ask him why?"

Brandt chuckled. "Yeah, yesterday when I called him."

Gabe propped himself up on his elbow. "He's still alive?"

"He is. I asked him, why go through all that when he'd suffered so much. He said, 'I just watched my granddaughter graduate from high school.' Twenty extra years or more, and he says the issues and problems were less important than his family. When I made that decision, I hadn't seen much in my future. No family, no one I wanted to stay around for."

"And that's changed?"

"You tell me."

Gabe lifted one side of his mouth. "You've got me. I know a month isn't a long time but—"

Brandt cocked his head. "My dad proposed to my mom after three weeks."

"Whoa, let's not jump the gun. I mean, what I meant to say…. I don't think that…."

"I didn't say I was going to propose, ya jackass." Brandt laughed when Gabe frowned heavily. "You're too cute."

Gabe grunted and crossed his arms.

Brandt puckered his lips and made kissy noises. "Come on. You know you want one."

Gabe looked askance, trying not to laugh at Brandt's ridiculous expression. Just to get him to stop, Gabe kissed him quickly.

"Told ya."

"You did." Gabe's smile faded. Being able to laugh and joke were good. Helped with the whole entire tragedy and loss.

"How'd it go with Randy?" Brandt took Gabe's hand and ran his thumb over his.

Gabe blew out a breath. "I gave him a choice. Accept my letter and we move into the house with the twins or tear the letter up, stay in the house, and be their dad." The part of him that was about want and self-satisfaction still questioned the sanity of that decision.

"And?" Brandt's voice was so tender and gentle. Gabe moved closer and rested his head on his shoulder.

"Tomorrow the twins go back to live with their real father. I'm not sure if we'll be a part of their lives or not." That was the heartbreaking reality he'd have to live with if Randy decided he didn't need help. Guilt that Gabe hadn't taken them and run was there, but taking the twins away from their father would have been a heavier weight to bear.

"I'm sorry. I know how much they mean to you." Brandt stroked Gabe's hair, the action comforting and relaxing.

"Thanks for not saying I did the right thing."

"You already know you did. Doesn't bear repeating." Brandt kissed his head and snuggled closer. Gabe could what-if in the future. Right then he was happy right where he was.

CHAPTER 27

BETSY SHOWED up bright and early with donuts, all wide-eyed and cheery. The twins had woken Gabe and Brandt at the crack of dawn. When Gabe told them they were going home, their excitement was immense. They hadn't stopped since. Brandt was currently on his back on the floor, legs straight up, giving them each airplane rides. Gabe sat on the couch, practically curled around his cup of coffee, extra hazelnut cream because he deserved it. Betsy sat in the chair, smiling as Maddy tried to make an airplane noise.

"Attention, Plane Maddy, this is the tower. You are cleared for landing." Brandt bounced her around as she laughed hysterically. "Turbulence! Watch out for the turbulence!" A few more shakes and he lowered her to the ground.

Gabe shook his head. "Make sure you don't get too winded."

Brandt waved a hand at him and cleared Mikey for takeoff.

Betsy looked to Gabe, giving him a thumbs-up, then pointing to Brandt as she mouthed, "Good catch."

Gabe snorted and took a drink of his coffee. As if he didn't know that.

"What time are you dropping the kids off?" Betsy swirled her coffee. Gabe thought that was an annoying habit.

Gabe looked at the clock. It was only nine. "Not until after eleven. Last night, Randy was—" Gabe looked to the kids and, when they weren't looking, mimicked the tipping of a bottle to his mouth. "Giving him time to sleep."

"That poor guy. I can't imagine what he's going through. Do you think he'll be all right with the kids?"

Gabe shrugged. "He will, or he'll have to ask for help. But I know he won't let anything happen to the twins. He really loves them."

Brandt let Mikey down and begged the kids to stop, even though they asked for more.

Gabe stood. "Let's all go and eat. I made you guys' favorite. Scrambled egg and cheese cups."

The kids raced into the kitchen and sat at the table.

"Need some help, big guy?"

Brandt looked up at Gabe slyly and nodded. Gabe held out a hand and was almost pulled over by an amused Brandt before he was off the floor.

"You did that on purpose."

Brandt shrugged and went into the kitchen. Betsy looked overly amused and followed Brandt. Gabe followed and went to the stove. He pulled out the muffin tins and plated the food while Brandt and Julia set the table. Gabe set the plate in the middle. They were all seated, and the kids dug in. Mikey grabbed his and took a big bite.

"Damn. These are really good." Brandt ate one in two bites.

"Yeah, I came on the right day," Betsy said.

Before Gabe could take a bite, there was a knock at the front door. He sighed heavily. Brandt raised his brow, but Gabe shook his head. He went into the living room and opened the door.

"Randy? Oh. Good morning. I thought you might sleep in today." He looked awake and ready to face twins in their terrible twos.

He dug his hands into his jean pockets. "Nah. I've been up for hours. Cleaned up the house and got some food."

"All before 9:00 a.m.?" Was he trying for the title of super dad?

"I'm used to getting up early."

"Come in. We're just eating breakfast."

Randy stepped inside and glanced around the room. "Nice craftsman cottage. You own this?"

"I rent. Not sure where I want to land just yet."

Randy nodded as his gaze darted about the room, and he rocked on his heels. "I wanted to ask you and your... um...." He pointed to the kitchen. "Your partner...."

"Brandt."

"Yeah, Brandt, if you wanted to come to dinner tonight. I got some steaks and beer. I thought we could work out a schedule, you know, with the kids. I have some nights I have to work late, and... I mean, if your offer to help still stands."

Gabe's mouth gaped, and for a moment, he was speechless. Not what he'd expected. "Yeah. Sure. I can help at night or after school. Anytime. I usually work from nine to four. I can even help in the mornings."

For the first time since Gabe met him, Randy gave a slight smile "I'd appreciate that. It's going to be hard on them, coming home and

Karen not being there." His voice sounded tight and forced. "I think having you around will help them."

"Thank you."

Randy snorted. "Don't thank me yet. Someday you might wish you hadn't offered."

Gabe knew the answer to that one already. "Never."

Randy looked longingly toward the doorway to the kitchen, where the sounds of chatter from Mikey and Maddy could be heard. "If you need more time, I can come back. I don't want to take the kids away from breakfast."

"Randy, let me pay you back the favor of dinner early. Come eat with the kids."

He appeared hesitant, then said, "Okay."

"Head on in. I'll be there in a minute."

Seconds after Randy disappeared into the kitchen, Gabe heard squeals and shouts of delight from the twins. "Daddy!"

Gabe's legs felt weak. His heart pounded in his chest. He sat on a chair. His biggest fear had been Randy saying no and shutting him out of the twins' lives. Until that moment, he hadn't realized how much of that fear he'd suppressed.

Brandt squatted next to him. "You okay?"

Gabe took his hand, so strong and reassuring, so right. Brandt gazed at him with those hazel eyes that had snagged Gabe at first sight. "I am." He ran his fingertips over Brandt's cheek and was rewarded with a coy smile. "Do you know how much I love you?" The immensity of that adoration, that love, was hardly contained within him.

Smiling gently, Brandt pulled Gabe to his feet and wrapped his arms around him, their bodies touching from chests to thighs. "You may have mentioned something, but remind me."

"More than anything." And that was an understatement.

Brandt cocked his head and took on a look of suspicion. "Are you trying to butter me up because we're going to be part caretakers of two children whose untapped energy supply could power an entire army?" Brandt ran his hand down Gabe's back, sending a shudder through him.

"You're begging for the job, and you know it."

"I will need some reimbursement for my services." Brandt waggled his eyebrows and rubbed their groins together suggestively.

Gabe snorted and smacked him on the shoulder. Brandt grabbed his hand and slowly brought Gabe's fingers to his lips, his gaze unwavering.

He lightly kissed Gabe's fingertips, sending waves of tingles through him. "I love you too, Mr. Reynolds."

Gabe grinned as Brandt brought their lips together. That touch still sent shots of electricity through Gabe's lips and down his spine After a moment's hesitation, Gabe fell into the kiss, ready for a lifetime of kisses with Brandt. Happily ever after might not be easy, and there were no guarantees, but Gabe would take what he had over that any day.

JAKE C. WALLACE started writing from a young age, but took a break for marriage, kids, and college (in that order). A few years ago, he rediscovered his passion for writing stories and ventured out into the brave new world of publishing. He has published several novels and short stories. Recently, his novel *Jerricho's Freedom* was a finalist in the Rainbow Book Awards.

At night and on the weekends, Jake writes about all things men, believing there is nothing hotter than two men finding and loving one another, whether for a night or forever. An avid reader of M/M romance, Jake loves a good twist of a plot, HEA, HFN, or tragic ending, and has over two thousand books in his library. He also writes what his best friend calls HUNKs (Happy Until the Next Kidnapping). In his daytime hours, Jake works with individuals with autism and behavior issues. He is owned by a beautiful partner, three kids, and two grandchildren. He lives in northern Vermont.

Website: www.jcwallacebooks.com
Facebook: www.facebook.com/jcwallacebooks
Twitter: @jcwallacebooks.com
E-mail: jcwallacebooks@gmail.com

JERRICHO'S
FREEDOM

JAKE C. WALLACE

As prince of the Anzuni demon clan, Jerricho's entire life has been planned for him. At twenty-five, he will become the crown prince of the Anzuni, marry a man chosen by his parents, and bear his husband's children all without choice. If that wasn't enough, he must remain a virgin until his wedding night. To do otherwise would spark an unimaginable scandal.

With only ten months until his twenty-fifth birthday, the walls close in on Jerry, and the realization that he will lose his small apartment, his job at the library, and his freedom hits hard. But that's nothing compared to losing the man he loves. Rex is a smart and sexy construction foreman with a keen interest in demon "mythology." When Jerry and Rex give in to spending one night together, their indiscretion can't be kept secret for long. But that's only the beginning of their problems.

Someone wants to harness the power of Jerry's bloodline and his ability to conceive—someone with designs on horrifying experiments, sex slavery, and murder. Jerry and Rex are at the mercy of power-hungry sadists. With no one left to trust, they must fight for each other, their freedom—and their unborn child.

www.dreamspinnerpress.com

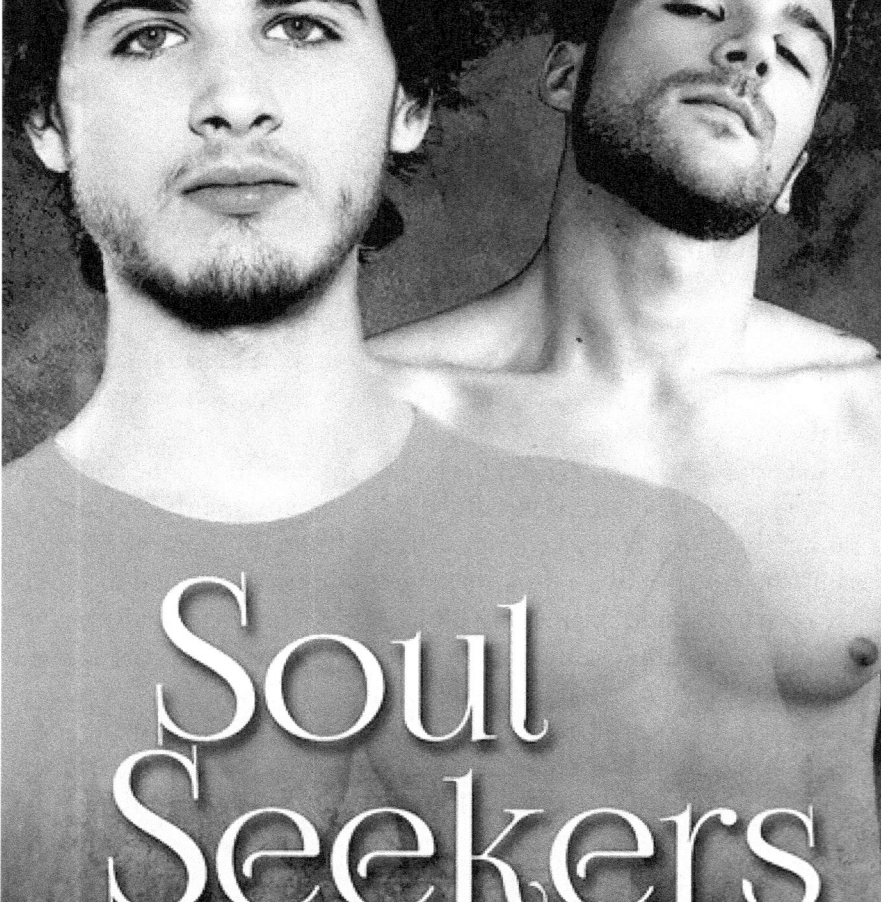

Soul Seekers

JAKE C. WALLACE

Nineteen-year-old college student Levi Reed has spent his life with hollow emotions and a darkness so deep that he's convinced he's losing his mind. He'd give anything to feel something, anything, real.

When a mysterious stranger appears, Levi is convinced the man is trying to kill him. When he's near, Levi experiences head-crushing pain and something surprising—real emotions for the first time. Jeb Monroe is arrogant, self-assured, closed-off, and handsome, but he isn't the harbinger of doom Levi assumed. Jeb's mission: help Levi find his missing soul.

Levi is pulled into the secret world of Seers and Keepers, those born with the innate ability to manipulate souls and tasked with balancing the negative energy they can produce. Levi learns he possesses a rare gift, and he's in danger. As Jeb and Levi grow closer, they discover a group of zealots who want to harness Levi's power to cleanse the world of damaged souls. Everyone Levi cares for is threatened unless he agrees to become their tool of death. But agreeing could spell the destruction of humankind. With no one to trust and nothing as it appears, it's up to Levi to save them all.

www.dreamspinnerpress.com

JAKE C. WALLACE

NEW VAMPIRE JUSTICE: BOOK ONE

DARE
TO LOVE
FOREVER

New Vampire Justice: Book One

With pain and loss in their pasts and evil threatening their futures, two vampires will find a love that lasts forever… if they dare.

Carson Locke is dangerous, even by vampire standards. A rare Tabula Rasa vampire, he can wipe the mind of those he bites—human or vampire. Because of this, he's lived his entire life in isolation. When his family is murdered, Carson runs from those who want him dead. Injured, starving, and about to be executed, he meets Commander Lincoln Samuels, an officer in the New Vampire Justice police force.

Lincoln, a Sanatore vampire, possesses the gift of healing. The moment he encounters Carson, broken and terrified, trying to steal blood to survive, he is compelled to help the other man—despite the risk to himself. Their bond creates something the world has never seen, but others have plans for Carson and his destiny was written long before he was born. He'll either become a tool to control the vampire world or, with Lincoln by his side, find the courage to fight and become its savior.

www.dreamspinnerpress.com

A CHANCE FOR US

NEW VAMPIRE JUSTICE: BOOK TWO

JAKE C. WALLACE

New Vampire Justice: Book Two

Love between a young man with a broken mind and the jaded New Vampire Justice officer who cares for him might be the last hope to stop a human-vampire war….

Justin Masters is stuck in a nightmare. Waking after seven years in a catatonic state, he falls desperately in love with the straight NVJ officer who saved him. Between that and dreams of being tortured and taking pleasure in the pain, which bleed into his waking hours, Justin's sure he's starting to crack.

The growing unrest in the vampire world should be Max Kincaid's focus, but Justin's struggle, along with Max's confusing feelings for his ward, have him reeling. When Justin's attacked, his resulting needs might be more than Max can fulfill, but he'll be damned if anyone else will touch Justin.

As the NVJ investigates humans missing from a high-end bite club, they uncover a deeper plot that traces back to Justin. If those who want him have their way, there will be bloodshed. Justin and Max are in a fight to save Justin not only from those who would use him, but from his own mind.

www.dreamspinnerpress.com